Citrine

Kyla Breene

Content Warnings

This series deals with heavy topics.

Check the content warnings!
kylabreene dot com/triggerwarnings

Spanish Translations

Eli is not a native speaker of Spanish. Like many children of expatriates, she was never taught and only picked up a few phrases. Most of them weren't meant for mixed company. :)

Curses/insults

- **Hijo de puta** - son of a bitch (this can be used as exclamation, or an insult, just like it is in English).

- **Uy, qué care-chimba** - Ugh, what a dickhead (literally: Ugh, what a penis face)

- **Que te folle un pez** - Screw you (literally: I hope you get fucked by a fish)

- **Los cojones** - bullshit (literally: the balls. Generally said to call someone out. "¡*Los cojones*! I don't believe it." Eli uses this term more broadly.)

- **Diablos** - damn (literally: devils)

General exclamations

- **¡Madre mía!** - Oh my! (literally: my mother)

- **¡Qué asco!** - Yuck!

- **¡Qué rabia!** - Aargh!

- **¡Basta!** - Enough already/stop it!

A note on species and politics

There are a lot of alien species in this series. This will help you keep track of which ones you have come across so far.

Manticorid: once empire seeking, now mostly living peacefully. The origin of manticore mythology on Earth.

- **Abstainers**: A sub-sect of manticorids with a strong political presence in Session. They believe venom is dangerous and cut off the tip of male manticorid tails at birth.

Genali: The slimes we all love to hate. Opportunistic, with a specialty in exotic goods, including people of all species.

Braceaaer: The origin of Little Green Men mythology on Earth. Violent, small, and much stronger than they look.

Drakonid: a dragon/dinosaur-like species that was once a servitor race to the manticorid empire.

Wroahk's species name is unknown, and who knows when he will share it (if they have even named themselves or he bothered finding out).

ELi

Trigger warning: physical abuse on page in this chapter.
"You're far too pretty to spend all your time with us," Ms. Janis tells me. "And what's wrong with the boys if they haven't seen how sweet you are and made sure you stopped working yourself to the bone?"

I give her a big smile. "Now, now. Just because you have all the men wrapped around your little finger doesn't mean I have your skills."

She tilts her head back, her silver braids shifting and her dark eyes sparkling as she lets out one of her deep laughs. "My dear, you have every drop of the same charisma."

I snort out my disbelief. She's my favorite and I admit we spend longer than necessary getting her ready to start her day. I like hearing all her stories, getting updates on her great-grandchildren, and the gossip about the latest silver-haired fox she has panting at her door this week.

The movement on the screen pulls both of our attention back to the nature show she has on. "What do you know about that one, Eli?"

It's an adorable little fuzzball and I let what I know bubble out, pleased to not have to keep myself in check around her. "That's a jumping spider. *Phidippus otiosus*, maybe? People call them the cat spider because they'll stay on your hand."

She whacks me on the shoulder, her usual response to show me she's impressed, though it took me a few times to figure it out. "How do you do it?"

I know it's rhetorical, since she asks it every time, so I just give her another grin.

"Your parents must be so proud."

My heart falls, but I keep the smile on my face and change the subject. "What's Darian up to? And the girls?"

She tells me the same stories she told yesterday, unfortunately, so it doesn't distract me from the sudden pit in my stomach.

From comments I've received, most think my big smiles and willingness to listen means I've led a blessed life. People like me know that a shocking number of the kindest people come from the most pain. Because we went through hell and had to decide to become harder or softer.

I chose softer and sunnier as my armor.

I don't really think of myself as all that kind, but others see what I want them to see.

My pocket buzzes again, just like it's been doing since I clocked in and started my rounds. I didn't recognize the number as I left my grocery clerk job for this one, but I bet it's the same one. I go to wash my hands as she continues her story and take a quick peek.

Yes, the same person and I've missed fifteen calls. I'm about to turn off the phone completely when a text pops up.

Eliyana Smith. Stop ignoring me.

Only one person has the audacity to think I'm a Smith and not a Martinez.

"*Diablos,*" I mutter under my breath. "How did she get this number?"

My hands are shakily tapping the screen as my mind tries to remember how to block a number when another message comes through.

It's an emergency. I need you.

"Just ignore her, Eli. Block the damn number," I hiss out.

I finally remember how, but my finger just hovers over it. My whole body is shaking now, heart in my throat as it pounds, but I can't make myself do it.

My *padre* loved her once. Would he be disappointed in me if I ignored a call for help?

I snort. "She ignored all of yours."

"What's that, dear?" Ms. Janis asks from the other room.

"Oh, nothing, just hit my hand on something."

She goes back to her recounting of how smart her grandson is, the same one she's been trying to set me up with, but I can't listen over the roaring in my ears.

Memories of pain and terror, warped by my subconscious attempts to protect my young mind, try to surge up, but I shut them down before they gain traction.

She never touched me, but she never stopped my stepfather. That it stopped short of sexual abuse was the only blessing. Words and fists hurt enough as it is.

I owe her nothing.

He isn't here. I swear. Just want to see you. Miss you.

My traitor heart squeezes and my eyes fill. How can you hate someone and love them at the same time? Why, oh why, do I miss her?

I'm typing a message before I can think better of it.

How long is he gone?

As the indicator lets me know she is replying, I recognize it's a terrible idea. I also know I'm going to do it anyway.

This better not get me fired or I won't even be able to afford that hinky bed share arrangement I just landed with the freaky chains coming off the bed.

* * *

She still smells the same. Chantilly perfume—far too liberally applied—cigarettes, weed, and fear. I know better than to squeeze her as we hug. Grunts of pain when I came to live here as a teen quickly clued me in to how often her ribs are broken.

Her bleach-blonde hair is piled high, hairspray making it stiff. Her heavy makeup makes the grooves that betray her age seem even deeper. She's far too thin.

She isn't wearing her usual long-sleeves and so I can see the bruised imprints of his large hands on her biceps.

Makeup and clothing cover up a lot, and my mind snags on the fact that she isn't hiding the evidence from me. I doubt it's unintentional.

It doesn't take long to see past the facade of their happy lives to the evil underneath. If you bother to look. Telling people about it taught me... not to.

People don't want to know. Not really.

I move away from her and sit down at the kitchen table. As much as I love seeing her, my body is signaling to me in every way possible that I should leave. Now.

I ignore it and don't leave. Just like she never has. My fifteen-year-old self had the courage, though. She's screaming at me to not waste the opportunity she gave me, but I'm an adult now.

I can do this.

Still, this is the first time I've been back here since I chose to be homeless. Any other time I've seen my mother, it has been in public places. My heart's pounding and I have to keep my hands in my jeans so she doesn't see how much they're trembling.

"What did you want? My next shift starts soon."

She huffs. "You work too much. How many jobs now?"

"Just three. Mostly."

I bite off my desire to tell her about them. About how tired I am. Or how I wish I had remained in school. She'd only get defensive and tell me I shouldn't have left.

As if I could have stayed.

I wish I could tell her how messed up it is that the streets were safer for me than her so-called home or that I found kinder people in alleys to huddle up with for warmth.

But of course, I don't.

She's picking at her nails, sitting back in her chair as she lights up another cigarette.

I don't keep the disgust off my face, but she ignores me. She knows they make my allergies go haywire.

Coupled with the music she always has blaring, it's a recipe for sensory overload.

I won't be able to stay long.

"I want to leave him."

She's said it all before, so I just keep my mouth shut. She'll ask for money next.

"I just don't have the cash."

I cross my arms in front of me and raise an eyebrow. When she reaches out to me to gain sympathy, I notice the track marks on her arms. That's new.

"I've given it to you at least five times. I haven't saved up again since the last time."

She slumps. "I thought you got a raise at the store?"

How the hell did she know that?

"I work a cash register. A raise barely pays for a cup of coffee. How about you start working?"

She shivers. "You know he'd never let me do that."

I let out a sigh. He controls everything. Most importantly, what money she has access to and what she can buy with it.

That he lets her buy drugs is just another way to keep her under his thumb. My empathy has been engaged, against my better judgment.

"I can spare a couple hundred. Just grab a bag and I'll take you somewhere."

She's shaking now. "I can't just leave all my things."

She isn't ready. She will probably never be ready, and no one can force that decision.

I had to make the choice for myself, and she'll have to do the same. If she ever decides to take the risk and accept the fear of starting over, I'll do whatever I can for her.

Anything she has will be mine, but not if it's going to destroy her.

I stand up, the chair rasping along the ground as my knees push it back. "I have to go to work."

"Please! Can you just send the cash? I'll figure something out."

I glance back to the evidence of hard drug use peppering her arms.

"No. I can't do that. If you want me to take you somewhere and pay for a few nights, I will. But I'm not giving you cash."

A low voice growls from behind me, instantly making my body lock up. "What the fuck, Noreen?"

Did he see my bike? I left it a block away, just in case. Stupid music. I should have turned it off when I came in.

Shit.

He must have snuck in. A waft of air brings the smell of his aftershave and my stomach heaves. I can't help but turn to him. My instinct to never let him behind my back is too strong to not override my desire to never see his face again.

He's livid. The same mask of rage that always preceded a blow... always there for something we did wrong.

No matter how trivial the offense, always that same level of anger.

"I knew you were up to something; you bitch. My buddy said to use cameras, and I fucking defended you. Said you would never betray me."

"You can't—" I try to say but he cuts me off.

"Don't you dare try your fancy talk on me, you ungrateful fuck," he hisses out at me.

I wasn't planning on it. It's not like he's ever listened anyway.

His fists clench and my mother keens out a low cry. "Of course I wouldn't! I was just trying to get some money. For that new bike part you want."

I whip my head over to her, my heart clenching. Is that where all my money has gone? To him?

Damn. That feels even worse than thinking she spent it on drugs.

"Don't you fucking lie to me, whore!"

He takes three long strides over to her and punches her hard on her left cheek, driving her to the ground.

I'm instantly shaking, no longer able to keep my cool as memories flood back. I've never seen him hit her there. He always chooses somewhere that's easy to hide. Just like he did for me.

He kicks her while bellowing out and I rush forward to pull him off.

At just over six feet, he is a good six inches taller than me and much broader. It takes him little effort to shrug me off, ensuring there is plenty of force behind it to send me reeling back.

The back of my head clips the edge of the counter as I fall.

In the few moments I take to shake it off, he's busy kicking her. She's curled up with her knees up and her arms over her head to protect her most vital areas.

He's going to kill her. It's never been this bad.

I'm scrambling up and headed back to their bedroom without conscious thought. The gun is where he always keeps it and I snatch it out, pull the slide to load it, and rush back to the kitchen.

I raise it just like my *padre* taught me and bark out a warning. "I'll shoot. Back off."

He spares me a quick look. "You don't have the balls, girl."

He finds out just how wrong he is after he makes contact with her hip, and she screams out.

The retort of the Glock is almost deafening in the small kitchen as I squeeze off a couple of shots. Two answering wounds bloom on his chest as he staggers back toward the mudroom, a look of disbelief on his face.

Then my mom is screaming, but for another reason altogether. "No, no, no! Don't die, baby!"

She has her right arm pulled tight to her. It's visibly broken. Her face is streaming blood, and yet she's applying pressure to one of his wounds with her good arm.

Desperate to save the life of a man who was trying his hardest to end her own.

I'm still standing in shock, my arms at my side, the gun still in it, when I hear the sirens. My heart jumps, urging me to flee, but that would be the worst thing to do right now. He was going to kill her.

Surely that will be obvious?

I put the gun on the ground near the hallway and move to the other side of the kitchen. As far away from my sobbing mother as possible while also moving away from the weapon so they don't shoot me on sight.

From there, it's a blur of movement. Cops come in and secure the weapon. Paramedics work on my stepfather. They move my mother and me outside.

She resists them, screaming the whole time, but once we get out, she whips around to me, pointing.

"She was the one who beat me. Arrest her!"

The words feel like a knife in my back as I stare at my mother, disbelief etched into my face.

"I was saving your life," I spit out. "Why would you say that?"

I feel like shaking her and take a step forward, but two officers grab my arms, their grip like iron.

I strain against them, desperate to close the distance between us. No clear idea of what I want to do if I get to her. I just need to make her see sense.

"She's lying!" I shout, locking eyes with her.

I thrash in the officers' hold, my muscles burning with the effort. Her light brown eyes, so much like mine, avoid my gaze. Blood streaks her eyebrows, a stark contrast against her pale skin.

The blare of the ambulance has already drawn the neighbors into the street, their stage whispers cutting through the air like the earlier gunshots.

My voice softens, pleading. "Why are you doing this to yourself, Mom? Why?"

Over her shoulder, paramedics wheel my stepfather's body out on a stretcher. His eyes flutter open, lips moving as if in prayer. He's still alive.

I should have aimed for his head.

She glances back at me. Guilt flickers across her face. A ghost of the mother I once knew. Yet, she turns back to him, her choice clear.

As the officers drag me toward a squad car, the betrayal settles in my chest. The weight of it all bears down on me, and a single tear traces its way down my cheek.

After they roughly push me into the back seat, I stare at the white zip ties contrasting against my olive skin.

I'm a criminal.

Wroahk

This rhelld will be my most challenging kill yet. I can already taste its flesh but stop myself from letting my teeth clack together in anticipation.

I keep myself moving through the water, my tentacles tasting the surrounding water, letting me know where to go.

I catch a flash of green limbs in the distance, along a reef I have hunted many times, though it is contested territory.

Another glance and I can tell it is a female, signaling in my direction, ready to lay a clutch.

No. I ignore her.

A rhelld would be far too difficult to fight if I were missing limbs. She will have to find another male willing to risk death just to offload his seed.

I have a better sort of hunt and turn my attention back to the trail teasing me through the water.

I see a flash of red and move my limbs so they propel me toward it, elated that it has moved into more shallow water.

I will soon have it trapped, though I would prefer to remain out of the warmth and sunlight. It tries to dart away again, but it is tiring, no match for my endurance.

As I close in, it releases one of its fins, hoping I am one of the many mindless creatures that would take the small meal as a distraction while it flees back into the trench beneath us.

I ignore it, though I see other opportunistic predators are already tearing it apart.

If it drops any more fin layers, it won't live much longer. I push through the long blue weeds close to the shore, scanning for another glimpse of it, tentacles splayed out to detect any disturbances in the water.

It isn't swimming now, using the weeds to hide, but after a moment I can detect its heart, pounding away in delicious fear.

I drift toward it slowly, savoring the last few moments of this day's long hunt, reaching out slowly toward where it is trembling behind a layer of weeds, pulling my gills tight against my body in preparation for its last defense.

I snatch the large red body toward me, ignoring the clicking screeches it makes, moving slowly away from the poison it has dumped into the water around us.

Just as I move it to a safe distance, and prepare to break it apart and feast, something punches down into the water from above.

I freeze. What new predator is this?

Something gleaming pierces the rhelld and I'm yanked up out of the water before I'm able to release it from my hold.

Once the spray of water clears, I see a giant pink... something in the sky. Floating there, just like I would under the water. It's... wrong. Nothing large moves through the sky.

Before I can puzzle it out or get away, it attacks me with its own tentacles, except there are far more of them than any creature should ever have, and when they pull against me, they feel nothing like flesh.

I try to tear into them, but they won't break and instead leave long cuts and gashes as they squeeze me into a smaller and smaller shape.

Then it pulls me into its maw, the rhelld screaming out in pain near me, its multiple rows of black eyes rolling as green blood pumps out of it and down into the water below us.

I try to fight against the hold, but only manage to swing myself through the air. The wind already biting into me and drying me out.

I'm spinning wildly as the creature pulls me into its mouth. I scream out my defiance as it prepares to eat me, but once I get inside its mouth...

I see other creatures. None of them look like they have been chewed. Do they live inside it? Cleaner fish?

I don't have a chance to figure out their role before one of them holds out a limb and coats me with something vile, every sucker sending me information about it I would rather not know.

My vision darkens as my stomach heaves.

Eli

Something's wrong.

I mean, more than just the fact that I've been arrested. We're heading out into the desert instead of downtown, where they should book me.

I've been there plenty of times on loitering charges to know this is bull.

The thought of confronting them about it makes my heart pound, but it's getting progressively more remote.

I clear my throat. "Where are you taking me?"

They ignore me, and it pisses me off. "My mom's going to wonder where I went. You can't do this!"

The one with the buzz cut scoffs at me, finally turning to engage. "Right, you little bitch. Clearly, the woman who accused you of beating her is worried about you."

"I didn't!"

He laughs. "That's pretty obvious."

The one driving lets out a long breath. "Are you sure about his one?"

"Yeah, I pulled up her record real quick while they pulled out that deadbeat. Just another nobody that no one's gonna miss."

His comment is like a punch in the gut, and I sink down into the seat, the zip ties cutting into my wrists in a sting to match the sick feeling in my chest.

He's right. I'm a nobody. I had plans to make a mark on the world. I had someone who loved me and believed in me. Both long lost.

Now I'll just be another statistic.

Someone who didn't show up to work, but everyone knew it was bound to happen, so they won't think about it more than a few minutes, likely just angry they have to figure out how to cover for me.

Hell, all I had was a bed share arrangement and it'll probably take her weeks to realize I haven't been around.

No one will even notice.

I blink back the tears and try again. "Where are we going? What are you planning to do?"

They don't answer, just go back to talking about some stupid football team. Soon after, we pull onto a gravel road, and I know I'm screwed.

It's a cop car, so the doors are locked. My hands are cuffed.

I'll just have to hope they kill me fast and there's no torture involved.

I'm feeling lightheaded as we bump down the road, my empty stomach sending waves of nausea up to somehow make the whole experience just one more layer of terrible.

"Why?"

Again, they ignore me. Cops and I haven't always had the best interactions. Partly because of my homelessness, the other part because I look like an immigrant, but many of them have been kind.

Helped me out, even, but these two are obviously among the scum that give the whole profession a bad name.

I give up trying to talk to them and instead look at my surroundings. The miles of baked ground, low scruff, and intermittent cactus aren't making me feel good about my odds if I try to run.

Another mile, with no plan formed, and we stop. I struggle when one of them pulls me from the car.

"Calm down, sweetie," he tells me, making me wish I knew how to break his stupid neck.

I struggle against the cuffs, desperate to get away, but it's futile.

"You'll like it," the one on my left mocks.

Before I can say anything more, the mocking one throws a thick cloth over my face, muffling my screams, then they drag me across some gravel before pushing me roughly against something hard.

Judging by the feel of it and the sudden pain of splinters, it's a wooden fence post. Big hands push me down until I smear all the way down it, my hands scraping along the wood until I can feel blood flowing.

Then they use another zip tie so my arms are tied around it, continuing to ignore me yelling at them. Then both car doors close. I scream at them again, but my only response is the sound of tires kicking up rocks.

No one comes and I eventually run myself out of energy, the hot sun leeching me of the ability to even keep myself upright.

It's like some sort of mockery of the sunshine cape I imagine around myself when I need to get my panic under control. What I get for trying to run away from reality all those times.

Now it's burning me alive.

I'm delirious by the time I hear the strange sounds, though I do notice that it is blessedly cool now. Far better than hours of endless heat and the fear of suffocating under the thick fabric.

When I smell some sort of gas and feel it pushing me toward sleep, it's a relief.

Wroahk

Voices hover over me, but my entire body aches too much to respond. I try to grunt, but even that feels like an effort. My lungs are burning, unaccustomed to being used. I never liked surfacing or the heavy feeling of my body outside of the water.

I can't understand them. My eyes won't open so I can see them, but I can feel their disgusting limbs all over me. My tentacles won't respond to my commands to crush them.

What is happening?

Am I dying?

They're probing at the drum covering my left ear and a searing pain comes as something is pressed against it until it breaks through. Then they're dragging me onto a surface with sharp edges and a smooth top, the rough motion jarring my senses.

Suddenly I can understand their wet, garbled speech. "He'll be perfect for the auction. One of the matrons will throw all kinds of credits at us when they see both of those thick things. We can market it as a fuck hunt."

I try to grunt again, still unable to move any part of my body. I only hunt for myself. Never for others.

"Check the orders, Shriveled Skull. He's meant for the hunting ground."

"What? I just gave him a translator, upgrades for his libido, and the usual healing suite. The full package."

"I'm not dying because you can't read orders. Leave what nanites he has out of the report and get him in the chamber."

"Tell me that next time, Desiccated Testicles. I hate having to sequence suite removal. I'll just remove the translator, and no one will know."

I finally get my eyes to respond so I can see my enemy. They are blurry at first, but then I see wet gray skin, but not like my own. Instead, they leak some sort of pink substance.

I don't see gills, and their bodies look like they would sink. Drowning is a good option then, though that won't be satisfying. Their eyes look vulnerable to plucking out with a well-placed sucker, but I don't see any bones to break.

Ripping them apart a piece at a time will be the best way to kill them slowly. I commit their profiles to memory, along with their scent.

I hope their screams will be just as wet sounding as their voice.

The surface I'm on tilts, spilling my limp body into a confined space. It's too smooth to be a cave, and it smells odd.

"I hate the big ones with lots of limbs," one of them grumbles as I feel my tentacles tossed in with me one at a time.

The other one lets out a grunt. "Why would they want him as a trophy, anyway? The aquatic ones just shrivel up."

They plan to hunt me for sport? Many have tried.

Once my body responds, I will leave this odd cave and tear them apart so they know that no one ever succeeds.

"Let the hunters figure it out. We'll be rid of him as soon as we get the chamber sequenced. I'm extracting the translation nanites now."

Soon after that, I can no longer understand them.

They throw in the last of my tentacles, this time one of my mating ones, nicking the more delicate skin with some sort of claw. I look forward to finding out if their blood tastes sweet.

A clicking sound is followed by a hiss and as much as I resist it, I can't stay awake.

***

"This is disgusting," I mutter, perched on the edge of the lake, my tentacles twitching in discomfort.

Chilled freshwater laps at the shoreline, which differs from the shadowy depths I am accustomed to. The freshwater doesn't suit my skin, sending an uncomfortable itch crawling beneath the surface.

I wish to go back to the familiar embrace of salt water, where I can hide and hunt my prey with ease.

Even if it is a complete disdain, I have to admit that this lake is livable, if barely. The warmth of the water grates at me, but I live through it, knowing I have little choice in the matter.

"For how long?" I question with a sigh.

My back presses against the rough surface of one of the rocks lining the edge of the lake. Green tentacles stretch out into the water, some lazily drifting while others grip the rocks with a firm hold.

My aquatic-blue skin—perfect for blending in with my native environment—contrasts against the rough brown rocks as I let my lower body submerge in crystal water.

The rhythmic lapping of the waves against the shore lulls my senses, while the melodic chirping of not-food in the nearby trees fills the air. Too hard to catch and not even worth the trouble.

Their sounds rasp at my nerves, and I wonder if it might be worth flinging rocks just to silence them.

My gaze catches the horizon where the lake meets the purple and green sky. I take a moment to take in the scene before me. The lake stretches out, its green-blue waters shimmering in the sunlight. It's waiting to swallow the sun, the light dimming.

Beneath the surface, myriad fish dart and weave, their movements a mesmerizing dance in the water. As I observe the aquatic life below, I can't help but feel a sense of detachment.

Unlike these darting creatures, I am an amphibian, straddling the line between land and water. It's a distinction that sets me apart. Our species are superior, of course.

A sudden commotion in the water draws my attention. The fish that were swimming in languid movements, now leap into the air with frantic desperation.

Their struggle for survival is a worthless effort for something so short-lived.

I narrow my eyes as I spot the green menace making its way toward me. This one is different, larger and fiercer than the others. It stares at me intensely, revealing its intent to harm and eat me.

These creatures ruled the lake before I arrived, and so they still challenge my dominance, slow to learn.

How could they possibly think of me as an easy meal?

I twitch one of my upper limbs at the thought, the graspers flicking a dismissive gesture, mocking the very idea that these creatures could overpower me. A world far harsher than this one shaped who I am.

Still, the predator moves with lethal purpose, its sharp teeth gleaming under the water. I can see its muscular form rippling as it swims, each movement precise and deadly. Its predatory eyes are fixed on the tentacles trailing behind me.

"You will lose," I taunt, graspers flashing insults at it.

With a flick of my tentacle, I ward off one of the approaching creatures I have named Many Teeth because of their rows of sharp fangs.

This one certainly leaves quite an impression. The beast hesitates, tries to bite me again, eyes narrowing as it assesses me. I relish its uncertainty. It knows, despite its menacing appearance, it stands no chance against me.

Even if it finds another of its kind to attack me together.

"Go on, swim away," I mock, watching as it leaves me alone.

It knows better than to challenge me again. I am the sole threat of worth here, and these waters are now my domain.

So, here I am, stranded in this place, a lone predator adrift in a sea-less stretch of unfamiliarity. Even in this strange and hostile environment, the instincts of my people remain unchanged.

Survival is all that matters, and I will do whatever it takes to ensure that I emerge victorious in this deadly game.

Memories of their attack grip me, its hold tightening like a shenrase's jaws. Anger surges in a fizzling that demands release. I punch the water with all my strength with my most powerful tentacles, sending shockwaves rippling across the lake's surface.

The warm liquid splashes against my skin, but it does nothing to soothe the rage churning inside me. I pull back up their musty scent, their slick gray skin and those limbs that would make them helpless in the water, though everything else about them suggested they should have been aquatic, just like me.

To be captured by such a weak species...

I remember the voices, the rough treatment, the feeling of utter helplessness.

It defied the laws of my nature as a creature.

I hate fresh water. All it does is twist my memories, pulling them in an endless tide. I get out.

I writhe along the edge of the lake, my tentacles dragging lazily behind me. On one side, the dense forest encroaches upon the water's edge. On the other, jagged rocks hold back the water and mark the domain of the land-dwelling creatures.

Droplets of water cascade from my body and splatter onto the murky, dry plants that line the shore. The sight before me differs from the barren landscape on the other side.

Here, vibrant green plants sway in the gentle breeze, punctuated by bursts of color from others that dot the terrain. Small creatures flit through the air, their delicate wings make fluttering sounds.

Nothing like the movements and sounds underwater. Foreign and wrong.

It's just another patch of land I never wanted to visit, indifferent to my presence.

What's the point of it all if you can't eat it?

I continue my trek along the water's edge, my thoughts blank. The world around me holds no temptation, no significance to survival. It's just another obstacle.

As I move farther away from the water, the sounds of the forest fade into the background, replaced by the hum of small crunchy things that don't taste good and the occasional chirp of a flying creature.

I pay them no mind, my senses attuned only to the hunt.

A sudden thunderous crash shatters the peace of the scene, jolting me out of my stalking. My gaze snaps toward the source of the disturbance, my tentacles instinctively tensing in readiness.

It is far away, but I can still make out enough details. Rocks fly and a puff of dust rises.

I cock my head at the intensity, my curiosity piqued by the chaos unfolding before me. Shards of something glint in the sunlight as they scatter through the air, propelled by the force of the impact.

My eyes widen as I catch sight of a small figure tumbling out of the wreckage, their form obscured by the billowing dust and debris.

"The sky sent me my enemy," I breathe out.

A potential source of sustenance lies before me, hopefully devoid of the ever-present taste of mud.

Without hesitation, I abandon my path toward the forest and turn my attention to the rocks, drawn by the promise of fresh food. The thought of hot blood fills me with a dark thrill.

As I propel myself through the water, my tentacles undulate with controlled power, lifting me toward my target.

The anticipation courses through my veins, driving me forward with an almost primal urgency. Every instinct in my body screams for me to close the distance, to claim my prize before it slips away.

With each stroke of my tentacles, I draw closer to my quarry, my anticipation building with each passing moment.

As I approach the rocky shore, I can feel the excitement bubbling within me. What awaits me on land? With eager anticipation, I begin to climb the rocks, using my tentacles to propel myself upwards.

Then the scent hits. It wafts into my gills, registering in my brain in a way I've never experienced before.

Normally, scents hold no sway over me, but today is different. This scent stirs something within me, awakening sensations I've never known. It was as if I could truly smell for the first time, and the effect it had on me is... unexpected.

Terrible. The smell is terrible.

"It's disgusting," I growl, my voice tinged with disdain.

I can't comprehend how something so foul could permeate the air around me so completely. It hangs heavy, assaulting my senses. It feels as though some putrid stench has tainted the very essence of the world around me.

I shake my limbs in disbelief, trying to rid myself of the offensive odor that seems to cling to my skin like a suffocating shroud. But no matter how hard I try, I can't escape it.

"It's like... like something rotting," I mutter, my stomach churning at the thought. It even makes me forget about my meal, which has never happened.

My tentacles try to flick off the smell, the putrid odor clinging to the air like a suffocating fog. My gaze darts frantically, searching for the source of this repugnant scent, but it remains elusive, hidden somewhere.

It reminds me of my enemy, the ones who took me, but isn't quite the same.

I lose vital time that would be better spent climbing in my attempt to be rid of it.

Then, from the other side of the stones, I hear it—a tiny grunt, barely audible over the gentle lapping of the waves. My eyes widen in alarm as I realize that I'm not alone. My meal, who fell from the streaking silver shell, is nearby, concealed from view by the rugged terrain.

Ignoring the smell, with a swift and decisive motion, I allow my tentacles to lift me, propelling me upward with effortless grace. Liquid trails behind me, droplets shimmering in the sunlight as I ascend the rocky outcrop.

Each jagged edge of the stone presses against my slick skin. The rough texture of the rocks scrapes against my flesh. It Is a sensation that is both exhilarating and uncomfortable.

I ignore the discomfort, my focus fixed on the mysterious presence that awaits me above.

And then, finally, I reach the top.

With a surge of effort, I pull myself over the edge, my eyes scanning the rocky terrain for any sign of movement. And there, huddled against the base of a weathered boulder, I see it—a figure cloaked in shadow, its features obscured by the dim light of the setting sun.

There is my prey.

Eli

My eyes snap open as I wake up from a nightmare of blood, my mother screaming, gray blobs, and pain.

Except the pain is still here, throbbing through me and stealing my breath. I take several gasping breaths.

"Where the hell am I?" I breathe out, scanning the surroundings. This looks like an even worse nightmare.

The sun's harsh glare stings my eyes, and I squint in pain until they adjust to the sharp light. Trees stretch in a line on one side, while on the other, jagged rocks jut out like shark's teeth.

The sky, a pastel purple instead of blue, shocks me.

My throat burns as if I have swallowed acid. My head throbs with a relentless, concert-like pounding. I gasp, the air scorching my lungs, and force myself to sit up, wincing as pieces of glass dig into my skin.

I grasp a shard of glass in my thigh and yank it out, the sting barely registering as my eyes widen in shock.

Struggling, I push myself off the gritty, brown sand, my legs trembling beneath me. My head feels numb, disconnected from my surroundings, until a glass fragment catches the light, and I see my reflection.

Long, yellow hair flows over my chest. I tear my gaze away from the reflection to confirm it is there, then back to meet my reflection's eyes. They're no longer the light brown I remember; instead, they gleam back at me in a bright shade of yellow, a little darker than the unnerving hue of my new hair.

"What the hell?" The words come out as a whisper.

It's like looking at someone else's body, yet every sensation confirms it's mine.

"Why am I naked?" The question slices through the fog of confusion clouding my mind.

My entire body throbs with a dull ache. Even my nipples are sore, and my legs protest with every movement. There are deep scores across my legs and arms, throbbing in an insistent rhythm.

The trees don't look right, a too-bright sort of green with foliage of an odd texture. The sun doesn't even feel right on my skin, even the sand isn't the right color. I feel vertigo starting and my limbs are shaking.

It's all becoming too much, and I have to imagine my cape of sunshine wrapping around me so I can push through. Keep doing what needs to be done.

I grimace as I struggle to stay standing, feeling the sharp sting of the scrapes on my skin.

Leaving the ground only makes it all worse, since I'm now dizzy, but it does give me a better view. There is some sort of silver contraption, pretty much just the right size to hold a human, mangled on the rocks.

My mind races for a moment.

I'm beat the hell up and woke up right next to something that looks like King Kong picked it up and smashed it in a fit of rage.

I glance up at the sky.

Or it fell. A really long way.

"*Dios*," I mutter, not liking the few options left to quick deduction. Or the alien feeling of my new, yellow hair.

I move painfully over to the silver vehicle, noting the soft red padding inside, then see a touch screen. A tap brings up alien letters my mind seems to think I can read, but a moment later they disappear, and I'm left wondering if I just hallucinated.

A quick touch to my head reveals a bump, so it is quite possible.

No, I'm not. There is a lever that my mind says is marked as an emergency exit, but the letters are in the same alien language.

I try tapping on the screen again, hoping to glean some helpful information, but it's dead now. Or it never worked to begin with. A groan of frustration mixed with pain vibrates up from my stomach, which only makes my head hurt worse.

I strain to recall how I ended up here, but the memories slip through my fingers like sand. All I can grasp onto is the image of the officer's taunting face, a memory I push away with a pang of anguish.

I was supposed to be in jail, but somehow, I was kidnapped?

"I need clothes," I mutter, my breath forming a thin fog in the chilly air.

Almost instantly, a black material expands from the thin belt around my waist, wrapping around me. The sudden change startles me, and I yelp, stumbling as the fabric adjusts to my body.

"*¡Madre mía!*"

I reach out a trembling hand, expecting another hallucination, but I feel a smooth, vaguely latex-like material under my hand.

Driven by curiosity, I command my clothing to dissolve and it leaves me exposed once more to the strange reality I find myself in. A yellow triangle marks the juncture of my thighs, a symbol of the inexplicable changes that have overtaken me.

Surveying my altered form, I can't help but notice the differences that extend beyond my canary yellow hair.

My breasts have swelled beyond my already generous C cup, which is just great. More back problems in my future. My hips have further widened from their already curvy shape, but it's the strange tightness in my belly that disturbs me the most.

It feels artificial, as if it doesn't belong to me. I liked the womanly swell of it before, which was hard earned after years of rough living.

"What exactly happened?" I mumble to myself, my fingers pressing into my throbbing temples. "*Dios*, don't tell me I'm the only one here."

I ignore the tinge of guilt that comes with hoping someone else is sharing this screwed up situation.

But still. I can't go that long without talking to people. The compulsion to speak as a way to center my racing mind and anxieties is already growing.

Taking over clear thought and reasoning.

I pull my arms close and imagine they are coated in sunshine so I can think it all through. My body is different, the environment is all wrong. I don't recognize any of the plants or bugs I've seen so far, and it's a hobby of mine to memorize them.

"Toto, we're not in Arizona anymore."

I can't quite say it yet, but I'm starting to wonder if I'm even on Earth anymore.

My movements are cautious, each step deliberate as I walk through the uneven terrain. Suddenly, something catches my eye.

The sun's rays reflect off a glint beyond the jagged rocks, and I realize it's a lake.

Trees tower overhead, their gnarled branches reaching out like skeletal fingers against the ominous rocky formations. Sharp brown rocks protrude from the ground, their surfaces mottled with patches of green, purple, and yellow lichen.

I swallow hard, the dryness in my throat becoming unbearable. "I'll have to find water."

No way is that lake water safe to drink.

As I press forward, the long shadows cast by the trees and rocks stretch across the dusty planet. With the failing sunlight, an eerie chill hangs in the air, causing me to shiver.

I cast a wary glance around me, my heart hammering in my chest. The dense purple and green foliage behind the rocks obscures my view, heightening my sense of claustrophobia.

Every nerve in my body is on edge. Yet, despite the unease, there's no sign of any presence other than my own. Alone in this strange wilderness, it seems.

Even as I think it, I can't ignore the sense that something lurks just beyond my line of sight. The rustle of leaves and the faint whisper of wind through the trees only serve to amplify my unease.

Memories of childhood adventures flicker through my mind. I remember getting lost in the woods as a child, only to be rescued by my *padre* within minutes. A faint smile tugs at the corners of my lips as I reminisce about the warmth of those moments spent with him.

But the smile fades as quickly as it came, replaced by a surge of longing and sorrow. If only he hadn't left the world. I wonder how different my life would be.

Tears prick at my eyes, threatening to spill over, but I quickly shake my head, banishing the unwelcome emotions.

"This is not the time, Eli," I murmur to myself, steeling my resolve.

With a deep breath, I close my eyes and center myself, preparing to face whatever lies ahead. When I open them again, I take in my surroundings one last time.

Behind me, the forest looms like a dark, foreboding presence.

To my right and left, the trees are lighter in color, reaching up to thirty or forty feet in height. Ahead of me, the landscape shifts abruptly to a jumble of rocks, each one a different shade of brown, illuminated by the kaleidoscopic patterns created by the sun's reflection on scattered shards from the silver vehicle.

"*Hijo de puta.*"

I've hardly ever been able to use the few Spanish phrases I learned from listening to my *padre* since I didn't know which contexts are socially acceptable. Doesn't seem like it matters right now. It sure felt like an excellent time to use one of his favorites.

"Yep. Son of a bitch."

I move along the rocks, careful to not fall against their sharp edges, nervous that they block my view. A sudden gust of wind whips through the air, enveloping me in a cloud of dust.

Blind and disoriented, I struggle to regain my bearings.

When the dust settles, I find myself face to face with a creature perched atop a rock, its gaze locking with mine.

It has six green tentacles. Its torso is sleeker than a human's, with two arm-like structures extending from its shoulders.

It has one finger and a thumb on each hand, with a webbed structure in between. Fin-like structures rise from where an elbow would be, but it doesn't look like it has bones.

Its body is like that of a streamlined human male, but with shark-like skin that looks smooth and shiny. Its face is broader than a human's, with a wide mouth filled with sharp teeth like a dolphin's.

It doesn't have much in the way of lips surrounding that row of jagged teeth.

Its eyes are black, cold, and predatory, reminding me of a shark's gaze. There's no hair on its head, just smooth skin stretched tight over its skull.

"*Los cojones!* What the fu—"

Fear grips me, paralyzing my limbs. One of the tentacles flick toward me.

I flinch, losing my balance and turning my ankle on a rock. The world spins, and the ground rushes up to meet me.

Wroahk

My tentacles are poised to scoop up the creature before me. But before I can reach out, the bright yellow eyes meet mine, wide with terror.

Something makes me pause as it takes in my form with frantic, darting eyes. Then it slips from the rocks, tumbling to the ground below with a dull thud.

I study the fallen form.

Her bright yellow weeds cascade around her, a stark contrast against the muted tones of the rocky terrain. As I study her, I notice the small, delicate frame of her body, far more curved than the females of my species.

The creature is a female and injured, red blood trickling in tantalizing rivulets on her brown skin.

Another whiff of air drifts my way, carrying with it the unmistakable scent that invaded my senses earlier. I recoil, realizing with a start that it emanates from her.

From the smell of her, I can tell her flesh would be vile.

She is best for the Many Teeth.

I descend the rock so I can grab her. As I scoop her up onto my tentacles, I can't help but notice how small and fragile she seems in my grasp. Her body is delicate, almost childlike compared to the robust forms of my species.

Even our young ones are larger and more formidable than her. It's almost laughable how easily I could crush her with a mere flick of one long, twisting limb.

I lift a long tentacle to do just that, excited to see her spill more of that red blood, even if it will probably make the air even more foul. My limb quivers in anticipation as I try to bring it down to strike her.

I just... can't.

Instead, I climb back up the face of the rock with her and back down the other side toward the lakeshore. Her body is limp as I hold her above the rock, the vast expanse of the lake spreading out in my periphery.

I thought the sky had sent me something extraordinary, but all they sent was a dainty meal.

And a nasty one at that.

She's not even the enemy I have sworn to kill. Useless.

I sigh, extending my tentacles to drop her into the lake below. The sunset is already on its way, casting an orange glow over the water. Just as I'm about to release her, she moans.

Her eyes flutter, then open wide and bewildered as she takes in her surroundings before she focuses on me. Those same disgusting eyes I saw earlier. They make my skin twitch with the desire to have her away from me.

She lets out a string of words I don't understand, along with sounds I would guess are pain, as she tries to escape me.

"You make no sense," I tell her, not even sure why I'm bothering speaking to Many Teeth's food.

She gasps, a grasper darting to her throat, no longer trying, and failing, to push off my suctioned grip, "*Madre mía*, being alone was way better," she says, using the clicks and calls of my own people.

How?

A surge of rage follows her exclamation, since it is said in the stolen voice of my people. I gather myself to crush her in retaliation, but once again, my body betrays me, shifting to hold her more delicately instead of crushing her against the rocks until she never moves again.

It's then that I notice the yellow weeds coming from her head again, and a wave of disgust washes over me, though I tell myself that's all it is.

I become stiff, hesitating for a moment longer than I should.

Her eyes, so vivid and terrified, hold me captive. For a single thrumming of my blood, I find myself unable to follow through with any plan, beyond holding her.

What am I doing? She's unworthy of my hesitation. Yet, something in her gaze stops me.

I tighten my grip, trying to shake off the unease creeping into my mind.

Instead of dropping her, I lower her onto the lake shore. Her eyes never leave mine, a mix of fear and something else flickering within them. Once she realizes I'm not going to crush her, she sits up straight, her graspers moving over her oddly sharp, rigid limbs.

There's a look on her face I can't quite understand, but it gnaws at me.

Maybe she is just dirty, and that is why she smells so terrible. Maybe I will keep her to myself and prepare her, so one day, I can crack her bones and eat her with satisfaction.

The idea feels right, a way to reclaim my control over the situation. I'll keep her, fatten her up, and when the time is right, she'll be a meal worth savoring.

My graspers twitch at the thought as I watch her drag herself to the edge of the lake. It's clear she can't move correctly; the fall must have injured her. Vile red blood seeps through her tight covering.

She cups her graspers, which have far too many digits, and dips them into the water, drinking frantically as if she hasn't had anything to relieve her in a moon's passing.

Each gulp is desperate. Her eyes are darting around, scanning her surroundings for any signs of danger.

How has she not dried out?

I survey her. She's small. Harmless.

The worst thing anything could ever be, but there's something intriguing about her desperation. Her bright yellow weeds fall over her face, sticking to her skin as she drinks.

Distressed. Maybe that's why I am drawn to her.

I always did like the despair prey get in their eyes right before the kill.

Once she's had her fill, she wipes her mouth with the back of her grasper and looks directly into my eyes.

I notice something that makes me pause. There's something about her eyes I finally recognize. Something I wouldn't expect in prey that knows it is beaten and is simply waiting for their death.

The female is angry.

Eli

I'm relieved as the hideous creature finally drops me on the shore of the lake. Screams still want to bubble up out of me, but at the same time I'm numb.

And aroused, somehow, at the same time.

Something is definitely wrong with me.

The water glistens invitingly, and without thinking, I try to stand up and walk toward it. A sharp pain shoots through my right ankle, making me wince. The injury must have happened during the fall.

I sigh and drag my body across the mushy grass toward the water's edge. My throat is burning, parched beyond anything I've felt before.

I need relief.

Even though I don't know if this water is safe to drink, I have to take the risk. It's so clear, like a pristine mirror reflecting the lavender sky above. I can see fish swimming in it, some even resembling those found on Earth.

The creature watches me with predatory eyes, but I can't worry about that now. I cup my hands and scoop up the water, drinking it like my life depends on it. The cool liquid soothes my throat, and I can't help but gulp down more.

I feel the water slide down, bringing a wave of peace.

I look up at the freak with murder in my eyes afterward, but it just cocks its head, studying me. I don't even know how to process the fact that some sort of octopus-shark-dolphin-man just talked to me.

With water in my body, I go back to what I should have been doing right away and keep crawling down the shore, desperate to get away from the freak. I've seen that sort of violence in someone's eyes before and you should never stick around.

It quickly becomes obvious that it's hopeless as he easily keeps pace with me. After a few more sharp rocks bruise my knees, I give in and shift onto my butt, feeling numb again.

My mind doesn't want to deal, and I look back at the water.

"*Dios*, I took water for granted," I breathe out, staring at my reflection in the clear lake.

This new version of me doesn't disgust me quite as much as it did the first time I saw it. I have accepted that this is no dream.

This is reality. A cruel, unyielding reality.

I might as well take it all in, though I'm not quite ready to embrace it.

The lake stretches endlessly, blending into the horizon. Dense forests encircle it on three sides, their dark silhouettes reflecting in the purple-tinged water. Plants and insects of a dizzying array of colors catch the fading light in a luminous glow.

On the fourth side, jagged stones jut out, and perched precariously on one of them is the ship I assume I came here in, hanging as if only a strong wind is between it and a fall.

My eyes trace the path from the crash site to the creature.

Its tentacles spread out like the villain in that Spider-Man movie, Doctor Octopus—green and filthy. His dolphin-like blue body looks soft to touch, not that I ever want to feel his skin again.

A memory of the way his tentacles writhed over me like slick snakes intrudes and I shiver. I bet my skin still has circular patterns from where he was suctioned to me.

Gross.

Then our eyes lock.

Those shark-like eyes pierce through me, and arousal surges in me, quickly followed by anger. I'm pretty certain he was hunting me. Everything about him screams that he plans to kill me. That he's toying with me and enjoying my pain.

He's a monster. I shiver and gulp.

Why not just do it, then?

I drag myself farther away from the water, still feeling the sting of my injured ankle. My throat feels better, but the rage bubbling inside me overshadows any relief. I glance back at the lake, then at the creature.

Its tentacles twitch as if waiting for my next move, ready to keep following me if I try to escape again.

I can't get away, after all that I've done to keep fleeing in my life, and now I'm trapped. There's cracks starting inside, breaking my usual control, but I can't seem to pull up my sunshine to help me disassociate.

"You were going to throw me in there," I spit out, my words dripping with venom, even though I doubt he understands English.

"It's because of you I have this injury," I point angrily at my leg, the pain pulsing with each beat of my heart.

His expression remains impassive, devoid of any flicker of emotion.

I suppose taunting him isn't the best idea, though can it really get worse than something planning to kill me?

Then he speaks, his voice reminding me of whale song. "You stink."

I can understand him. But why?

Thinking back, I realize I was making the same whale squawks instead of English, and I realize it really can, in fact, get worse.

"Better than ugly," I hiss out at him.

He blinks at me. Slow and with menace. "A voice stealer."

The threat in his voice is clear.

I scramble to get myself away, my eyes scanning the ground until I find a sturdy tree branch.

I grab it, using it as support.

The pain in my ankle flares up, but I grit my teeth and push through it. I tried to flee, and know confronting him is foolish, but I can't live in fear.

I've been through worse.

I think back to when I left my stepfather's house—another bastard who thought he could control me. He thought I would stay in fear, just like my mother.

Then I picture the blood blooming on his chest and wait for horror to follow, but it doesn't. He had it coming.

I open my mouth to tell him to go away, hoping that it will make him stop following me, but no sound comes out.

Despite my bravado, a surge of anxiety flows through me at the thought of challenging someone. That never ends well, and here I am mouthing off to something that looks like it was made to kill.

Revels in it, even.

Stop being stupid, Eli, I chide myself.

I watch, wide-eyed, as the creature's thin lips move, forming each syllable of whale song with chilling precision. "You can't keep my words, my voice," his tone is low, but there's violence in his words.

Tentacles start to move against him, as if they are trying to dislodge something, and the sight makes me gag. Then one of his arms with its weird pinchers start scratching at his skin.

"I will kill you. Some day." His tone is calm, but beneath the surface, I can sense the simmering anger.

My mind stutters to a stop for a long moment.

His gaze roams over me.

Then he turns away, a clear dismissal as he turns toward the water. He dives into it, launching himself with his powerful tentacles, his movements fluid.

Every movement screaming predator.

I assume the itchiness of his blue skin drove him to seek relief in the water. His head pops up soon after, two of his long green tentacles lifting toward me in an unsettling way.

Instinctively, I take a step back, dragging my injured leg along with a stick for support, as he swims nearer to the shore, his alarming presence looming closer with each stroke.

"I will crack open your skull and feast, but not today."

His words hit me like a physical blow as he revels in my reaction, his satisfaction evident in his expression.

"Fear. That is good," he comments.

Of course I'm scared.

Which isn't helped in the least bit when he disappears into the water. There's no way I'll even see him coming.

I put two bullets in the chest of my greatest fear and have no regrets, but is this my punishment? To have him replaced? With something worse?

My leg is screaming at me, and my limbs are shaking too hard with memories of terror to hold me upright anymore. I already tried to get away, and I should try again, but everything hurts.

Instead, I sit down, the movement jarring a moan, then painfully pull my legs to my chest and make my body as small as possible.

Flashes of memories. Broken bones. Screams of rage. Accusations of doing things wrong just because I knew it would make him angry. Him hitting my mother because she couldn't make me perfect.

It was always our fault. Each wound earned, whether physical or verbal.

He was wrong. I know this logically, but it doesn't change the association. The pounding fear and the tight chest.

I did nothing to earn such violence in my old life. What could I have possibly done now?

Mere existence?

No. A line needs to be drawn at some point. I'm sick of feeling scared. It might be the hardest thing I have ever done, but this terrible, violent creature won't continue to make me feel small.

He's either going to kill me and eat me, or he isn't. Nothing I say or do is going to change it.

If there were an award for the rudest, scariest person in the world, he'd win it. Hands down, but that doesn't mean he gets to win by making me cower.

For the first time, I might actually believe those words I've been telling myself since I was thirteen years old.

People are only as scary as you let them be. You can't control them, only the way you respond.

Is it fatalism? No clue. I just know that suddenly I feel a lot better than I have in a very long time.

8

Eli

I don't get to think about it or analyze this new feeling before he's back again. Looking just as pissed off, and just as deadly.

Fear tries to bubble up. From my experience, I know it's mere moments away from boiling over.

Then I think back to him ordering me to not steal his voice. In other words, don't talk.

Hijo de puta, no way.

Despite the knot of fear tightening in my stomach, I refuse to let his threats intimidate me. I've had enough of that for a lifetime. I spent most of my life trying to avoid conflict.

Look where that got me.

My subconscious screams at me to back down, to avoid provoking him any further, but I need to embrace this change in the little bit of time I have left to live or I've truly let every bastard in my life win.

My voice rises as I challenge him. "I've had enough of people like you. If you plan to kill me, then just do it."

I watch his reaction keenly, my heart pounding in my chest. He's massive. He's made his intentions really freaking clear. He starts rising from the water, his tentacles making him tower above me before he's even on shore. His alien face twisted in rage.

I'm going to die.

Suddenly I can't take it.

I fled an abuser, lived on the street, pulled my life back together a little more each year... for what? Just to be on this *maldito*... terrible planet? With this monster?

Something in me snaps.

Irritation bubbles up inside me, mingling with the fear that threatens to consume me, and in a moment of defense, I do something I know I'll soon regret.

"*Uy, qué care-chimba*," I mutter, then yell it in English to help fortify me further. "You dickhead!"

I rise shakily, my whole body protesting, though not as loudly as before.

I grab a handful of pebbles from the ground, my fingers trembling with adrenaline as I take aim at his dickhead face.

Each stone punctuates my frustration and anger as it pelts off his smooth skin.

With a growl that makes my stomach turn upside down, he reacts like an enraged beast. The dangerous sound echoes through the air and I wonder if it is just me and him on this island.

It's a primal sound, one that triggers a surge of fear within me, reminding me of my vulnerability in the face of this powerful creature.

Indeed, I am weak, but as they say, fake it till you make it.

"*Hijo de puta*," I curse again in Spanish.

I wish he knew I was calling him a dickhead son of a bitch.

Finally, one of my pebbles strikes him squarely in the eye, which he barely closes in time. A small victory in the face of overwhelming odds.

It only serves to stoke the flames of his fury and the part of my mind that usually helps me avoid really stupid actions starts to reassert itself.

His growl intensifies, reverberating through the air like the roar of a hurricane, all howling wind and destruction. I find myself frozen in place, my heart pounding in my chest as I await his next move.

"Stop," he bellows as he makes his way toward me.

I can't back down now. Everything my *padre* taught me about bullies, which I abandoned in all those years of trying to stay small to avoid being hurt, comes rushing back.

Never let them see your weakness. They are all cowards inside.

I can see the intensity in my *padre's* black eyes as I remember, and it fills me with confidence.

Or more stupidity, but I go with it.

"You think you can scare me?" I retort, my voice trembling with adrenaline. "You think you can just threaten me and expect me to give in to fear? I'm not some helpless victim you can push around!"

I have definitely lost my freaking mind.

Of course he can push me around. He has a million limbs, and they all look like they could snap me in half.

None of that shows as I take a big breath, then scream back my own inarticulate hurricane cry. Sounds a human should never be able to make, and they somehow make me feel bigger than I am. Stronger.

If he kills me, at least it will be on my own terms. I've allowed myself to be far too small for far too long.

It got me nowhere but arrested one moment and here the next.

My mind pulls up an image of my stepfather on the stretcher and I wait for the horror to rise, or to wonder if he's still alive, but there are no regrets. My only regret is how long it took me, and that he might not be dead.

It was easier than I thought and maybe I need to stop underestimating myself.

Yes. I'm done.

He stops as I run out of breath and the whale hurricane sound ends in a whistling wind, his eyes narrowing as he regards me.

He makes a dark, grating sound, and it sends shivers spidering down my spine.

"A fierce challenge," he admits, his gaze never leaving mine. "You lack the strength to do it."

Diablos. What did I just say I would do?

Doesn't matter.

I square my shoulders, refusing to show any sign of weakness, though I'm burning with curiosity to know what I just said to him. It didn't feel like words.

"I would do even worse," I challenge, my voice steady despite the tremor in my hands.

He makes the grating sound again. Laughter? "If you expect fear, you will be disappointed."

With a sudden burst of movement, he lunges forward, his tentacles whipping through the air with terrifying speed.

He didn't even need to leave the water.

Shit.

I stumble backward, narrowly avoiding his grasp, my heart pounding in my chest as I try to keep my footing on the uneven ground.

Before I can even process what's happening, I'm drenched, a force pushing me to the ground as if a floodgate opened. It knocks me to the ground, more bruises added as I hit jutting rocks.

The water envelops me, soaking me to the bone, leaving me dripping and disoriented. Is this some sort of childish game of pool splashing on freaking steroids?

Better to use his tentacles that way than to crush me, I suppose. But it doesn't help make me any warmer.

"Useless shitty clothes," I mutter, imagining burning them in my rage.

And then, as if to make matters worse, I feel his eyes on me, his gaze burning into my skin as if he would really eat it alive.

I glance up to see him emerging from the water, his massive form towering over me like some ancient sea monster. His eyes are wide with surprise, his expression unreadable as he takes in the sight before him.

And then, to my horror, I realize why he's staring at me so intently.

"Shit! Shit! Shit!" I curse, my heart racing as I realize I'm now completely exposed.

There are no clothes on my body.

It reveals every contour in stark detail. I can feel his eyes lingering on me, tracing the lines of my curves with a hunger that makes my skin crawl.

And then, as if by some cruel twist of fate, I feel a flush of heat spreading across my cheeks as his gaze lingers on the most intimate parts of me. An answering heat between my legs follows, just as persistent as the first moment I saw him.

What the hell? Nothing about him is the least bit attractive. Nothing.

I want to scream, to cover myself up and hide from his penetrating gaze. My mind is blank. I can't move, can't tear my eyes away from him as he stands there, a silent predator watching his prey with lust.

He could do whatever he wanted to me, and there's nothing I can do to stop him. And I'm aroused?

I don't know how.

I don't know why.

To my surprise, instead of advancing toward me, he remains where he is. And then, without a word, he turns and moves back into the water, disappearing beneath the surface with a sense of finality that leaves me feeling strangely hollow.

I lay there for a moment, my heart pounding in my chest as I try to make sense of what just happened.

My hands are shaking as I get myself upright again and look around for something to defend myself. Anything.

A sharp rock catches my eye and I grab it, holding it tight to my chest, surprised when my suit shifts and I look down to see a new pocket for it.

I let out a snort, then imagine it in a better location for my makeshift knife.

Have I escaped unscathed, or was this just the calm before the storm? Only time will tell, but one thing is certain—I'm in far deeper trouble than I ever imagined.

9

Wroahk

What just happened?

I sit on the edge of the lake, my mind swirling with frustration, and I can't shake the feeling of unease that's settled over me because of an encounter with a harmless creature. I heave, bile at the back of my throat, as I remember my attraction. My fascination.

She is food.

I take a deep breath, trying to calm the storm of thoughts raging in my mind. As I glance toward the other side of the shore where I left her, I notice that dusk has begun to settle in, painting the sky with streaks of orange and pink. The stars twinkle overhead, casting their soft glow upon the land.

"What did she do to me?"

The air is filled with the hum of not-food, their chirps and buzzes creating a cacophony of sound.

I watch as she sits on the edge of the lake on a stone, one lower limb dangling off a rock and the other pulled up close to her.

She has a yellow hunk of the long weeds from her head in her graspers, separated from her body now. I'm puzzled for a moment, then I realize she's using it to wrap her injured limb.

Even though she's within my gaze, mere moments away, I know she can't see me. I've hidden myself behind a prickly dry plant, keeping a safe distance between us.

It's ridiculous.

Here I am, the predator who rules this place, reduced to hiding like a coward, but I had no choice.

I had to distance myself from her before I did something I would regret. Like touch her, and not as a precursor to violence. Why would I want to do that?

Twice now, I've been on the verge of killing her, yet something held me back. I don't even have words to describe the feelings in my chest. There's a nagging sensation in the pit of my stomach that tells me I made the right choice, but everything else in me is screaming at how wrong it is.

I close my eyes and try to push away the memories of her exposed body, the way her light brown curves glistened in the sunset. It's infuriating how she's managed to intrude on my thoughts.

But why? Why does she affect me at all?

I've encountered countless creatures in my lifetime, but none have ever stirred anything within me, aside from brief, violent encounters during mating season.

Everything else is food.

With a frustrated growl, I push myself up and move along the edge of the lake. I need to clear my gills. Distance myself from her disgusting presence.

She is like a haunting cry, rippling through the water and resounding over and over in my head.

What am I doing? I'm allowing myself to be consumed by thoughts of her when I should be the one killing her.

With a determined scowl, I force myself to focus on the present. There are other matters to attend to, other creatures to hunt and conquer. I can't afford to be distracted by her any longer.

Still, I can't tear my eyes away from her as I watch not-food lighting up around her, casting a warm, golden glow upon her face. The flickering light illuminates her features, highlighting the curve of her cheeks and the softness of her lips.

"Her teeth," I mutter to myself, my voice barely a whisper, but still echoing my disdain. "So polished, so blunt."

As I continue to watch her, a fresh wave of disgust washes over me, mingling with this terrible inability to look away. I can't believe I'm even entertaining such thoughts about her.

She's just an insignificant creature, unworthy of my attention.

Despite my best efforts to push the feelings aside, they linger, refusing to be ignored.

It's infuriating, maddening even, to find myself drawn to her in this way. I've had my fair share of females from my species who came to me, but I never clung to them with my mind like her.

I never thought about them—any more than they did me—after we quenched the mating fever.

And yet here I am, unable to tear my gaze away from this pathetic creature, feeling a strange tug in the pit of my stomach that I can't quite explain.

Something finally clicks inside me.

As I watch her playing with the insects, a realization dawns on me. It is simply the usual need for entertainment. I enjoy it when my prey challenges me. When they put up a fight.

It triggers a chemical rush that heightens my satisfaction when I finally consume them. Perhaps that's why I'm feeling this strange pull.

Here in this strange place, I've encountered nothing that's put up a real challenge. They've all been easy prey, too stupid to offer any real resistance. She's different. There's something about her that ignites a spark of excitement within me.

My eyes are fixed on her. The golden glow of her hair merging with the flickering light.

"The satisfaction will be worth it."

I ignore the fact that it isn't my stomach that stirs in anticipation, but my two mating tentacles.

With a deep breath, I sink into the water, feeling the familiar warmth envelop me. The water takes on a deep blue hue, then gives way to the welcome darkness below.

If only I could make myself descend into it.

I watch her silhouette on the other side of the shore, her movements graceful and unaware of the danger lurking beneath the surface. I will let her settle and then I'll strike.

My graspers flick in anticipation, but then I see movement in the water.

A silhouette of Many Teeth emerges, floating toward the edge where she sits, moving itself along with small movements of its long tail so it doesn't betray its presence. It is night, so it isn't moving as confidently, though I can still see it clearly.

That's why most hunting happens in the dark.

The female is oblivious to the danger. Too weak, and obviously too ignorant, to survive, this loathsome, soft thing.

The Many Teeth must have tasted her blood when she was washing in the water. My eyes narrow as I watch it move closer, its sleek yet heavy body gliding through the water slowly.

Yes, I want her for my meal, but I want to see how she will fight a Many Teeth.

This will also give me a sense of the capabilities she has, if any. I feel a thrill of excitement at the prospect tingle along my many limbs. The anticipation of watching her struggle against one of the deadliest creatures in the lake is making me bounce in the water as my tentacles whirl.

With a twitch of my limbs, I follow the Many Teeth.

I keep a safe distance between me and the creature to ensure it won't notice my presence. I swim silently, my movements fluid and practiced, staying just out of its detection range.

The water is murky, the only illumination coming from the faint glow of the bugs on the shore.

As the Many Teeth swims closer, I stay behind, watching intently. We are already near the branch that she is dipping in now. At the water's edge for no clear reason I can discern.

Her silhouette is framed against the glow of the not-food. The Many Teeth's rows of razor-sharp teeth glint faintly in the dim light, a silent promise of death.

The Many Teeth slows further. Just below the surface where it can't be seen. She's crouched near the water's edge on a stone, her grasper dipping into the water to continue rubbing at her skin.

The creature is just beneath the surface, its eyes locked onto her as it prepares to strike.

Will she notice in time?

Will she be able to fight it off?

Knowing that I will witness her struggle, her desperation, brings a fresh thrill.

The Many Teeth is almost upon her now, its body coiling and uncoiling in the water. I can see its muscles tensing, preparing for the final lunge. My eyes flick between her and the creature, my own breath coming in shallow flutters of my gills.

This is it.

As the Many Teeth is about to lunge, I can't help but wriggle my graspers in impatience. They still when I see her moving away from the edge toward a tree near the forest's entrance.

Disappointment makes my limbs hang loose in the water, but she may return.

The Many Teeth waits for her on the edge and so do I.

10

Eli

There is nothing worse than asking for peace all your life, but when you finally have it, you just do not like it. Right now, I feel the surroundings creeping on me as the sun dips below the horizon. Darkness starts taking over, and the stars twinkle brightly above me.

I place another large leaf from the trees in a pile. They are more like prickly feathers than any leaves I'm used to, but I had to make do.

The only good thing right now is the sweet little fireflies helping me see. They are far larger than ones on Earth and keep glowing and dancing around me as if I'm fascinating to them.

Maybe I am.

There's sticky sap on my hands and I return to the softly lapping water to clean it off.

An eerie chill runs down my spine as I put my hand in the ice-cold water, but what catches me off guard is a pool of bubbles just a few inches away from my hand on the sleek lake surface. I quickly retract my hand, abandoning plans to wash and move toward the tree near the forest entrance.

He's probably watching again, but it's best to stay away from the water until daylight either way.

Using another tree branch as a cane, I look around, my eyes scanning the area for anything that might help. That's when I spot a tree with foliage similar to a coconut tree right at the edge of the lake. The broad leaves look like they could cover my body and provide some warmth.

I approach the tree, limping little by little, though I could swear my movement is improving. Maybe something was out of alignment and it shifted back.

"Let's hope this works," I mutter to myself, reaching up to grab a large leaf. It's surprisingly tough, and I have to put all my weight into pulling it down.

The leaf finally gives way, but to my dismay, I lose my balance and tumble backwards. I fall into the lake with a splash, the cold water instantly soaking through my clothes.

Luckily, the lake is shallow at the edge, and I don't go under. I scramble to my feet, shaking off the shock. As I push my wet hair out of my eyes, something catches my attention—a glint of light on the water's surface.

Squinting, I see what looks like a turtle shell shimmering under the moonlight.

It looks unlike any shell I've ever seen—larger, with a strange iridescence. I'm mesmerized by the sight for a brief moment, but then remember I'm not on Earth and start to scramble away.

Suddenly, a ripple disturbs the stillness of the water. My heart skips a beat. I freeze, every instinct screaming at me to run away, but it's too late.

The water erupts in a violent splash. The turtle-like creature bursts forth, its maw opening to reveal rows of sharp, gleaming teeth.

"Shit!" I gasp, stumbling backward.

The creature lunges at me, and I barely dodge to the side, my adrenaline surging. I turn and bolt toward the shore, my mind racing. The water slows me down, my injured ankle screaming in protest.

I can hear the creature thrashing behind me, its movements sending waves crashing around me.

I reach the shore after only a moment, my breath coming in ragged gasps. Just as I think I'm safe, a searing pain shoots through my scalp. I scream, realizing the creature has caught my hair in its jaws.

Panic surges through me as it pulls me back toward the water.

"No!" I scream out, clawing at the ground with my free hand.

I throw a hand behind me, hitting whatever I can reach with my fist, trying to dislodge the creature. It hisses, the sound like steam escaping from a pressure valve, and tightens its grip.

Desperation fuels my struggle.

I twist and turn, trying to free myself. My mind races, searching for a solution. I remember the makeshift knife I fashioned from a sharp stone earlier. With my free hand, I reach into the pocket that formed as soon as I thought of one and pull it out, my fingers trembling.

"Get off me!" I scream, stabbing at the creature's snout.

The blade connects, and the creature releases a guttural roar, jerking away from me. Its grip loosens, and I yank my hair free, stumbling backwards and falling onto the shore.

"*Diablos*," I yelp.

As the turtle-like creature lunges at me again, it leaves the water, its entire body surging onto the shore.

In the moonlight, I realize my mistake. This is no turtle.

It's an alien alligator, and a massive one at that. I fling my body to the side and its jaws snap shut with a bone-chilling clack, missing my face by mere inches. I feel the wind from its bite, the raw power behind those jaws terrifying.

The creature's eyes gleam with hunger as it lands, its huge tail slapping the water, causing a violent splash that drenches me further.

I crab walk backward, panic clawing at my throat. It's preparing for another attack, its body coiled like a spring, ready to unleash its force.

Before I can even think to move, the alligator lunges at me with even greater force.

"No. no..." I huff.

My heart pounds in my chest, and my legs feel like they're made of lead. The monstrous predator is almost upon me, its jaws wide open.

I close my eyes tightly, preparing for my fate, but it never comes.

I open my eyes. It's being held by a tentacle.

Six more, strong and sinewy, shoot out of the water and wrap around the alligator, halting its attack. The creature thrashes violently, water churning into a frothy chaos around it.

I'm frozen in place, wide-eyed and unable to comprehend what I'm seeing.

It's him.

The creature who left me earlier, the one who threatened to crack open my skull and feast on my brain like some sort of zombie kraken.

He's holding the alligator back, his tentacles constricting around the predator's body, keeping it from reaching me. I watch, gobsmacked, as the scene unfolds before me.

"*Dios*."

The alligator lets out a guttural roar, its powerful tail whipping through the water, sending waves crashing against the shore. The tentacles flex, tightening their grip, and the two titans begin their epic struggle.

The alligator twists and turns, trying to free itself from the killer's grasp. Its jaws snap viciously, trying to bite down on the tentacles holding it. The octo-man lets out a low growl, his upper body half-submerged in the water, using his strength to keep the alligator contained.

It's a savage battle, the kind you only see in nature documentaries or horror movies.

The alligator manages to get its teeth into one of the tentacles, tearing into the flesh with a sickening squish. The octo-man roars in pain, his grip faltering for a moment. But he quickly recovers, using another tentacle to deliver a powerful blow to the alligator's head.

Dark blood begins to mix with the water.

The sound of the impact is brutal, a wet, meaty thud that echoes across the lake. The alligator's eyes roll back in its head, but it isn't done yet. It thrashes harder, its claws raking through the water, trying to find purchase.

The tentacles are relentless, though, wrapping tighter and tighter around the creature.

I can see the strain in the octo-man's muscles, the determination in his eyes. His face says he's fighting not just for dominance, but for survival, though it doesn't seem like he's in danger of losing.

The alligator's thrashing grows more desperate, its movements more erratic. It's losing blood fast, and its strength is waning.

With a final, savage twist, he slams the alligator's head against a rock jutting out of the water. The impact is devastating, a sickening crack that sends a shiver down my spine. The alligator goes limp, its body floating lifelessly in the water, blood oozing from its wounds.

He releases his hold, his tentacles retracting back into the water. He's breathing heavily, his body heaving with the effort of the fight. The water around him is a gruesome mix of blood and foam, the aftermath of the brutal battle.

I can't tear my eyes away from the scene. This terrifying creature who threatened my life just saved me from certain death. The realization is surreal, almost too much to process.

He turns to look at me, his eyes narrowing.

There's a flicker of something in his gaze—anger, frustration, maybe even curiosity. He's covered in blood, his own mingling with the alligator's. He's wounded, but he doesn't seem to care.

He moves toward me, and I back away with a shiver and a gulp.

"What... why?" I manage to sing out between stammers, my voice trembling.

I can't find the right words to express the whirlwind of emotions I'm feeling.

Rage sweeps over his features.

"If you cannot defeat that, how could you ever hope to defeat me?"

He says the last word in a bellow, then lifts the dead alligator out of the water and uses his tentacles to break its back. Then he flings it. I can't even see where it lands, I just know it hits the water a short while later with a splash.

My body's shaking at the wanton violence of it.

"I don't want to defeat you, I just want to be left alone. Why help me?" I ask again.

He doesn't answer. Instead, he studies me, his eyes scanning my face as if searching for something.

"You are a useless hunter," he mocks me.

I swallow hard, my throat dry. The adrenaline is still coursing through my veins, making my hands shake. I picture the dead alligator sinking down into the lake, its once fearsome body now a lifeless, bloody husk.

A shudder passes over me, and I finally remember all those manners my *padre* taught me.

"Thank you," I say, the words feeling inadequate.

With a start, I realize they don't translate. That I spoke them in English, which his look of confusion confirms.

I try again to say my thanks in his language, but I can't. My brow furrows, but I can't figure out what that means right now.

He saved my life, despite his earlier threats.

He grunts again, the sound odd when spoken in whale tones, turning away from me.

I watch as he moves back into the water, his body blending into the darkness. The lake is returning to its eerie calm, the only evidence of the battle is the slowly dispersing dark blood. I'm left standing there, soaked and shivering, my mind racing with questions and fears.

Alive for now, but what does he plan to do with me?

I look around at my makeshift shelter and at the top of the rock I was trying to climb to see that glinting of metal. Should I move back to the silver vehicle?

I let out a sigh. I don't think I can make it to it, since he moved me up and over a large stand of rocks to move me toward the water.

Was his plan to drown me?

Anxiety grips me, and I let out a frustrated groan. Tears well up in my eyes before I can stop them. I wish I could go settle into the red fabric of the silver chamber and pretend none of this is real, but I can't.

"Great. Just what I need. Getting emotional now," I mutter to myself.

As if that has ever helped.

I shuffle farther from the edge, grabbing the broad leaf I gathered and moving it as far from the shore as I can manage with my injuries. Above me, the stars twinkle brightly in the clear night sky.

A surge of loneliness hits me. This is too much to handle by myself.

"Miss you, *padre*," I whisper, hoping somehow he can hear me, watching over me from wherever he might be. Whatever comes after death.

The weight of isolation presses down on me, right along with the grief. Not as fresh as it once was, but a wound that never heals.

Then I sense something—I'm not alone anymore. My pulse quickens as I see him emerging from the water, his presence a strange mix of terror and an unexpected sense of safety.

Despite our tense history, there's something about him that makes me feel protected, despite his scary as hell threats.

He approaches with purpose, and before I can react, his tentacles wrap around me, lifting me off the ground. Panic surges through me, and I start to struggle.

"*Hijo de puta*, put me down," I gasp, hitting him as hard as I can.

My fists pound against the sinewy tentacles, but it's like hitting a squishy wall.

"Stop making your noises or I'll drop you," he growls, his voice a low, menacing clicking song that freezes me in place.

His eyes, cold and unyielding, meet mine, and I know he means it.

With surprising gentleness, he sets me down on a higher, more stable rock. From here, I have a better view of the moonlit surroundings, a vantage point that makes me feel safer. Able to monitor any potential threats.

"Stay away from the water," he commands.

After a moment, he speaks again. "I am the only one allowed to hurt you."

The way he says it sends butterflies all over my body. It is an odd mix of fear and something else I can't quite identify—something that leaves me feeling even more aroused, and I hate it.

I don't know how to react to that sensation, and it confuses me. I'm going insane.

Clearly.

He turns and slips back into the water, leaving me on the rock. I notice one of his tentacles is injured, a nasty gash from the earlier battle. Concern tugs at me despite myself.

Then it pisses me off.

"You can't order me around," I yell after him, trying to regain some semblance of control.

"I just did," he retorts, his voice carrying clearly over the water.

I watch in disbelief as he tends to his wound. He blows on it, then takes mud from the ground, rubbing it on the gash. To my astonishment, the wound closes, healing before my eyes.

"What the hell?" I whisper, more to myself than to him.

This creature is full of surprises, each one more confounding than the last.

I settle back on the rock, my mind racing.

His words echo in my mind. Was it a threat or a twisted form of protection?

I lie back, staring up at the stars. For now, I'm safe, at least as safe as I can be in this alien world. The night's events replay in my mind, and sleep feels like a distant dream.

Tomorrow, I'll have to figure out my next move. For now, I'll rest and try to gather my strength.

I close my eyes, the image of him tending to his wound lingering in my mind. It makes me realize that my own are healing faster than they should, though nowhere near as fast as his.

Is it something in the air? Another mystery to figure out later.

Why the hell did he have to put me up on a rock? I get up, trying to find a safe way down, but can't figure it out.

I settle for trying to keep myself as close to the center as possible.

11

Wroahk

As dawn becomes morning, the ray of the sun hits the water, and darkness recedes from the shallow basin. I lurk beneath the surface, my tentacles floating and my senses alert as the creatures in the water begin their journey for the day.

After a patient wait, prey comes close enough and my tentacles snaps out just in time, capturing it and snapping its spine.

I repeat it a few more times until I am sated. Despite all this, the female laid out on the rock ledge still slumbers. The creatures of this world have awoken, and the ruthless cycle of life has begun, yet she remains in stasis.

I raise my head slightly above the water to observe her again.

Her consciousness fully departs as she sleeps and she becomes unaware of the world around her, despite the constant danger.

Weak, unpolished, clumsy. Not even the females of my species can be described as such. In fact, they are powerful hunters, each able to hunt independently, as is expected of any living being. Why do I continue to watch her when I have never paid the slightest attention to the females of my species?

It's best to avoid females. This lack of interaction is a survival mechanism that has kept the males of my species alive for a long time. We know just how dangerous interacting with the female of our species is and we do not do it to survive.

With her, it's just... different. Strange. Indescribable. I am drawn to a pathetic creature because she is female. She has long since no longer been food in my mind. I do not want anything to hurt her. I want to keep her in my sights all day and never let go.

I am losing my grip on reality.

It makes no sense to me, regardless of the fact that she is harmless. Unlike the females of my race, she cannot crush me in an instant or bite my head off. It's disgusting.

She has no strengths. Her sickly yellow hair is a terrible trait underwater. For a creature who is neither poisonous nor huge, she draws a lot of attention as prey. She makes a lot of unnecessary movements as well, screaming when she's in danger and using those bony limbs to get away in the loudest way possible.

I'm sure she would be a terrible swimmer. Using two limbs instead of several seems like a critical flaw. I can't imagine how horrifying I would look without my tentacles, and she seems to stumble around with just two.

A shiver passes through me at the thought of being so limited.

She has no sense of self-preservation, and a bottom feeder has more survival instincts than she does. If she dives under alone, she'll be gone in two bites.

I swim closer, still looking for an answer. All night I have stayed close to the shore, exhibiting my presence to the other creatures in the water as a deterrence, so none of them come close enough to snatch her away.

My fierce protectiveness over her scares me.

It's the first thing that ever has, and I feel the rage building again as I wonder what she did to me. How she took my voice.

Suddenly, I remember my enemy, and how I could understand their voice until they took it away. Did they do more to me? Are these new impulses because of them?

They must be.

My tentacles twitch with my desire to make them scream, and I taste the water yet again for any hint that they may be near.

Nothing.

So, they have changed me, but why in this way?

She should be here, with my limbs wrapped around her as she sleeps. I let out a hiss at the thought.

It's ridiculous, what they have done.

The night was long, and my eyes never closed in rest. My mouth tingles as I remember the taste of her blood in the water.

The metallic taste that settled on my tongue pulled up an insatiable curiosity. If it had been the blood of any other prey, I would've reached out to tear them to pieces and devour them until there was nothing left.

I must know why she is different.

And yet, I am disgusted at myself for feeling curious about a being so weak I can't be bothered to kill it. When have I ever been curious about anything or anyone?

Not that I have spent any length of time with anyone since leaving the violent pod of my youth.

Her eyes flicker open, but the next moment, she drops from the rock ledge I propped her on. I hear a crack when she falls and watch her scream out.

A bubble of breath escapes my lips to see yet another example of stupidity.

She attracts the predators I chased away earlier, but I spread out my tentacles to look bigger and scare them back down, picking one and throwing it against a nearby rock to make sure they don't come up.

I hope she does nothing else to harm herself as I swim back to her.

Inside me, there is a teeming discomfort, as if I'm not pleased that she feels pain.

She makes me doubt myself. Some part of me wants to perceive her differently and another part of me yearns to rip her apart.

No. For this creature who makes my thoughts as muddy as the lake shore, I only have a clear, if peculiar, dislike. This wanton curiosity and a lack of physical hunger for her is unacceptable.

There is nothing I hate more than change.

12

Eli

I half expected to wake up the next morning surrounded by the black silk curtains of my latest bed sharing arrangement. Reality is rather cruel, and the chill of morning runs through me, making me shiver.

I crack open one eye. The purple skies fill my vision, reminding me that I am stranded among the stars.

My perspective of the world shifts quickly as my eyes open and soon after, my body connects with the ground. I hear the loud crack and slap my relatively unhurt hand against my mouth to stop myself from screaming.

It didn't work like I wanted, and I scream loud enough it echoes across the water.

"*Hijo de puta.*"

Of course, it's a bad idea to sleep on an elevated surface with no soft landing. I knew that, just like anyone does, but I didn't plan on falling asleep. I didn't even decide to go up there in the first place, that bastard.

Why put me on a place I can't get down from?

My chest rises and falls as I try to control my breathing.

I broke my arm while trying to wake up, and there are cuts all over me again.

Is there any relief for a poor girl thousands of light years away from home? My entire body trembles uncontrollably, pain spreading from my left arm to the rest of my body. It hurts like hell and my mind spins from all the pain.

"*Basta! Basta!* Enough," I hiss out through my teeth.

I'm in uncharted territories where alien alligators wait for the slightest move of my body. Even the wind blowing seems like a threat.

I heave again, blinking my eyes to clear the wetness in my vision. I'm dizzy, but I can't afford to faint. Dealing with a broken arm is much better than dealing with being hunted down and eaten alive.

But damn, does it hurt.

Dios, what am I doing? Sitting on the rocks feels like being stabbed in the butt by a thousand small needles, and that alone activates the pain receptors in my arm.

With no clinics and no way to make a splint by myself, I can only bear the pain. Adrenaline will only take me so far, even though I am literally a walking target. I rest against the rock and hold my arm in the position that hurts the least, sighing.

With a broken arm, internal bleeding is the biggest of my worries. If I can't help my arm heal properly, I'll be dropping dead from an embolism soon.

I sigh again, my gaze resting on the lake. It ripples peacefully, like it isn't inhabited by dangerous creatures that want nothing more than to tear my skin apart.

A manic cackle tries to build as a light breeze runs through my hair, a shiver following it, joining the trembling of pain.

I force down the bile making its way up my throat. My body still feels strange, but if I'm alive, a broken arm, a sprained ankle, nothing can stop me from...

Wait, my ankle, I realize with a start.

I stretch my leg and flex it, rotating it from side to side. I try to get up to step on it, but the pain in my arm makes my body recoil. My arm is screaming out at me, but my ankle only has a dull ache. I can't believe it and keep rotating away.

In all my years of existence, I have never heard of someone who could heal a sprained ankle in a night.

Have I become... inhuman?

A shiver tears through my body, but it is not from the pain this time. That single thought, coupled with my environment, makes my hope dwindle. I am on an alien planet, just floating on another piece of rock through the universe, alone and hurt.

Well, not totally alone. There's the octo-man.

I remember his long tentacles reaching out of the depths, grasping at me. An echo of the visceral fear I felt staring at him rises, and my instincts scream at me to flee. I can't see him, but I can feel something watching.

A face flashes into my mind. He's been dead for a long time, but the memories of him, of a happy childhood, have always been the catalyst to keep me alive and sane. My *padre*.

Despite the pain, the abuse, the suffering, I keep moving forward because I want to believe life is worth living. He taught me that, and I won't fail him now just because reality shifted.

I need to get up and find somewhere away from the shore, somewhere I can find something better to eat and tend to my wounds, clean myself, and figure out why my ankle healed in just a night.

"Move, Eli. You can't stay here," I growl out.

A manic laugh bubbles up and I try to move again. Nothing.

There's a splash in the water, like something's moving toward me. I'm not the least bit curious to find out what it is.

There's hope for me yet, somewhere in this place. I just need to find it.

"Get up!" I urge myself again.

My legs are weak. I'm barely holding on to my consciousness and my sanity. There's still danger in my immediate surroundings.

My uninjured arm reaches for the nearest rock to pull myself up and redistribute my body weight. It doesn't work at first, but I'm persistent. I try again and succeed one minor pull at a time, rousing my entire body to my feet.

I stagger, but the fear of being impaled by sharp rocks keeps me on my feet.

I move, placing my hand on the nearest rocks to keep me going. I can barely see anything, but just keep shakily shuffling along, fresh injuries from the fall making themselves known with each step.

One leg at a time.

The sounds of waves crashing behind me and the vivid sense that I'm being watched keep me moving. My vision is clearing up. I'm getting somewhere at last.

13

Wroahk

I can hear everything.

The sound of her muscles coiling. The ridiculously colored weeds on her head flying in the wind. I don't need to see her before I sense her. I am attuned to every movement she makes, and it feeds back to me, a habit, but only used for hunting.

This is not that. My tentacles twitch and my gills flare.

That I am keenly aware of her every movement annoys me. There's a sort of simplicity in her movement, yet the coils of her muscles tell a different story. I know now that there's something wrong with her.

I just don't know why it concerns me so much.

From the moment she awoke to the moment she fell from the rock, my eyes never strayed. My tentacles move instinctively as I'm drawn to her and they coil around, waiting for a moment to leap at her.

Instead of spreading my senses all around, as I should if I want to survive, they're all latched onto her right now.

I do not scold myself anymore, preferring to think I am enjoying the thrill of a hunt. There's no hunt when she's ever so slow, and ever so heavy. She leaves a sign that she's traversing the world, an awful behavior for prey.

Most erase their presence or make themselves invisible or try to make themselves bigger or blending into their environment. Not her.

She's searching for something.

A cornered prey is hardly ever mobile unless they are looking for a hiding place. That would explain it, though I wonder where she'll find one.

I watch her, aware of her labored breathing. It's erratic, which doesn't make sense to me either. If she doesn't breathe, she'll die.

Such an off-putting thought. I don't want her to die. Why don't I, a hunter, want my prey to die? Why am I paying so much attention to her?

She's repulsive, and yet as I look my mating tentacles pulse, though I carefully ignore them, using my other limbs to keep them contained.

I hear the words she mumbles under her breath, but I cannot understand them. The words run from her mouth often and it seems like she's talking at herself. She is so strange it makes me unwilling to continue my pursuit.

When she moves too far away, I follow.

I see her struggle to rise, her small eyes searching. Such pointless struggle, especially if she plans to hide.

Her blood leaks through as she walks, leaving a trail as she drags herself among the rocks, using them to keep her body upright.

I hear those useless teeth grinding together as she moves farther away from where she started. She's slow, but she doesn't stop.

She keeps moving along the shore, carefully shifting her limbs so the one is pulled tight to her side isn't touching any of the rocks. This only slows her down, and it only looks reckless from where I'm watching.

If she wants to arrive at a safe space soon, she must stop wasting her breath and her blood.

Her slow walking angers me, so I take my eyes off her and swim toward the other shore, deeper and farther from her. I reach out a grasper and climb up to the surface, feeling the warm air on my body. It feels much too odd.

I dislike it as much as I dislike being around that female.

There isn't much to see on land except more rocks. I don't know what I'm looking for, aside from seeking something else besides obsession.

Then I remember the gust of wind that knocked me over and how I met the female. The thing she arrived in is still there. If she finds it... I don't want to think about that.

Quick action is needed if I want to avoid drying out. It takes very little time to reach it.

This silver shell that brought her here. To me. It is the source of my misery. I growl as I stare at it, remembering the violent graspers that tugged at my body and the haziness that filled my head.

I still don't know much about what happened to me or how she got here. All I can think of is how angry I am and how disgusting the feel of this air is on my skin.

My tentacles wrap around it, flinging it into the lake. It lands with a loud splash, causing fierce ripples to spread along the surface of the water. That type of chaos is enough to draw in more predators, but I don't care.

With quick writhing movements, I join it in the water.

I watch it sink and make sure it doesn't resurface, following its descent to the depths. It goes out of view into the trench, and it brings a small satisfaction.

The presence of that female maddens me. Every breath she draws grating against my senses. I don't want to see her anymore, so I stay underwater, trying to remind myself of my dignity as a hunter.

It doesn't work very well.

I keep wondering, what if I lose sight of her? What if I never understand why I can't hunt her? When did I lose my will as a hunter and become curious about my prey? Why do I focus so much on her when everything else is novel to me?

I must return, the dread of losing sight of her crawling up my tentacles, up my back, and onto my scalp.

The ripples on the surface of the water are calm as I make my way back to the other side. I swim through the lake silently, stretching out my tentacles to feel for any nearby predator. When I don't feel any, my body drifts to shore, toward the very female that enrages me.

Of all the things to be curious about, why such a weak and unfettered thing that draws predators to herself with every walking step? The wind carries her scent into the water and even I can feel their excitement for a rare prey. I certainly haven't seen anything like her before.

Is it because her upper body is similar to mine?

There's an infinite number of excuses I can come up with, an infinite number of questions I can ask. The trail of blood excites my tentacles as they taste her scent and my body reacts when I'm near her. How could something vile be so exciting?

This isn't the excitement of a hunt anymore.

Even if she is weak, my reaction to her is proof she is a different kind of danger. One I don't yet understand, but if I am to survive her presence, I must.

A good enough reason to keep trailing her.

14

Eli

My pace is slow, though at least I'm not leaving a blood trail anymore since my wounds have somehow already closed. The hairs at the back of my neck are raised so I'm aware I might be in danger, but I'm still moving. I won't stop until I'm safe.

I don't know if it's simply my imagination, but the pain in my arm dulls as I keep moving.

The rocks littering the shore make it difficult to move with a broken arm, but I am able to make a fair distance from the jagged array of rocks. Now that my vision is clearer, I can see how far I've gone and spot an alcove.

I walk closer to it and relief floods my mind.

There's an entrance to a large cave nearby, but the extending darkness doesn't welcome me into it. I can hear the wind whistling and water dripping deep in the cave.

I'm not curious enough to fall for a horror movie cliché.

No need to make my situation worse, yeah? I decide to search for an alternative, a safer shelter for the night that doesn't scream *death trap*.

I look past the cave and find a cove with promising depth, and make my way into it instead. Water washes over my leg as I enter, but the water is shallow, and I can see all the way to the end of the cove.

Soon after, I enter a thick forest of trees with bright green, feathery foliage and purple bushes. Light barely filters in through the canopy the farther in I go.

There are a lot of things I'm worried about. I'm on an alien planet, with no idea if there are vampire bats or bloodsucking insects lurking around. My eyes shift endlessly, and I crane my head around, but no clear threats jump out at me. I keep moving through the trees when my eyes catch something.

There's an incline that leads to a flatter area of tall grass and very tall trees. It's surrounded by sheer rock on all sides that don't lead to the lake, rising to form a hexagon-type rock structure that protects it from wind and hopefully lurking predators.

As I stare at this wonder, I see the sky slowly getting dark.

I push my way farther toward the rock formation, wanting to gain distance from the water.

I glance at the distance to the cove, hoping it will deter that octo-man from barging in here. My body says he is still stalking me.

I don't like the feeling the least bit.

My stomach grumbles, reminding me I've been moving and healing non-stop with no form of nutrition. It's not like I can hunt like the octo-man, not that I want to, nor can I forage on an alien planet with strange looking trees.

I can't even climb to catch fruit with a broken arm. Not that I've seen any. Or that it wouldn't just poison me.

I sigh, leaning back and closing my eyes.

The sound of the wind whistling through the leaves of the giant trees and grass is soothing and I clutch my limbs to my body, praying to anybody that would hear me to let me live another day undigested.

Bugs chirp and chitter around me, flying around in the tall grass, their calls creating a discordant disharmony. They sound odd and look even odder. Their flight patterns, and shapes subtly wrong.

Maybe I can eat bugs, I muse.

That would be a grand way to stop being vegetarian. I look at one of them nearby, a black body with an iridescent red sheen, a dozen prickly looking legs.

Nope. Not that desperate just yet.

I survived homelessness before, albeit in a far different environment. I can survive living on an alien planet.

It isn't the same though. I miss sleeping on a bed and I miss at least knowing where my next meal will come from, even if it's a cheap diner meal.

As my thoughts continue to drift, the raucous cacophony of the bugs eventually lulls me to succumb to my exhaustion. Fear still runs rampant in my veins and my eyes are still focused on the entrance of the cove, waiting for the octo-man to rise from the water.

However, I have little strength left.

My eyes feel heavy as I remember I need another way to protect myself now that my only weapon is gone. Figure out food.

Stay alive. Live another day.

15

Wroahk

My eyes open from restless slumber and my body springs back to life. I unfurl my tentacles and twirl them, trying to get rid of the stiffness.

Though I've staked my territory, the Many Teeth in this water are more than willing to dispute it, unlike the creatures of my world who know better.

A moment later, my mind is back to the female. Watching her flail around is as unexciting as trying to figure out why I feel strangely drawn to her, but both must be done.

Ever since I saw her, she's all I can think about.

The sun isn't up yet so the lake and its environs are mostly quiet. It wouldn't be difficult for me to slip away. If I search enough, I can find another suitable lake and a more abundant source of food.

Maybe even find a river that leads to an ocean. It was my plan before she arrived, so I should get back to it.

I won't have to deal with the frustration of staying beside this female anymore.

I say that, but my mind rejects the thought of abandoning her, even though it is exactly what should be done to the weak. They are dead weight, but I feel... reluctance.

The few times I've felt reluctance before did not coincide with this curious feeling I have now.

I go looking for food, swimming aimlessly until I come upon what looks like a nest. I sense them before I see them. Floating near the nest are two Many Teeth with their eyes closed. I can tell they're sleeping. If I swim closer, their eyes will snap open.

I can't bring myself to kill her. Why don't I use them? I can be rid of her and them in one breath.

I like this plan. She must perish for this feeling of uncertainty to leave me. Since they are just floating around, catching them isn't that hard. All I need to do is carefully extend my tentacles and disable their body's defenses, trapping them between my limbs.

The best place to catch them is the midriff, wrapping my other tentacle around their snout so their teeth remain shut until I need to release them.

I do so before I change my mind. Holding two of them at the same time is the difficult part, but I manage, making a dash for the surface, ready to unleash terror on her while ignoring the thrashing of the Many Teeth.

As I approach the surface, ready to find her and throw them on top of her, one of the constantly thrashing creatures breaks free for a moment. I catch a glimpse of the long and sharp rows of teeth the creature possesses, and my body involuntarily stops.

The image of her being torn into pieces, chewed up by this creature, flashes through my head and anger surges through me.

No. She is my prey. Mine to eat.

The hold of my tentacles loosens, and the creatures free themselves. They growl at me, but I growl back, a clicking call meant to inspire terror, scaring them into turning tail. They swim away, a warning growl floating behind them.

My prey? No prey requires this much special attention.

It is probably the work of those poor excuses for sea life slimes. Those things poked and prodded me for a long time.

If I see them again, I'll rip them to pieces immediately.

As I watch the Many Teeth disappear from view, I decide to look for her. I can still remember the path she took and can still feel her presence. I slink around the rocks, hyperaware of how sharp they are.

I soon see her, surrounded by tall grass, resting against a tree. The wind bites at my skin and my tentacles shrink, begging for water. Even though she's a few steps away from me, I cannot claim my meal. The feeling of dryness creeps up from my tentacles to my throat as I feel the moisture escape my skin, pushing me back toward a source of water.

I follow the path out of the cove, bypassing it when I sense a nearby source of water in the large cave. If she is going to be so near it, I should search it for threats. I enter without hesitation and soak in my tentacles, shivering as the disgusting feeling of freshwater makes my tentacles throb.

I hear a low rumble behind me, but I am slow to react. I growl in pain as something clamps onto one of my tentacles, massive teeth glinting back at me. In my distraction I forget that I cannot sense movement above the water the same way as within it.

Two of them surround me, nipping at my tentacles, taking the ends off two of them, their maws open and ready to attack. I throw my uninjured tentacles out, hoping to disrupt their rhythm. They attack with their jaws, but I snap them shut, and then wrap their jaws in a crushing grip.

My body feels weak. I stayed on land too long, following her trail.

She caused this.

I roar, snapping one in half. The other one whimpers and thrashes around, dragging my tentacles around the rocky cave. I snap its spine without hesitation and shiver in disgust as I tear off chunks and its flesh fills my belly. It's revolting but it's all I have to eat.

I miss my home.

When I roamed in my saltwater domain, I truly underestimated the feeling of freedom and the opportunity for variety. Now, I'm stuck eating disgusting freshwater creatures that do more than fill my belly. I sigh, flicking the rest of the blood off my tentacles.

They're damaged now and it'll take some time to recover. I need something more nutritious to heal.

I wonder how she'll taste. All that brown skin probably means she tastes just like the rest of the mud dwellers. Will the taste of her blood energize me?

Before I realize it, I'm wandering out of the cave, throwing the dead Many Teeth into the water so they don't foul the cave as they rot, then head back to where she was.

My body feels heavy and sluggish, barely dragging me quietly across the grassland. I am more vulnerable on land. As my eyes narrow on her, I reach my webbed graspers toward her, imagining my teeth sinking into her neck and her warm blood inciting the hunger that I lost.

It happens again. My tentacles stop just short of her neck, and I'm looking over her without the intention of causing harm.

The wind carries her scent to my suckers, and I realize she smells... less terrible. In fact, her scent rouses my mating tentacles. Far from hunger for blood, I feel a deeper, more primal instinct.

16

Eli

I can barely feel my body as I wake up, hazy and hungry. A throbbing headache follows my slow return to consciousness, making me want to go right back to being unconscious. My mind flickers between confusion and awareness, but I know I shouldn't go back to sleep.

Someone's watching me. Closely, not too far away. Probably him.

My eyes snap open when the sound of a stick breaking pierces my consciousness. Just a few steps away from me is the giant octo-man staring at me unflinchingly. A strangled scream escapes my throat, and he finally moves, his tentacles driving him backwards.

My scrambling movement does nothing good for my throbbing headache and it feels like my skull is about to split in two. However, this is my chance.

"Wait!" I call despite myself.

He pauses and looks at me with his usual annoyance. At least that is what I think I read from him. He stands frozen in the same spot, the annoyance on his face shifting to accusation. I blink my eyes open, keeping my gaze on him.

"You stole my voice. Why?" he accuses again.

"If I knew the answer to that, buddy, I wouldn't be in this position, now would I?" I reply dryly but he doesn't look amused.

I decide to try again. He thinks I'm prey, yes, but I need to understand what's going on. I've never spoken this language before. I can't even call it a language since it's just mostly whale-like noises and dolphin-like clicks.

Talking is my life-blood, though so I'll take any form of communication I can and I want to know more.

"I don't know why I can speak your language, either. Something strange is happening to my body. This is not how I usually am."

I can't tell his facial expressions accurately, but I know I caught his attention. He growls at me lowly and I look down at his feet... tentacles. They're squirming on the grass, the force of his weight crushing the blades flat.

I have to crane my head up to look at him as he is quite tall, though judging by the way he has his tentacles arranged, he is using them to push himself into a more threatening position. Not that he needed help to look freaking scary as hell.

I keep my observations to myself and continue to communicate with him.

"Look, this isn't my home planet. I don't know where I am or how I got here. I'm healing faster than I normally would and my hair... it's different. My body has been altered."

His gaze briefly dwells on my hair before it moves down to my face, still silent. Somehow, I feel like I'm being judged by him. It doesn't feel nice to be judged by an alien, any more than all the looks I used to get when I was on the street.

As if I would have chosen that for myself, just like I didn't choose this.

"Do you know where we are? Is this your home?"

"No."

His tone is bitingly cold, which seems like a feat since he is clicking and singing. When I make similar clicks they don't sound quite so... violent.

Still, I'm grateful he even bothers to respond. He could just as well reach out to snap my neck, but he's staying in the same spot. Is it even a he? I just assumed. With that aggressive attitude and possessiveness, as well as the deep voice, I'm sure about it.

I don't like making assumptions about gender, but something tells me he won't answer me if I ask, and he will probably get angry that I want him to reveal anything about himself.

"Thank you for saving me last night."

He cocks his head at me, and I realize thanking him didn't translate. Yet again.

Try as I might, I can't convey the words to him. I let out a long string of synonyms, then move on to Spanish, but none of them come out as clicks or song.

What kind of language doesn't have a word for gratitude?

Everything about him is just so weird. Those shark-like eyes seem to stare into my very soul, impatiently waiting for me to cease this conversation.

"I didn't mean to save you," he responds.

That shocks me, leaving me unable to respond. What does he mean by that? I saw him snap that crocodile-like creature in half with my own eyes. Was it because he was initially hunting the creature and saving me as a snack?

Is that why he propped me up on the rock I broke my arm falling off? Did he expect me not to get down from there and to wait for my death?

"So, why did you?" I manage to ask.

"I don't know why. You did something to me."

"I'm not capable of anything like that."

"I know you did," he growls. "Stop lying, female."

"I'm not lying," I say, fighting the urge to scream out in frustration.

He looks more frustrated than me, though. "I would have preferred to eat you than keep you alive."

I know what he's saying, but the implication of his words sends a shiver down my spine and a lingering warmth between my thighs. Although the feeling isn't unfamiliar, it's confusing.

How logical is it to be aroused when a terrifying and frankly rude creature tells me he's going to eat me? It's not, but every single time I see him it surges again.

It's sick.

"Something is really wrong with my body. My body is... excited, even though my brain thinks differently about you."

He understands the meaning of my words and snorts.

"You have such a weak body. It is no wonder you can't control it."

Those are his parting words as he departs from the grassland. His tentacles leave a trace in the grass, the proof for my questionably conscious mind he was truly there, and this interaction was not a figment of my imagination.

"*¡Que te folle un pez!*" I yell after him as he leaves.

I wince almost immediately, feeling my head recoil from my headache.

As I hear the crashing noises of his movement stop and a splash as he enters the water, I remember what the direct translation of that was.

I hope you get fucked by a fish, I recite in my head.

Absolutely perfect, if I say so myself, although I can see my *padre's* look of censure for being so crude.

If anything deserves crudeness, it's this situation. And this infuriating person.

If my arm wasn't throbbing, I would appreciate a good belly laugh.

I don't have the luxury.

I'm not used to swearing at somebody or telling them off. In fact, I don't think I've ever cursed someone out before. It feels strange to my tongue, like burning coal rolling off it the more I push the words out.

However, I feel a strange kind of relief.

As a service worker, bowing my head and swearing under my breath just fit me more, but this is a new world.

Maybe it's time for a new Eli.

Still, it takes several long minutes to push aside the anxiety of being rude to him to the back of my mind so I can focus on more important things. I rotate my ankle again and find that it healed fully through the night.

After shakily rising, I realize I can walk properly, and my leg no longer even hurts.

I still don't know how I'm healing so fast, but my arm still sends spikes of pain if I try to use it. Whatever it is, it should get to my broken arm soon. Judging by the angle it's at, it would probably not be a great thing if it was healed right now.

I look around, searching for what to use as a cast to set my arm or it'll heal crooked.

Using the enormous tree as leverage, I steady myself, wincing as a sharp pain shoots through my arm. My eyes scan the area and lands on foliage thick with fallen branches, vines, and sticks.

I move toward it, thinking of how I would make my cast. I sift through it, pulling out a branch to make a splint and a vine to wrap my arm, and some sticks to support it so my arm will heal properly.

It'll take some work and imagination, but I will make it work.

17

Wroahk

Slinking out of the cove she has claimed, I venture back into the dark cave. I can taste the remnants of my blood and feel my tentacles healing from the earlier attacks.

I sigh, resting my back against the moss in the cave and dipping my tentacles into the water and using them to splash more across my body.

It moisturizes me, taking away the feeling of thirst and dryness I've had since I got on land.

I don't know how that female exists solely on land. From what I've seen, she prefers to stay above the water and rarely ventures near it, making her a completely foreign concept to me.

There is land on my home, but it is only occupied by thoughtless beasts. None of them can speak, let alone steal my voice.

I can't fathom staying above water for an extended period. It's not something I ever thought I would have to do, and then it's something I vowed I never would after almost dying from being beached so far from water by my captors.

The cave is still and quiet. I don't feel anything else in my immediate environment, reassuring me that I've at least scared off the Many Teeth to abandon their nest and not breach the area on land.

If she is my prey, the surrounding area is my territory. I know better than to let other predators roam freely around it.

The large cave just beside the cove has a much larger opening I can fit myself into, and from that opening, I can watch her closely. If I walk just a little farther, she'll be within my reach. My tentacles twitch agitatedly as I hear her voice. It is rather loud, and she might as well be notifying the surrounding predators of her presence in the area. My presence is the only deterrence she has.

I didn't understand her words, or why she would want to talk about how I killed the Many Teeth.

She wasn't praising my skills. She wasn't talking about her own weakness. It was like she was trying to tell me she liked what I did, but there was a meaning beyond that I know I am missing.

I don't like feeling like a fool.

I truly did not mean to save her. It is forbidden, especially considering she was on land.

My body moved before I could understand what I was doing, and I was reaching out to break what was trying to steal my prey from me. My instinct to hunt, my most basic and useful instinct, felt like it was snatched from me in an instant and I was moving to use it to protect her.

Still, it doesn't explain why I didn't kill her myself afterward. It was like I was being controlled.

I move to the front of the cave and look back at her. As usual, she's doing something strange.

She gathers parts of the trees with one limb, stopping and panting for a few minutes before she continues to walk around the large trees. She picks up more parts of the trees before she goes back to settle at the base of the large tree.

I can't figure out why she's doing something as useless as that. Will she continue to get more bizarre? Driving me to insanity, even as I think I have a grasp on her strange behaviors?

The sounds of her groans pull my attention back to her. She's trying to dampen them, clamping her lips shut. I hear her labored breaths all the way from the cave, making my ear drums itch.

She's trying to tie her limb to a tree. Why? Is this a trick?

It's going on for too long for it to be, and it looks far too painful for deceit. She's a weak creature who needs to rely on her mobility to escape from predators. Tying herself down is a terrible idea.

She moves her grasper slightly, moans in pain and shakes her head, whispering words I can't understand under her breath. She doesn't seem to be making any progress, and her energy will only dwindle the more she tries.

Why do such a useless thing? Is she trying to pull my attention? Is this a trap mechanism for her species? Why must she be so impossible to understand?

I move closer to the cave opening, a moment away from breaching into where she is. I haven't absorbed enough water, and my tentacles are still healing. Yet, my body doesn't seem to listen as it leans into her voice, desperately trying to escape my self-restraint and move to her.

I cannot let that happen.

She stops again, breathing heavily. It's irregular and I'm beginning to question how she's even still conscious. It's hard for prey to endure extended pain.

Is it to attract my attention? Does she want to control my body? Get a predator to do her own hunting?

I don't know nearly enough, and I keep watching, despite the struggle within me. She holds one end of the vine in her teeth and the other with her free grasper, taking slow, deliberate breaths. She pulls both ends of the vine and the most gut-wrenching scream erupts from her throat.

I've heard prey scream many times as I sunk my teeth into their flesh, enjoying the sounds of their terror before the life departs from their eyes. I should enjoy her screams, but I don't.

I need her to stop. Right now.

Her entire body trembles as she falls to her knees and pants. Why is she going through all this pain? I look at the limb she has tied to the tree and see it's the one that looked broken before.

What's the use of her actions? She can just shed it and grow it back. It might be better for her to cut it off. It is what I do for all my limbs.

Then a prickle of awareness creeps over me. Of... fear? What if she can't?

She uses her free grasper to feel the one tied to the tree, shivering as she does. I can tell it hurts, but she is relentless. Her expressions makes it easy to tell that she's going through more pain than she can handle.

So why do it? I have protected her all this time. Why does she want to harm herself?

She pulls against the tie again, screaming out in pain. Her face contorts, bodily fluids leaking from her eyes, which roll in their sockets, brimming at the edge with more fluid. My desire to go to her fights harder against my restraint, but I prevail once more.

Just barely. I shouldn't care. I don't care.

She mutters something under her breath again, moving her body upright as she slowly moves one end of the vine to her mouth. It is strange to watch, like time is moving slower than it should be. She rests her back against the giant tree, her eyes barely open as she pants. My grasper clenches unconsciously, even though she isn't doing anything.

Her voice gets louder as she speaks to herself in the same strange language, pulling the vine with her teeth, holding it taut like she's giving herself strength, then moves back to where she was.

I recognize it almost too late. She's about to do it again.

She pulls again and screams, her voice becoming raw. Her groans rile up something in me, a burning urge I can't ignore, and no longer care that I don't understand. My instincts crash against my restraint like an overflowing river, and my body moves, ignoring the protests of my mind.

Nothing is allowed to hurt her. Ever. Not even herself.

With that in mind, I lunge out of the cave, fully set on stopping her before she hurts herself even further. Every rational thought in my head screams at me to stop, to consider my dignity. Time slows again as I'm rushing toward her.

And then even my mind stops holding me back. I have decided to protect her, and I will be as effective and ruthless at it as I am in my hunting.

Not even she will stop me.

Her face looks pale, like all the blood has been drained from it as I get close to her.

I like my prey intact and healthy, for a good chase. I cannot chase her with a faulty limb, neither can I fully gorge myself on a proper meal.

Yes, that feels right. This is what I will keep telling myself. That she's a meal worth saving.

From the moment I move onto the dry, scratchy weeds, the burning behind my throat reminds me I shouldn't stay for too long, shouldn't linger. However, the rest of my body is intent on writhing to her.

I'm caught between a cliff and a deep plunge, and I already chose to jump. There's no stopping it now. I know I'm choosing to interact with this female.

Whatever happens next, I am sure it is a decision I will regret.

18

Eli

Gathering the twigs, vines, and sticks I needed was the easy part. My heart fills with dread at the thought of readjusting my arm by myself. I sigh, looking at the crooked arm through blurry eyes, wondering exactly how I got here. I have never had the opportunity to reset a bone, neither did I think I would have to.

The most exciting thing that happened in the grocery store I worked in was somebody getting buried in cartons of chips after knocking over the supply boxes. Then, I was glad it wasn't me that made such a huge mistake. Or that time I spilled cleaning fluid on a carpet in my night job.

Not exactly worth this sort of karma. Oh, wait. I guess I did fucking shoot somebody, even if he deserved it.

The thrill of standing up for myself weaves together with saying *fuck* and it makes me feel... powerful.

Huh.

I know I'm spiraling to distract myself from the pain, but I let myself keep at it. It's excruciating and my heart is pounding in my ears to let me know just how close I am to passing out.

Every move feels like I'm being stabbed with a thousand needles. Falling from a bike or getting hit by my stepfather just doesn't compare to this kind of pain. What he broke there were at least doctors to fix when I 'fell down the stairs.'

My body screams at me to give up, but I know I haven't gotten the bone in place, so I'll have to keep pulling until I do. Just the thought of it is enough to send shivers down my spine.

The wind blowing through the trees doesn't help to regulate my body's temperature but the feeling of being watched still lingers, leaving my nerves frigid.

Thanks to my blurred vision, it's going to take a lot more than blind faith and instincts to help me set my bone back. I seriously need help. If I keep pulling, the sheer pain is going to knock me out.

My efforts are still not enough.

There's no one I can ask for help. As far as I can tell, I'm the only human here, though I can't risk saying that out loud because of how real it'll feel. I can't stand being the only human stranded on an alien planet.

Who will I talk to so I can keep the nightmares at bay?

There is someone else, my mind points out, but I can't fathom asking him for help.

I'm barely even conscious and I'm injured. An easy meal. I'm not going to be eaten alive in my most vulnerable and pathetic state. Even in the best-case scenario that he doesn't eviscerate me, he won't help me.

He already said he didn't intend to save me, unless it's for an afternoon snack.

After another failed attempt I know I can't do it. I don't know what I'm doing. My vision is blurred, fear is pumping through me, my teeth are chattering with cold.

There's nothing in my stomach, but it still feels like I'm going to throw up.

I breathe shakily, urging myself to get it together when I feel something wet and rubbery wrapping around me and pushing me forward so there is slack in the line I'm still stubbornly pulling against, a ragged, animal scream tearing at my throat.

Tears sting my eyelashes, blurring my vision further, and my body flinches with even the slightest touch on my injured arm. The only thing keeping me going is adrenaline and sheer will.

"Why are you harming yourself?" I hear him ask in a deeper tone than before, the echoes of his song reverberating through me now that he has me pulled up against him.

I doubt my own ears, wondering if the hallucinations have started.

There's no way it's him, especially not asking that question. Is this really the end of my pathetic life? No, it can't be. I can't go like this. I can't...

"Respond, female!" His voice resounds in my ears again, quicker.

Angrier.

"I will not allow you to hurt yourself!" he screams at me in whale clicks, just barely penetrating my pain induced haze.

My mind finally recognizes that he's here in the flesh. I tear my eyes open and see him looming over me, an arm gripping me tight up against him, tentacles on my broken arm. I gasp, feeling ripples of pain go down my arm.

Does he want to tear off my arm as a snack? What does he want and why the hell is he yelling so much? I'm in so much pain, and he's just being an asshole.

The adrenaline blinds me, and I do something I would never have done before, considering the massive headache I have and the fact that he towers over me easily.

"Shut up!" I yell, nothing like my usual self.

Surprisingly, it works, and I take a few panting moments to gather my shattered mind.

When I feel more in control, I speak again. "Stop screaming at me. My arm hurts and I need to shift the bone back or it won't heal properly or worse, I die from an embolism."

He contemplates on my words. "Will it hurt more or less if you do this?"

"It'll hurt a lot now, but it'll heal later and hurt less. I'll be able to move it properly for the rest of my life if I shift it into alignment, but it won't work right if I don't. This is necessary."

"Let me see your other grasper."

I assume he means arm. I raise it, shivering when his smooth, two-finger hand moves over my arm, pressing it in a few places. He looks deep in thought, although it's probably my imagination.

He reaches for my other arm, inspecting it and pressing it like he did to my other arm. I react immediately, muffling my scream by closing my mouth and snatching my arm away.

This asshole, what the hell is he doing?! It was bad enough when he held it the last time, but pressing on it is a different thing.

"What the hell did you do that for?" I yell at him, trying to hold my injured arm away from him.

I'm in pain and he's stronger than me. It's impossible to stop him, though I do try to wriggle away. His tentacles wrap around me, trapping me. It's not like I can move much, but his hold is rough, making my pain worse.

He looks at me for a second, holds my arm, and twists it.

The scream that bursts from my throat sends knives of raw pain along it, blending with the agony in my arm. Blackness takes over my vision.

I wake to him shaking me. The tears come right after, gushing down my cheeks like a waterfall. I heave, my vision waning. I look down at my arm blearily. It was cruel and fast, but efficient. My arm is back to its original position.

He holds it in place, waiting on me. "What do I do next?"

Through heavy, sparse breaths, I gesture to the splint. "Tie that on the arm."

He does as he's told, using a combination of his hands and tentacles, not gentle in the slightest, though thankfully I don't have to teach him how to tie a knot. Not completely primitive, it looks like.

Still a stupid ass, though, I grumble to myself.

Now that my arm's back in position, it hurts less, but it's only a matter of degrees. He uses his webbed hands and the tip of his tentacles to fix the splint in place, tightening it roughly.

I fight the urge to curse at him, lest he change his mind on helping me. Once the splint is in place, my body goes slack with relief. I feel the wet, leathery feeling leave my arm as he retracts his touch.

I'm amazed that he's capable of listening to instructions. Of something more than threats and violence.

He helped me freely. I don't know how much he cares, but I know he doesn't want me to hurt myself.

Why would he care if I'm just a walking meal? I don't know what that means just yet, but I'll play it safe. As long as I'm not an afternoon snack, I'm fine.

He lets me go, ensuring I have my feet under me before releasing the hold he has on my waist. I sway, but I don't fall.

In the tense atmosphere, my stomach growls to break the silence, my hunger the main source of my dizziness now. It makes him frown, like he's offended by the sound.

I haven't eaten since I woke up in this hell and the hunger is becoming more apparent with every passing second.

It's really a miracle I haven't passed out yet.

Just as I thought that, my body staggers. He catches me before I fall to the ground, his face contorting into something that is not quite anger.

"Even your insignificant weight is too much?" he taunts.

"I haven't eaten."

"No self-respecting person will allow others to hunt for them."

"No need. I don't eat food."

He looks at me, confusion now clouding his eyes. I am getting better at reading his expressions. The word *meat* doesn't translate into his language because what I meant to say was, I don't eat meat. I'm a vegetarian.

"Meat," I say in my language, although my voice sounds strange.

I try again in his language. "Food. ¡Qué rabia! Food! That's not the word I'm trying to say. What I'm trying to say is I don't eat the flesh of living creatures."

"That's the only thing that is food."

"Well, I eat plants," I hiss out in an annoyed voice. "I just don't know which ones are safe to eat."

"You will have to learn about that on your own. I'm leaving."

I fight the urge to yell at his back. He helped me, but is so damn insulting I want to strangle him with his own fucking tentacles.

He doesn't turn around like I fear, soon disappearing from my view.

I heave a sigh of relief and look at my arm. Despite his gruffness, I'm thankful for what he did. It is already starting to hurt less. Still, I prefer him as far away as possible. Even better if he's not on the island. He's the most dangerous thing here.

I don't care if he leaves me alone. I don't. Conversation where I am the butt of every barb isn't worth it.

I let out a huff of breath. I know myself. If he comes around, I will still talk to him. Dammit.

I recall the memory of him breaking the spine of the alligator. If I'm left alone with those creatures, I will not survive. That chilling thought is a lovely way to begin my day.

I stroke my now-fixed arm, looking around. I'm still starving, yes, but I can finally get a chance to observe my surroundings now that I'm not wallowing in pain.

As I take slow, steadying breaths, the ache in my arm reduces to a dull throbbing and in a while, I can finally move it enough to move in search of food.

19

Wroahk

I feel stupid now. Rushing out to help her, I was ready to protect her again. Despite what my self-restraint was telling me, I was ready to abandon my dignity to protect her from herself. It doesn't even make sense to me, but I already did it.

Already decided I will keep doing it.

She wasn't trying to hurt herself. As I suspected, she can't regrow her limbs. That seems awfully inconvenient, but she's an entirely different being, so it must be what happens to her species.

Her frequent use of things around her surroundings must also be a trait of her species. Rather than use it to blend in, rest, or hide, she has a surprising number of uses for the things around her.

It's fascinating.

She isn't like the enemy I plan to kill. Maybe there is some other use for her other than her death. Though I don't know what, something in me must already have the answer.

I have never restricted my strength before, the way I had to when holding her arm to straighten it. I barely held on to it and a little tug on my part straightened it right up. She felt so weak, so tiny in my hold.

It would've been easy to break her, to tear her to pieces, but I didn't. Being so close to her, I didn't want to hurt her. Something altogether strange rose up in me. The need to... I don't even have a word for the opposite of wanting to crush something.

And then there is the sudden impulse to speak.

I can't remember the last time I've heard my own voice this much. Speaking above water for an extended period is difficult, but nothing I cannot accomplish.

It is speaking to her that's the difficult part. The inflections in her voice, the rapid change of emotions in her eyes and her breaths, everything is infinitely more complicated with her.

That conflict made me slink back into the lake and flee, this time searching out an underwater cave better suited to me than large one in the cove.

No sense in staying above ground. I fall back deep into my new cave and just lay about, trying to think.

Still, I feel restless. There are many things that lurk in this lake, but none make me as agitated as that female. The feel of her skin lingers on my graspers, and the freshness of her breath persists in my mind.

I don't think it'll be easy to just leave her alone or erase her from my mind. My tentacles itch as I think about her, the urge to speak to her rising in me.

I haven't spoken this much to anybody since leaving my nursery group, which I left quite earlier than my peers and I have seen little of them in recent years.

I don't know if I'll ever get the chance to see them again now, stranded in this place, not that we would have done anything beyond try to insult or kill each other.

Memories of the days of glorious competition for territory surface in my mind. Those who are slow, born without the instincts to hunt, who cannot swim properly, and those who are cowards, are inevitably eaten by other predators. Those, like me, who do what they must for survival, live, at least until age makes them weak.

Some of them extend their lives by creating nursery groups, though they ultimately die as the group ages.

Killing and eating each other to survive is natural. The competition always starts from inside the pod, a feeding frenzy of survival where the weak are culled and the survivors get the chance to live. There are always conflicts for everything, but that is just the natural order.

So why am I protecting her? It's not because I am aging and the idea of her being strong enough to extend my own life is ridiculous.

A hunter may hurl insults at each other whenever we win or lose, never help the other heal. Those were the limits of social interactions I had, the essence of conversations that mattered to me.

Or the cutting barbs I exchanged with the few females I plunged my mating tentacles into as I held their sharp teeth at bay. It was always a race to deposit my seed before a chunk of me was missing or a tentacle was ripped off. Just the memory makes my two mating tentacles start swaying and grasping.

Speaking with her involves none of those things, and I'm starting to realize that I might not... hate it.

I wonder what the yellow female will do if I try to mate with her.

The smoothness of her body does not compare to the sturdiness of the females of my species. Besides, she looks nothing like them, so it would be quite the challenge to find where to insert myself.

No. I hate her.

Looking at her fills me with disgust. Something about her is just wrong. She's too weak to resist me, the sure sign of a female who should never be allowed to breed.

She has no weapons to fight back. Her appendages are weak attachments that snap easily.

The thought is interesting, though. What would it feel like to mate with someone without the other person trying to rip off my head? To experience the pleasure that builds up in my mating tentacles as I release without having to protect my body?

The thoughts splash around my head as I go back to watching her. She seems to have found something to eat, nibbling on a few weeds. It hardly makes any sense, and I want nothing more than to shove something better down her throat.

However, I'm stopping myself, which is something I've never done before. It makes me feel strange, as if I've lost the very last part of me I could cling to after being taken.

Watching her does me no good, and it only makes me hungrier. She's injured and weak. I doubt just eating leaves will make her recover faster. My limbs itch with the desire to hunt for her, but I already said I wouldn't.

It would be a waste of prey, not to mention an insult to both of us.

She picks up more leaves, munching on them without regard. She shows no interest in the creatures buzzing around her or the ones soaring in the skies above her. Even if I consider them not-food, they might be enough to sustain her small form.

This weird female eats like a bottom feeder, never bothering to hunt for itself or leave its territory to find better food. She looks nothing like a bottom feeder, but perhaps that's why her teeth are so polished.

Does she really have no strength or will to fight back?

That makes her even worse than a bottom feeder. At least they can regrow their limbs or protect themselves against predators. All she knows how to do is attract predators to herself and steal my voice and senses.

   The only thing I can praise about her is her resilience. She clings on so fiercely to survival. It's almost... something. I don't know a word for it, but my mind keeps working at it.

20

Eli

I try to put my nonexistent foraging skills to the test.

A purple striped insect passes by me, looking a lot like a bee with no stinger. I decide to call it a purbee, which makes me smile, and then follow it, hoping it is as harmless as the name I gave it.

"Hello, little one," I croon to it to stave off the loneliness.

How long has it been since I talked to a human? Oh, right, it was those cops. Gross. The last enjoyable conversation? Then I remember it was Ms. Janis and my eyes well up with tears.

I should have taken that date with her grandson, lived a little. Learned to trust someone enough to let my mask slip. Now all I have is this crushing isolation.

I shake my head, focusing back on the purbee.

Where there are bees, there's pollen. Where there's pollen, there are flowers and fruits. It's basic biology and I am going to follow it. The purbee's path is straightforward, and I ramble along behind, finding a bunch of flowering trees. Thankfully, they're not high up or huge.

They look climbable, but I'm not exactly healed enough for that, though maybe by tomorrow.

Dang, that is still such a weird thought.

The bird-like creatures have picked off every good fruit, but the flowers being pollinated by the bees are still intact. The leaves look like they're being eaten by some other insects, my sign that it's probably edible. I have no other choice but to believe that.

It's either that or starving to death after finally finding a way to survive.

I start foraging, picking up some relatively intact leaves and flowers. The purbees are quite persistent, but I manage to pluck some flowers and remain grateful that they don't have stingers.

I wonder if I can find their hive for some honey as I search for fruit that the birds haven't decimated. There's only one or two, but it's enough for a trip when I have two working arms to climb.

I make my way back to the trunk of the tree and begin eating as the sun shines down on me.

My body screams at me to eat more, but until I know how I'll react, it's not a good idea.

After eating, I drift off to sleep, feeling my head grow heavier and heavier until I lose consciousness.

My eyelids feel like lead. They become heavier as I try to open them, and my body feels like it's floating. I barely filled my stomach and drift off to sleep despite myself.

When I wake up a short while later, there are the remnants of the plants I fed myself earlier. Seems like they didn't have a negative effect on me, so I eat all of it.

The taste is foreign and discomfiting, but I keep eating until they run out. I'm still hungry.

I sit up, feeling a dull ache in my back. Sleeping against a tree on the ground is terrible. It's been a while since I've experienced this level of discomfort, but it never really gets better. I suppose a layer of leaves is better than dirty concrete.

There's also the rising panic and anxiety that extends beyond being here. It's been too long since I've talked to someone.

I have never gone this long without talking to people.

A feeling of panic settles in the pit of my stomach when I realize I really am the only human here. I've never truly been alone, even when I was homeless. There are plenty of other people who were in the same situation, many of them incredibly caring individuals.

A lot of my pitiful earnings go toward visiting them and taking them things I know they like.

Talking with people is something I enjoy doing, must do, but here, the chance of that is slim.

Well, the option so far is one alien... person? Yes, I suppose, regardless of his terrible manners, he's still a person.

Just the thought of him makes my skin crawl and memories of my stepfather rise up, stealing my breath. Both of them predators of their own sort. Both of them angry.

But then my mind rejects the comparison. Octo-man is angry, true. He's the scariest person I have ever met, but that anger somehow lacks... menace. At least toward me.

A part of me knows that he is interacting with me in a way that runs counter to his nature. I think back to him screaming out his confusion after he protected me. Then it hits me. He's angry with himself more than he is with me.

Except, isn't that how it is with any abuser? They hate themselves, but can't direct that hatred inwardly, so they find a victim for it?

I shiver. He's already blamed me for it. I remember now. The usual prickle of fear rises when I think of someone being angry. My head feels light and my heart pounds.

Flashes of my stepfather's twisted features, and the emotional barbs, or the physical pain that always followed, flit through my head.

My shaking hands catch my attention. Am I really doomed to live like this no matter where I go?

I can't accept that. If I had someone to talk to, I could distract myself from the looming fear of doom that lives in my head constantly.

Surely there are other people here. I need to look for them, but how am I going to manage it with him always blocking me? Would he kill them if I found them?

My heart constricts. I don't know. He's said plenty of times he would kill me and he hasn't, but I can't say for sure that threat won't apply to someone else.

I could be bringing death along with me if I look for other people. My fists tighten and the desire to strangle him is as high as it has ever been.

Before I look for others, I need to tame him. I let out a snort.

Tame a violent octo-man with no form of gentleness in him? *Right, Eli...*

Except, is it true that he can't be caring?

He keeps saying he plans to kill me but doesn't. I assume he's only trying to convince himself by this point. Maybe if I can convince him that the way he feels isn't my fault, his anger will dissipate.

Abusers never truly help the people they are abusing, it's only to manipulate them. To get what they want. I just need to figure out what he's after. What motivates him...

I mean, it never worked on my stepfather, but I refuse to believe I am stuck in the same hell.

Or maybe I'm completely deluding myself and I really am so desperate to talk to someone I'd welcome a psychopath's company.

Before I can think more about it, I yell out. "Hey! Are you there?"

I realize I don't know his name. I can't be blamed for that.

Most people don't ask monsters for their names and horror movies don't count. When my voice echoes out, it isn't met with a response.

That's bull. I know he's watching me and purposefully ignoring me. He only comes out of his own volition.

"Hey! At least tell me your name."

Ignored again.

The bugs and wind are the only ones who respond to my calls, a cacophony rising in the grassland again. I look up at the trees and one look at the hanging vines gives me an idea. I reach for the lower hanging vine, wrap it around my splint and pretend to pull, screaming at the top of my lungs.

I hear him long before I see him. Before I can take a breath for another scream, his tentacles wrap around me, his stormy eyes bearing down on me.

"Why would you hurt yourself again?" he berates, pulling my arm back down. "I mended it. Stop!"

Even though it hurts, I smile at him, pleased that I got him here. I feel a familiar heat in my lower body as his tentacles wrap and caress my body, but I firmly ignore it, the craving for communication trumping my carnal desire.

And, also, ick.

"Can you tell me your name?"

He pauses and his eyes look like they are trying to bore a hole into my head. He speaks, making a whale sound that roughly translates to killer.

Hell no. There's no way I'm calling this brutish alien *killer*. He needs to soften some edges if he wants to make any damn friends.

What sort of cliché and egoistic name is that? It's way too arrogant.

"I'll call you Wroahk."

It's a shortened form of the sounds he made.

He doesn't look very pleased. "I don't like it."

"Too bad. My name is Eliyana."

He tries to pronounce it, but it comes out mangled and disorderly. I don't like it either.

"Just call me Eli," I say firmly.

He gives me what I assume is a deadpan look and just says no. There's really nothing else I can do about it. I can't threaten a tentacle monster that crushes alligators as easily as he breathes.

So, I decide to pivot.

"Do you know where we are? Have you seen others like us?"

"I do not know where we are, only that this place is dangerous. There are no others like us, but there are more like the ones who took me. If you move out of here to find any, you will not make it very far."

His blunt tone sends shivers down my spine. I can tell he's not lying. I know we're not on Earth, but the possibility of rescue just became very, very slim. I try to change the subject again, but my voice comes out very small.

"W-What do you do? For a career, I mean."

It's a dumb question so he looks at me weirdly. He has the name *killer*, so it should be obvious. However, the concept of careers really doesn't translate well, and he's left looking to me for an explanation.

At this point, I don't care anymore if he understands me. I just want to talk to someone. So... careers.

"Working at the grocery store was fun. The old people loved riding on the scooters and telling me stories about their grandchildren while trying to give me expired coupons," I chuckle, remembering the time I accepted an old newspaper from the nineties.

"They always had something to say. It was always 'back in my day', and you can see them relieving the memories of their youth. Some of them even drag their grandchildren to the store and try to introduce me to a few as dates," I chuckle again.

I used to live in survival mode, so I took those memories for granted. Not anymore. They're my precious memories.

Now I know what survival mode actually means.

"I don't understand," he clicks out.

"Of course you don't," I mumble under my breath.

"My kind are hunters," he ignores my mumbling. "Nothing more, nothing less. I do not care for anything else."

I let out a huff. "So brutish."

"I do not enjoy talking to you."

Well, that hurt. I can't believe I was excited to talk to him.

"Well maybe if you focused more on using your brain rather than just bludgeoning through everywhere like a dumb sea monster with only his tentacles to show for it, this conversation might be more productive for you."

He just stares at me with those emotionless shark eyes, remaining silent. The feeling that I won the argument fills my chest with pride. I stare him down, ignoring the large row of teeth that glint under his gaze.

He won't eat me, right?

His tentacles slip off me and he starts moving away. The fear of being alone overshadows my pride of winning, and I quickly speak up.

"It'll hurt me if I don't speak to anyone!"

Alright, that's an insult to all women, but whatever. There is truth in it though. I do feel like I'll explode if I don't talk to another person.

"Nothing can hurt you or I'll kill it," he growls.

Seeing his large row of teeth being bared in my face, hovering above me like they were going to chomp me in half, scares me for a bit, but then I realize where this big dude's inner struggle is coming from. He wants to harm me, but has decided nothing is allowed to.

I can work with that.

"You're the one hurting me by leaving," I point out, trying to keep my voice from shaking.

"How much does it hurt?" he asks, taking me by surprise.

It's probably my imagination, but his voice is softer, gentler.

"A lot," I whisper.

"You are a very strange creature," he says, his voice regaining its usual tone. "I cannot stay with you all the time. I have to hunt to eat and that means I will have to leave you."

He's being surprisingly considerate. I pick my next words carefully.

"You don't have to be here all the time. I can hold out when you go to hunt, and everyone needs some time to themselves. You just have to stay here and talk to me when I need to talk."

He looks me over and considers my words. As he does, I suddenly remember that the reason I am currently in this bit of grassland mixed with tall trees is because I was running from him.

Have I lost my mind?

Having him beside me, his large teeth clacking and his tentacles ready to squeeze the life out of me isn't a sane plan. Before I can retract my offer, he replies.

"I will remove that pain."

21

Wroahk

No matter what I'm doing, no matter where I am, my attention always returns to the female.

I've watched her sleep for the second night in a row yet the storm in my mind has yet to stop raging. It's doing nothing for my raging thoughts to be so near her, but the expression on her face when she sees me approach is something I've never seen.

I want to see more of it.

As I approach the grassland, I see she's now standing, like she's waiting. I can't stay too long on land, yet I cannot leave her here.

"Good morning!"

Her voice is high pitched, making her fumble through the clicks of my language. My grasper twitches with the desire to insult her, but I keep it still.

Her tone and body say she is happy, but it doesn't feel right. Like it's a trick.

She maintains her distance from me, and I can see every tense muscle in her body. She can't run far from me, but it doesn't mean she isn't going to try if I frighten her.

Why should I care? I won't have to expend much energy catching her. I don't respond to her greeting, though I do I wonder why she's excited.

"I have a feeling it's going to be a great day! I've already eaten and I'm ready for a little chat."

"We cannot stay here," I immediately say, trying not to prolong my time on the surface.

"Why not? It's nice here, and I have found a way to make myself comfortable after my arm started healing. Look, I made myself a little *bed*." She points to the base of the large tree and I see a rough compaction of the grass, mashed together like they'd been pressed on.

She looks proud of her ridiculous nest.

"I figured since the grass doesn't hurt my skin, it's fine if I create a little sleeping *bag* for myself. Anyway, why don't you want us to stay here?"

"I'll dry up."

Her eyes drift down to my tentacles as her mouth forms a round shape. She puts her grasper to her chin, and I can see that she's thinking. I'm tempted to just toss her over my shoulder and take her with me, but I cannot hurt her.

"*Okay*, let's go! It's not like I can say no to you, anyway. I'm just happy to be here with someone," she says, her face not looking like it usually does.

Is she lying? Yes, I think she is, but I don't understand why.

Sometimes she is very angry, and it seems real. Sometimes she is very happy, and it feels like a trap.

What would motivate her to lie about being happy?

I reach to carry her since she's very slow, but she moves out of the way, fear flashing across her eyes for a moment before her happy face trap is back. I retract my grasper and let her walk behind me, listening to her little gasps and mumbles as we head to the lake.

Much to my annoyance, I now must watch over this fragile thing constantly because it will die from not speaking.

Is there anything that won't kill it?

We settle along the shore on opposite sides with me watching her from the water. She nestles on a small stretch of sand and my upper body is slightly above the water. Her mouth hasn't stopped moving since we decide to move to the water.

"It's funny that the last face I saw before I woke up here was my *mother's*, begging for her *lover* to still be alive. She birthed me yet I was less important to her than the *hijo de puta* that beat on her every single day," she scoffs, anger brewing in her eyes.

She calms herself with a breath and continues talking, although I really wish she would stop.

"Maybe the reason I went to visit her that day was because I had *hope*, *faith* that the female my *padre* once *loved* and *cherished* was still in there, somewhere. He was such a good *man*." Her voice changes again, her face falling.

My tentacles itch, but I pay them no mind.

"My *padre* and she were *married* for a while when I was younger. I thought they were in *love*. I used to believe such *fairy tales*. It all came crashing down when they *divorced* and my mother got everything, leaving me to be with my *padre*. What could he do? He was an *expatriate* with no *family* around. He *raised* me as best as he could. He did everything to make me happy and even *encouraged* me when I got into the *gifted program*. *Padre* was the best and I thought we would live like that forever. Unfortunately, life is so cruel. He left me so early and passed away in a *work* accident."

Her voice is soft and passionate. She speaks fondly of this person she calls *padre*, her eyes becoming softer when she mentions the name. She also speaks of the person who birthed her. To know the person who is responsible for your existence is such an odd feeling to me.

"Who is this *padre* person?"

"He's... my *father*. He's the other person responsible for me being alive."

It's truly so odd.

"Your seed-bearer is dead?" I say.

She wiggles her face up and down. "Yes."

"I see. I understand that. Many of the males of my species do not survive seed-giving, or if they do, they die young and violently. But why does it matter to you that he is dead? It is normal."

"Like I said, he was *responsible* for me. He took *care* of me best as he could. He wasn't always good at it, but he tried his best. It doesn't always have to be how you describe."

"I do not understand. What other way could it be?"

"You find other people who look out for you, and you look out for them. You make a *safe* place, and you protect it together."

"I do not trust others. They will steal your kills and tear out your throat in your sleep if they can."

"Wroahk," she says, looking at me with something I don't recognize in her eyes. "Has anyone ever touched you without violence?"

"No."

"What? Your life has been very different from mine. I mean, my *stepfather* is pretty much a *bastard* who used to beat on me and my *mother* but aside from that, I met a lot of people who were *kind* to me."

Kind? I don't know what that means.

She must know that, because she pauses and does the thing where she's carefully selecting her words.

"That didn't translate. *Kindness*. It means for someone to look at you without an intent to harm or have someone speak to you with no ill will, usually to make you feel good and you do the same for others."

"That does not exist," I say, hoping to end this immediately.

She is as insane as I suspected.

"Can I prove you wrong?" she asks, her voice pitching up.

I can't deny my curiosity, though I know she has nothing to teach me.

"You can do whatever you like, but you will fail. I'm confident that it does not exist, this thing you speak of. You are a terrible hunter, so why would you know anything I do not?"

Despite what I say, the look on her face unsettles me.

22

Eli

My first impression of him was that he was a wild animal. Completely untamed, completely ridiculous. It's still true.

However, I can see some of that wildness fading, like the sheen leaving a brand-new car. He doesn't admit it, but I can see he's more curious, more conversational.

I don't know why I told him about my *padre*. Maybe I was trying to soften him. Maybe I was trying to see if I can find humanity beneath the monster that he is.

But when he said he's never been touched before, it stirs my empathy.

No one should live like that. Besides, I want to see if I can find humanity beneath the monster. Or, whatever you would call it, to bring out a softer side to his violence.

Clearly he isn't completely opposed to change or he would have simply murdered me within moments of finding me.

"Can you come out of the water, Wroahk?"

It's a lot to ask, since I know he needs to stay in the water to survive. However, I can't dive in.

The mere thought of it makes me shiver.

Those things are still lurking beneath the surface. I need to stay somewhere safe. He stares at me with what I can only assume is suspicion and slowly makes his way out of the lake and up to the shore. He settles just a few paces in front of me, his tentacles right at my feet.

The tip of the closest one keeps coming steadily closer, not matching the arrogant look of his features or the way the rest of his body is telling me he doesn't want to be around me.

I finally get a proper look at his torso, now that I'm not shifting terrified looks between his sharp teeth and tentacles that can crush things far larger than I am with little strain.

He's huge, yes, but also sleek and muscular. It's obvious he really does spend his days just swimming around and hunting. His teeth and his hands are built for it and I would imagine he doesn't need too much time hunting down his prey and devouring them, he must just... like it.

A bloodthirsty hobby, but it fits.

Just the thought of that sends shivers down my spine.

"So... if I touch you, do you promise not to hurt me?"

"Nothing is allowed to hurt you. Not even me."

My heart skips a beat. It beats even faster, bringing with it a rush of memories of the last time I felt this way. Do I really feel... protected? By this writhing ball of rage?

Huh. I do.

It's been such a long time, reminding me of my days as a love-struck, empty-headed tween who lived in daydreams, which were made possible by a loving father. I used to imagine a tall, dark and handsome stranger sweeping me off my feet.

Later, when my life turned upside down, I used to dream of a savior, a dark knight that would fight off the monster for me.

Because the shining white knight? Those don't exist

I abandoned those dreams a long time ago. My relationships never last because I annoy the men I'm dating with my constant talking.

Even when I know they're annoyed, sometimes because I do know they are annoyed, I can't stop talking, eventually running them off. My eyes go back to Wroahk.

"Is there anywhere you'd prefer I didn't touch?"

"No," he replies curtly. "You can't harm me."

"That's not what I..."

I trail off, since I doubt he would understand.

I'm trembling as I step over his sprawled tentacles so I can get closer to where they have him lifted up, looming over me.

He subtly lifts himself higher, and my lips twitch when I realize he must feel threatened.

Unsure.

It makes me feel powerful and helps me work up the courage to slowly stroke the tips of my fingers gently down one of his muscular tentacles, starting with the thicker top, and dipping down until I can't reach any more of it without stooping.

A shiver passes up the tentacle as I stop. A quick glance up at him and I see that his eyes are now locked onto the movement of my hand, following it with the intensity I would expect in someone named *killer*, but for a very different reason altogether.

I slowly move my hand over to another tentacle, doing the same. Shudders pass through him, but he doesn't pull away. Hardly blinking as he follows the trail of my fingers.

It makes me bolder, and I lift both hands, pleased that I've gained back movement in my broken one, toward his torso.

His eyes are still locked onto my movement as he sinks down. I'm not even sure he's conscious of the movement, mesmerized as he is by something as simple as a light, gentle touch.

It makes my heart hurt for him. Makes me want this to be something special. Maybe even something life-altering.

How did he even survive? Human children die without touch. What kind of childhood did he endure?

I move my hands and hover them over his chest, just in case he wants me to stop. After a moment, he moves himself forward, bringing himself into contact with my hands. I stop worrying about the issue of questionable consent if he doesn't even understand the concept of gentleness. His movement let's me know he likes it, even if I doubt he will ever admit it.

His skin is softer than I expected. Blue on his torso and transitioning to green for his six tentacles.

I move my fingers down his boneless arms, lingering on the shark-like fins jutting out the back of them. His arms feel rigid, but also flexible. Like another form of tentacle, but with a couple of fingers at the end of each.

I move lower as his torso transitions to tentacles, noting the lack of genitalia, but avoiding the area just in case. I look up at him. His shark-like eyes are staring intently at where my hands are, but his face doesn't reveal any emotion.

Just an intense focus.

I keep feeling along the thick muscles of his tentacles, the bumps on the tops and sides, around the suckers on the bottom, letting some catch my hand. I feel a shiver pass through him, and I know I've got him.

I look up with a smirk, but he's still just frozen, with his eyes riveted to my hands. I continue to stroke along him, my ever-present, unexplainable arousal surging. As I continue to sensuously trail my fingers along a tentacle, I get the urge to ask him how it feels.

"Wouldn't you do your part to live together with people if you had access to that?"

He doesn't respond. Just shakes himself, his eyes darting up to mine, looking far less arrogant. Maybe even... lost.

He slips back into the water and disappears. It's getting too dark for me to see if he has stayed around or if monsters... other monsters... lurk instead. In the end, I go back up into the cove and curl up under my tree.

In my bid to find the humanity in him, did I push him too far?

I'll find out soon enough. He doesn't stay away for long.

Evenings are way too dark in this place and my shelter is too revealing for me to harbor any confidence about my own preservation. I suppose, hanging out with him earlier was against my own preservation.

Despite my deep-rooted fear, I tried being friendly. It felt right and I wonder what he's thinking right now.

Laying on my woven-out bed, I laugh to myself. It's so funny, how far I've come. Lightyears, it seems, and now I am trying to explain the concept of kindness to an alien.

The weirdest days of my life, for sure.

I move my arm around a few times and feel nothing besides a slight cramp. The mystery thickens, with no one to provide answers. At first I assumed he knew more than I did, but something tells me that with Wroahk it really is a *what you see is what you get* situation.

He's from a primitive planet, with a primitive culture. I have far more to teach him than he even realizes.

It's crazy, but I'm looking forward it.

The grass blanket I tried to make for myself with leaves does barely anything to protect my body from the constant wind that flows through this place. I've only just noticed it now, since I have continually collapsed with exhaustion, but the birds don't stop chirping at night.

There's a constant cacophony of noises. I'm grateful, though, since it makes me feel less alone and far from home.

I toss around, staring at the entrance of the cove from where I am. After walking through this place for a while, I've created a trodden path for myself so I can always see my entry and exit, plus the additional bonus of finding myself a suitable hiding place.

Humans really are the destroyers of nature. I've only been here a few days, but I've already altered the natural state and ecosystem of this place.

My thoughts keep me from sleeping right away, but I eventually drift off to thoughts about Wroahk. He's the only one of his kind I've seen since getting here.

I did ask him if this was his home, but he said it wasn't. Still. Are there more under the lake? Do they all look as spectacular as Wroahk?

I feel ridiculous for just thinking about it, but his broad chest and wide shoulders are more impressive than human men. It's like finally seeing a man after flirting and talking to only boys all my life.

And I am the one teaching him. Letting him experience all there is to know about a gentle touch.

I imagine running my hand down his broad chest, caressing the curves of his torso and finding out if he's as big down there as I think he is. Wild fantasies of being curled up and folded by Wroahk fill my head as desire causes warmth in my lower body.

Damn. I lit a fire that I can't douse easily, and sleep tonight will not come easy.

"This is just sick, Eli. I can't believe I'm horny right now."

Worst of all, I can't relieve myself. Besides, survival is way more important than lust. I'm just hoping there are no more surprises.

23

Wroahk

The feeling of her short limbs over my own overwhelmed me.

I remember her asking if there was a place she couldn't touch, but I didn't think it would be a problem. I was wrong. It was too much and not enough all at once, and I don't know how to think through it.

It was a strange, enjoyable feeling. Such a simple gesture, yet I stayed there, transfixed, as I let it happen. Even as I remember it, my entire body trembles in pleasure, expecting more of her touch.

Needing it.

It's a far different type of starvation than any I have experienced before.

There's no sensible predator that exposes themselves like that to anything. It felt like she was reaching past my skin, down to the depths of my being. My distrust, my hesitation, all of it seemed to wash away when she touched me.

This must be her ability.

I've wondered how she survives having no useful physical qualities. It's quite insidious, this power she holds. She must have the ability to subdue someone without using physical strength or violence.

That might explain it. Her strange ability must affect my unwillingness to eat her.

No, it doesn't make any sense. How is it possible she subdued me before ever touching me? What is it about her? Her disgusting yellow weeds? Those round eyes? Her soft, fragile body?

The battle in my mind returns the more I try to understand what she is. An inferior version of me that dares to control me without having enough strength to match my own. A species that has to rely on... whatever that was to be able to survive.

I despise her.

She's the opposite of everything I stand for, yet her touch lit a strange type of warmth under my skin. It wasn't scalding, neither was it violent. It consumed me... *kindly.*

I let out a breath, and then accept the truth. I can't bring myself to hate such a thing. It's a unique sensation.

I don't know how I've lived my life without it.

I avoided my pod mates. I lived a solitary lifestyle and kept to myself because I always thought it was best.

And it was. I was the strongest, so I survived.

I lived everyday hunting and defending my territory. It was what I was made for and what I was meant to do. I lived every day like the last, not bothered by how large the outside world was.

Her touch was like a rough awakening. I was violently thrust into a world much bigger than mine, where the circle of life and death mattered, but not by avoiding the death of a single, very specific person.

If she has this, others might also provide it, so why not just kill her and search.

My tentacles clench at the thought, and I bare my teeth. No. It would never be the same. I know it.

The warmth of the sun, the precious caress of the ocean, food in my belly. All I needed for survival were hunting and defending my territory. All of that made sense to me before I met her.

Those are all that should matter. Not the company of another. None of this ever mattered to me before, but I will not let it go now that it is in my grasp.

Now, every part of my body craves her touch again. As new as it might be, it's now an instinct as deep and primal as my need to hunt.

It took all my restraint to not latch on to her and take her down to the depths with me so my newfound discovery will not be extinguished. The only thought that stopped me was that she cannot swim, and I cannot harm her.

Although her constant talking is annoying, she can do it as much as she likes as long as she keeps being *kind.* As long as the new world she has introduced me to doesn't collapse on itself, I'll keep listening to whatever she decides to communicate.

Even if it makes no sense.

Still, my mind struggles to accept it. I should drift with the currents, eating and killing whatever comes my way.

If I understood her correctly, she says *kind* touch comes from protecting the weak. The slow ones usually have no option but to starve to death. The moment you stop being strong, your death is almost assured.

This feeling of warmth she gives is pleasurable, but it also weakens me.

If I'm weak, then I will die. If I die, who will stop her from being hurt?

My life has become impossible now. I can't go back to a life where I existed without this feeling of warmth. I wish I still hated her, that I still wanted to fill my belly with her. Now, I have to stay in this shallow, hot water, feeding off bottom feeders to stay close to her just so she won't be hurt.

Her definition of harm is wider than mine. If she doesn't talk, she hurts. If she isn't in the presence of another being, she hurts.

I don't understand it, but I can tell from her eyes that it is true. The requirements of her protection are getting higher, but all of it seems to be worth swimming into the new reality she has provided for me.

It's still nonsense, but I think I'm starting to understand her confusing concept about staying with people. By protecting her, I can have access to her and her *kindness*.

From her words, it means more than those touches, but I don't know what yet. I can at least understand the concept, when it comes to her touching me.

Is that what she does to others?

No. She will not.

If anyone or anything tries to do that to her, I will have to squeeze them until every bone in their body cracks and the pressure makes them split apart.

I can almost taste the victory bite.

I leave her for the night, venturing deeper into the waters. There isn't much to hunt when the darkness takes over the skies but taking a swim helps me to clear my head and stay focused.

I've been taking more swims lately and venturing deeper than I've ever gone before.

I didn't have any desire to explore the waters I found before I met her. I only went just far enough in search of better prey. When I found none, I stopped searching and established the best and most advantageous territory for myself.

Since it's freshwater, it hardens on my skin and causes drag, but I can still out-swim anything in these waters. I can't hold it properly when I'm on land because it's nowhere near as refreshing as the water in the ocean.

All I can do is endure it until I can find something better.

Until I can find both of us something better.

Venturing deeper into the water, the pressure changes. The number of the Many Teeth increases the deeper I go in and I find signs of their nests everywhere. The droppings they leave after consuming their prey are plentiful, and I can pick up signs of their migration.

It goes deeper, but I don't like the taste of it down there. Fortunately, they're getting farther away from my cave and moving into deeper waters, where the pressure changes.

She won't run the risk of running into the Many Teeth so deep into the trees. I disgust myself by rejoicing in that, but I don't feel as guilty as I used to feel.

The yellow one is mine.

Instead of moving farther downwards and placing myself in the territory of the Many Teeth, I go upward instead. I reach the surface in a few laps and my head breaks through the water. It's colder now. The sky is darkening, yet I can feel something approaching.

Two somethings, both of them running and breathing harshly.

They are strange and I assume not native to this area. I move closer to the shore, careful to not make any sounds.

I lurk by the surface, waiting for them to approach. The heavy footsteps give away signs of their location, as well as the babbling I hear from the distance. As they get closer, I can see them clearly.

The reluctance to kill that I felt when I first saw the female seems to have disappeared. My violent thirst to hunt and kill come back in full force, demanding the blood and head of the creatures that have encroached upon the water.

Are they the ones that took me?

I swim closer to them, eager to find out.

The one in front is covered in weeds, just like my yellow female, except it is far shorter and a different color. They are also much larger than her and of a different shape. Not her kind, then.

I keep my eyes on them, monitoring them as they approach the shore, then try to snap my tentacles at them. But I can't. There is a similar aversion that has so enraged me with the yellow woman, except I feel no attraction to the hulking creature.

It isn't one of the ones who took me, so no rage builds at my inability to attack it.

I let it move on, six limbs running down the shore of the lake. The figure behind it has the same body shape that's started to seem less odd in the female, but smaller, without her head weeds, and a gray-green skin instead of her warm brown.

Not my sworn enemy, but maybe one like it.

When this one comes close, I assume I will also be unable to harm it, but I'm wrong.

My tentacles shoot up before they can get by, and I grab them in an instant.

Though they struggle, my hold on them is tight. I pull them into the water, taking them deeper and deeper until we reach the Many Teeth's territory. I toss them forward and watch in glee as they're torn apart.

A wave of relief passes over me. She hasn't destroyed my hunter's instincts.

24

Eli

I jolt awake, heart pounding. Mind racing, trying to take in my surroundings and still confused.

My dreams were in no way peaceful. It's been a while since I've had any, but this one was as vivid as ever.

I was coloring with my mom, when she was still my mom and *padre* was watching us while fixing something in the kitchen. Life was simple... peaceful even.

My dream turned into a nightmare as my stepfather appeared. Then I sensed something looking at me. The gaze was intense, like it was right behind me. I knew it was about to kill me right before I woke up.

A shudder passes through me when I realize someone likely is watching me, though I no longer believe he plans to harm me.

This time, my morning is ushered in by the sounds of critters moving around. I'm drenched in sweat, a terrible combination with the grass I wove to be my bed. I laid in a fetal position too long last night and stretch myself out. I turn my gaze to my arm and rotate it a bit, feeling a difference in the pain levels.

It is not my first broken bone, not by a wide margin, but I already feel weeks along in the healing process.

My dream and broken bone remind me of the years of beatings I received before I finally ran away. The days and nights I spent crying because he ruined the vestiges of the relationship I had with my mother and made my life a living hell.

My dark childhood transitioned into my dark adulthood. Homelessness, hunger, near-death experiences... all of that.

I forcefully push all those memories away and imagine my golden cape of sunshine draping over me. I can't let my heart get hard. My father would've never wanted that for me.

It wasn't always easy, but I have focused on putting on a smile, never complaining and rarely cursing. I bowed my head when I needed to and took an extra shift here and there so my coworkers would get along with me.

I was the ultimate pushover, yes, but there was no need for me to be aggressive when I had food to eat and at least shelter for myself.

Sunny Eli.

I glance down at my new garish yellow hair and laugh at the irony. Sometimes the universe listens, but not in the ways you expect. Or want.

I stand and stretch properly, rising to the start of a new day. The nightmare fading to the back of my mind, I look around the empty clearing. The birds are still up in the trees, and the bugs are still buzzing, but I'm the only human here.

Lost in the mist, struggling dearly to get back up. Nightmares are always mirrors of reality.

Feeling more stable on my feet, I head to where I found the plants the last time, hoping to find more intact fruits. The purbees seem to hold a grudge because they try to prevent me from taking more of their flowers, but they don't have stingers, so all they are is a bunch of pestering flies.

I take my haul back with one hand and sit by my tree.

I finally get the chance to calmly eat, this time filling my stomach.

As the sugary scent of the fruit fades, I wonder why I don't stink by now. I've been there for a few days. I should smell like something died. Maybe even worse, since I haven't taken a dip in the water.

Thinking of the water, I feel thirsty. I head out of the cove, walking toward the water, and I immediately feel his gaze on me. He's always watching, always waiting. I wonder if he even sleeps at all.

Ignoring him, I bend by the water and take a scoop, using my hand to drink it. I have the same logic for everything. If the food didn't kill me, I doubt the water can.

I seem to have a hyperactive immune system since I was taken. I don't know whether to be grateful or terrified.

I look at my arm. Okay, definitely grateful.

With my belly full, I call out to Wroahk. He comes almost immediately.

"Are you in pain?"

I realize he almost looks... friendly. Almost. Or at least not menacing, because his face is really just an expressionless mask. For him, friendly. In a mean, scary shark with sharp teeth and tentacles ready to crush you sort of way.

"The pain is gone now that your smiling face is here before me."

He's definitely not smiling, and doesn't even bother asking what the word means. I'm pretty sure his face can't do it, anyway. It doesn't deter me, though. He's the only one here, and after that nightmare, I need his company.

"The weather here is nice, but the nights are cold."

I continue rambling about the weather and something about global warming when my brain reminds me I shouldn't talk too much. He'll leave. Just like everyone else I chatter out of my life.

However, the world around me is still scary, and this is the only way I can soothe myself. My mouth just refuses to stop dropping words.

I used to be a quiet child, but during my adolescence, I started rambling. I don't know if it was because of rebellion or just a natural progression of my character, but it's compulsive now. That thought reminds me I can control anything I want, and I take a deep breath and just look out over the water.

It gets me talking about the refraction of light on water, and I just keep at it even when half of my words don't translate.

I'm talking more to myself, I know. When I was younger, my father used to tell me facts and sometimes, when we are both exhausted by the weary worries of the world, we'd sit on the porch and just watch the stars, imagining we could fly in the constellations.

I'm among the stars, padre. Just like we dreamed. It's just... nothing is ever the same without the people you love.

25

Eli

My arm feels surprisingly good as it swings along my side as I move to the lake shore.

Wroahk is there and I start chattering to him about how nice it is this morning, but I can tell he isn't listening.

I'm mid-sentence sharing what I've observed of purbee flight patterns and communication methods when he interrupts me.

"You have this strange idea about adults living and working together. How do you know people are better together? What if they're just weaker together?"

My mouth drops open in shock, before looking closer at his face. "You rarely ask me a question without looking like you're going to tear my head off. I like this change. Why do you ask?"

"Separation is the way my people have survived for a long time," he tells me.

I think back to what other things he has said. "So, you band together so your entire species doesn't die, but you kill the weak?"

"Don't the weak also die where you are from?"

I let out a bitter laugh, uncomfortable with how close he is to the truth. "It's not really like that. My species is based on the idea of dependence on others. One person can't do everything, so we form societies, little groups of people who work interdependently to make living about more than just surviving. From that, we got the idea of a family. There's a mother, a father, and their children. Or mother and mother, father and father... or found family, whatever. A nuclear structure is what I mean, a fundamental part of an ideal society. If this part breaks down, the entire society might as well be on its way to a total shutdown."

Judging by the number of words that came out in English, that was probably confusing, but the look on his face lets me know he understood at least some of it.

He might be violent and odd, but he is definitely intelligent.

"So, your species move around in groups?" he asks. "Like schooling fish that flit around, trying to confuse you."

I splash some water, my eyes roaming and focusing on the colorful fish dumb enough to swim close to him.

"Not exactly, but close enough," I tell him.

He whips out a tentacle and grabs one of the fish.

I grumble at him. "Don't eat the pretty fish. They aren't even a meal."

"I don't stop you from consuming those plants, so don't try to stop me from hunting. They are just bottom feeders. Why do you care?"

"I just do," I hiss out.

"Is it because you feel like them?"

I ignore the barb, knowing he's just pissed at me, and also don't comment when I see him let it go. Instead, I go back to trying to make him a smidge less violent.

"The concept of kindness I mentioned earlier is what makes up our species. The sense of empathy. Caring for others more than you care for yourself. Parents care for their children more than they do for themselves, and that leads to longer lives for all of us. They show kindness to their offspring, and that kindness continues for generations, meaning most of us live."

He makes his laughing sound. "If you abandon your offspring, they'll have a better chance at survival as an adult than if you keep coddling them to yourself."

My heart thumps in my chest. That's essentially what my father did, though not by choice. I flash back to that terrible day when I was pulled from my classroom, told to sit down, and then informed he had been killed in a workplace accident.

I shut down the memory before I spiral down into the same black hole of despair that consumed me back then.

Living with my mother was even worse than abandonment. I was most definitely not better off.

I shake my head. "No. That's now how it works. Offspring get the chance to be stronger while you protect them. And it isn't just parents that protect them. It's a whole community based on kindness."

I'm making Earth sound like a utopia, but he's confused enough as it is, and I ignore the part of my mind that hates breaking something so complex down into such an absolute.

I'm pretty sure no society actually works like that, but if he can get this, we can cover the thousands of exceptions later.

Way, way later. Or not at all if someone rescues me.

He doesn't look convinced. "You're saying that kindness has to be applied to everyone, and not just yourself, or it doesn't work? You could never trust everyone to do that. Why can't I just claim your kind hands like I have the rest of this lake?"

My chest constricts, and prickles rise up the back of my neck. My breathing turns shallow and flashes of so many near misses when I was on the street bubble up. Hands groping in the dark, having to run away, sometimes leaving behind the few things I had managed to buy.

I take in a slow, deep breath and glance at the sun, focusing on the warmth it provides on my skin, then I consider how to answer him.

It's likely a reasonable question from his point of view, but if I don't stop that sort of thinking all of this might turn very ugly, very quickly. His thought process is that of a predator, and he's trying to think of kindness as prey.

I'm convinced he's smart enough to see that it doesn't work like that, but I don't know how to explain it without him just dismissing what I have to say.

Then I see it, though the idea scares me.

He might be an alien, but he's still male. Just like human men, I bet he'll need to learn the hard way. I'm positive he doesn't want to hurt me. I think it might be time for one of those lessons.

Living with an abuser teaches you really quick how to manipulate any possible situation in any way you can to avoid being hurt. It's time to put those hard-earned skills to work.

26

Wroahk

She pauses, searching for an answer to my question. My eyes are drawn to her graspers, more fragile and breakable than mine, but I've felt them.

I know how they must be treasured now. Protected.

"*Kind hands* can't be won or taken, only *given*," she tells me.

"Why?"

She lets out a long breath and speaks again. "*Kind hands* must be offered, not taken, otherwise you get violent *hands* or if you're violent, you kill the possibility of there being a *kind* anything. You can't just seek to own somebody if you want them to be *kind*. Trust me, if you're *patient* and *gentle*, you will have more than if you try to take."

"So, your *kind hands* come at the cost of you endlessly talking?" I ask.

"Yes," she responds a little too eagerly, bobbing her head.

"I understand," I say, even though it would be much easier for me to simply claim my territory.

"It's a *deal* then," she says.

I stare blankly at her.

"A *trude?*" she asks.

I keep staring at her, not understanding the words coming from her mouth. She reaches out a grasper to me, eagerly looking at my face. I would take it as a gesture to fight, but she is not a creature of violence.

"Not that either, *huh? Dios*. This should be interesting."

She continues splashing water with her graspers, her expressions shifting before she speaks again.

"It's an *agreement* we have to make. I can't keep thinking you want to eat me every time you look bored, and you can't just hang around for no reason. Now that I think about it, you keep watching me like a *stalker*. I should get a *restraining order* against you."

She laughs that odd sound that doesn't sound like her normal self. It distracts me, but then I focus back on her words. I think I understand she wants me to stop watching her. No, I cannot do that. I know I won't keep myself away from her.

I peer at her. "What is the *agreement*?"

Her lips raise, I assume because she likes my question. "First, you've got to stop watching me all the time. It's like you're with me every second of the day. It makes it hard to do anything private."

"No. A Many Teeth would kill you."

"Many Teeth?" she asks, cocking her head to the side.

"The creature that attacked you."

"Oh... Well, they do have a lot of teeth. You do too..." her voice trails off as she stares at me.

"I am nothing like them."

"Fine, I know you're not," she clicks back, raising her graspers. "I'm just saying maybe that's not the best thing to call them. It might make them more irritable."

"I don't care."

"You look like you don't," she responds, her lips moving again in a way that doesn't seem natural.

"Still, it makes it hard to clean myself if you're constantly watching me."

I can't help spending most of the day thinking about her and therefore watching her. My eyes instantly find her, a need for her rising within me. I prefer to watch my prey, so nothing else steals it away or has the chance to.

She's mine to take.

"I'll keep watching you. No *agreement*."

She sighs in defeat. "Fine. I'll try to ignore your intrusive stares."

She seems to finally be done adding to the *deal*, good. "I have listened to you. You will give me *kind hands* now."

Something moves across her face as she hesitates, then she closes her eyes for a brief moment, stands up taller, then speaks. "No."

"There was a *deal*."

She moves her head back and forth. "No."

Anger starts to build, and I move out of the water. Her eyes widen, but she doesn't flee. I whip out a tentacle and wrap it around her wrist, then tug her forward, rubbing her grasper against the top of another tentacle.

Frustration builds in my chest, like I'm starving and my prey keeps alluding me.

She doesn't move, just stares at me. I put her other grasper next to the other, but she doesn't react. I gently move her graspers, rubbing them against me, but it just feels... like nothing.

"I told you, Wroahk. *Kindness* can never be taken, only given. It doesn't feel the same, does it?"

My grip loosens. "You will—"

She speaks over me. "Unless I move with intent, unless I decide to give my *kindness* to you, it will never feel the same. It's empty without my *consent*."

I release her and she takes a step back, pulling her arms close to her body and watching me intently. I look back down at her graspers.

That's not where her *kindness* comes from, I realize. It comes from somewhere inside of her. There is more to her than I can see, and I suddenly start to understand some of her power over me.

Is it a form of strength, but in a way that can't be seen or touched?

She takes a deep breath. "I think you understand now. The thing I want most of all is for you to ask if you want to touch me, not just do it. It's called *consent*. I won't touch you unless you ask. I will ask to talk, and you can ask for *kind hands*, but either one of us can always say no."

Asking for something. It's a simple yet strange concept. I don't ask prey if I can hunt or eat them. I've always done as I wished.

Except now I see that there are some things, very important things, that simply cannot be hunted.

"*Agreement*," I tell her, deciding to accept this new change to my life.

"Good. I think we will be just fine. Looking forward to *working* with you, Wroahk," she says with a laugh, this one sounding normal again, extending a grasper to me.

I look at it, unsure of what she wants me to do. She points to my grasper with her free hand.

"You bring up your *hand* the same way I did."

"No."

"Oh, come on. It's nothing hard. It's just a *handshake*."

Touching her grasper just seems so... dangerous now. And I fear breaking them, or not understanding *consent*. I still want her *kind hands*, and I need time to think about all of this.

I refuse her firmly and dive into the water.

After a quick hunt to clear my mind, I return to watch her.

She moves around doing her mysterious things as I think, my brain sick of how much of it I have been doing. She's wandering around, picking plants and following around not-food like they are the most interesting things she has seen in her life.

She doesn't even try to eat them. I don't understand the point.

I run through our conversation again, and the way she looked. Not like she usually does. Like a hunter does when they are trying to make it seem like they are looking at a different prey, all the while planning to kill the one to the side of them.

No, surely that would be something beyond her. She's ridiculous. Now she's climbing up into one of those huge plants now, pulling things from it and putting them in her mouth. Whatever it is, it looks disgusting.

The way she looked as I moved out of the water flashes into my mind. Like it was planned. Such an odd creature, but now I see I have underestimated her. She tricked me, making it seem like she was hunting something else, and I moved right into her trap.

My mating tentacles are writhing in the water as I try to understand just what type of hunter she is.

27

Eli

I can feel Wroahk's intense gaze on me from the water, though I already told him how annoying his staring is, but I suppose I can't do anything about it since he's protecting me. He's just lurking there, watching me.

His lazy floating is kind of impressive, but there's no way I will tell him that.

I swear he's even more interested in me now, which I suppose is a good thing. At least he won't try to eat me now. That doesn't mean he has stopped seeing me as prey. I'm constantly being watched and if I wander too far, he's always right there, reminding me I can't run from him.

All I can do now is coexist with the only other person here I can talk to, so I don't lose either my sanity or my life.

I highly doubt I would last very long if he wasn't here to keep away the Many Teeth. Fine, no chance.

We have a relationship, no matter how tentative. Although, I'm not sure if the whole 'kind hands' concept is a good idea. I mean, I told him it would bring me harm if I don't speak to someone. I knew he was talking about physical harm, but I was just blurting things out impulsively because I didn't want to be left alone.

My irrational decision arose because of my fear. As usual.

Our agreement is also imbalanced, since I get more out of it than he does. Sure, he didn't agree to stop watching me incessantly, but he's doing it all to protect me. He'll fight off the Many Teeth creatures for me and all I'll do is hug him? Kiss his cheek? Hold his hand?

It makes little sense, even to me. Then I remind myself that to him, it's probably like finding water in a desert. I feel for him, even though he's a terrible conversationalist, completely bloodthirsty, and his thinking is as alien as his looks.

I don't even know how I forgot to find a middle ground. Was I that desperate for protection? Is this what I'll do for survival?

Screw over an unsuspecting alien because he knows nothing about empathy and sexual arousal via touch.

And if I'm being honest with myself, I'm not sure I won't move on to other 'kind' things because right now, my body feels like one raging pile of unsated lust, and it'll only get worse the longer he remains by my side.

Like right now.

All he's doing is staring at my hands with his creepy shark eyes, and the heat from my lower body is threatening to overcome my senses. I'm turned on by an alien monster with tentacles.

It's insane.

My attention is like food scraps to a dog, only temporarily able to satiate its hunger. However, he's already clarified that to him, I'm just meat.

He must really be that desperate.

Oddly enough, to him, I'm meat... that no one is allowed to hurt, including himself. The octopus shark man seems to have a hard time reconciling it all, but I'm confident that the starved look in his eye will work to my advantage.

As soon as the thought occurs to me, I chide myself for being the type of person I've always hated. No matter the form or to whom, manipulation isn't acceptable. He's a creature that hasn't had the pleasure of experiencing any sort of affection, kindness, or love. There aren't even any words in his language for them.

My self-reflection comes with annoyance. I decide to come clean to him.

"Hey, Wroahk?"

"Yes? he responds in lazy clicks, still staring at me.

"Do you remember when I said it hurts me to be alone?"

His eyes flicker in an instant and he almost leaps out of the pool, suddenly alert.

"Are you still hurting?"

"No, no, it's not that. I just wanted to tell you that... I was lying. It doesn't hurt me to be alone. I just... don't like it and it makes me scared."

The emotions in his eyes flicker, but his tense body relaxes. "Scared? The only time someone is safe is when they are alone."

"That's not true," I shake my head. "There's safety in numbers."

"You're all just moving targets," he responds lazily, one of his tentacles coming out of the water.

"You know what, Wroahk? I won't argue with you. All I want is for you to spend time with me and protect me from those... monsters. But I shouldn't trade you my kind touch for it."

His expression flickers again, so I decide to clear it up right away.

"What I'm saying is that we don't have to bargain for it. Everyone deserves a kind touch, even you. So, what I'm saying is..." I stumble over my words, trying to find the right things to say so he can understand.

So far, he has been doing a good job of understanding.

"What I'm saying is that I'll touch you kindly if you ask. Just stay here and talk with me, so I'm not scared. I'm not saying this as a deal. I'm saying this as a sincere request. I need a companion, and I think you do, too."

He blinks slowly and I wonder if too much was left untranslated. "Do you understand?"

"Yes. You needed me to be with you, though I am not sure exactly why, and you used that to set a trap. You maneuvered me until you got what you wanted, just like a hunter would. I have never been prey before, and I do not like it, but I like to see you showing the ways you are strong."

He sinks back down to the deep, resurfacing a few moments later to look at me before diving back in again.

My mouth is still open in shock when the ripples of his movement disappear.

For some reason, the memories of my exes complaining about my endless drivel come back to my mind, and the contrast is stark. I can't believe it, but I think that's one of the best compliments I've gotten in my adult life.

I want him to come back up so I can tell him that and I look up into the sky at how crazy all of this is.

Without him there, it's silent again. I can't just speak to myself, or I'll go crazy... faster. Sighing, I turn my gaze back to the water. I shouldn't have done that. I hate his excessive staring, but being alone drives my anxiety to a fever pitch.

I hear a growl, probably coming from the farthest part of the lake and spring to my feet. I move away from the surface and run back to the cove, making my way back to my bed.

It feels quieter, more lonely.

The nights I spent on the streets come back to me in hurtful waves of nostalgia. The hot days and cold, barren ground at night, trying to find someone to huddle up with you know won't hurt you, and the impending fear that I'm going to be left to rot with no one knowing I ever existed or loved or lived.

Unfortunately, this fear has become much too real. Stranded on an alien planet, no one could really tell if I exist.

I was already a nobody back on earth. Maybe that's why I was easy to snatch up. All my dreams, my aspirations as a little kid, all gone now in a puff of smoke as an adult.

Before my eyes close, I feel a familiar gaze on me. Wroahk.

As annoying as he is, he sees me. In fact, he won't stop looking. If I went missing, he would definitely notice.

Too bad it took coming to a different planet and meeting the most violent person imaginable to prove those bastard cops wrong.

A smile graces my lips as I slip off to slumber, knowing I'm at least not alone.

28

Wroahk

I returned when she woke, pleased by the look in her eye when she saw me.

She never stops speaking. Even though her words fall like echoes, they are like a never-ending stream flowing relentlessly. I am sure the reason the fish have all disappeared is because of how loud she is.

Noise attracts predators and the reason this prey is still alive is because of me. This does nothing to bother her, as she is still speaking. She pauses sometimes to catch her breath and stares at me for a while before continuing. It is strange to see someone so dedicated to the act of conversation.

Although I agreed to listen to her, the cost for her touch seems high when she hasn't done so. She looks more content with my presence and the occasional brushes she does against my skin.

It feels like I'm being taken advantage of, even though she is someone who cannot harm me even if she tried. Her docility and mercy are just some of the many reasons I consider her species to be ridiculous. The more she talks, the more out of place I feel. This place is already so strange, but her words add a layer of alienation, filling my head with more thoughts and even stranger emotions.

"Honestly, I have never seen trees this big! We had some big trees back on earth, but I feel like I can use some of the leaves from these trees as a *blanket*! A *blanket*! Can you just believe how ludicrous that is? Honestly, not just the size of the trees is shocking, but the fact that I can breathe so comfortably here is, too. Trees back home assist in *aerobic respiration* using *oxygen*, but it's hard to even tell if what I'm breathing in is *oxygen*. Um, oxygen is an *element*... like a basic *unit* of all living beings. We're made up of things like that, from the biggest *whales* to the tiniest *bugs*. Speaking of *bugs*, the bugs here are colorful, too..."

Things like that.

When she speaks, it's hard to tell what she's talking about, especially when she easily switches topics in the same breath, moistening her lips with fluid from inside her mouth. My eyes focus on her lips as she does that, my throat feeling strangely dry.

The sparkle of excitement grates on me and my mind wanders to how good her moist lips will taste if I take a bite out of them. My eyes wander down to her exposed, fair neck and my throat feels even dryer as my body shakes with an urge that is not quite hunger.

Not a bite out of them. Just a small bite and a long taste.

"Wroahk? Are you good?"

That ridiculous name.

I don't know why she keeps calling me that, even though it sounds nothing like what I keep telling her. I respond to her with a strangled grunt and deviate my gaze from her body. My mating tentacles feel the urge stronger than the rest of my body and my eyes start to wander again, this time to the place below her torso as my interest waxes stronger.

"You're not saying anything, even though you can speak better than a few grunts and growls."

"I do not have the capacity to speak endlessly like you," I reply in clipped clicks, taking my eyes away.

She frowns and leans closer. "That is rather *rude*."

I don't know about *rude*, but I know I am right.

I don't respond to her, and she keeps on talking. She's chiding me, but her grasper hasn't made its way to my body. Even though that's why I'm waiting here, she refuses to touch me.

Her graspers are just a tentacle's length away, yet she's being careful with her actions, strangely stopping short of just brushing against me.

She's driving me mad.

I have an intense urge to just grab her grasper and force her to touch me. I want to relish yet again in the soft and serene feeling I felt when she touched me for the first time. Even though it affects my mating tentacles so much, I want to feel her *kind* touch.

I crave it. I want it now.

I tilt my head to the side. "Is there more than just *kind hands*?"

She laughs. "Oh, a lot more. Even better things. But that's not something I'm offering... right now," she says, slapping her grasper over her mouth like she is trying to keep more words from escaping.

It pulls my attention sharp to her, since she seems to prefer if they flow as fast as possible.

Right now, she said. So maybe in the future.

Yet, as I watch this soft, small being, I remember her words. If I want her *kind* touch, it cannot be taken by force. It must be given freely, which I find ridiculous.

Everything worth having is taken with force. Everything.

But, no, the one thing I crave is something I cannot have if I use my strength. It disturbs me, but the consequences of losing something fluttering so close to me is more terrifying. I watch her face soften as the subject of the conversation changes again.

"My *padre* was one of the most upright *gentlemen* I knew. He was *soft* and *kind*, even when he didn't need to be. He always says a female needs to be treated like a *princess*." She looks happy, her voice trailing off as she immerses herself in yet another memory.

Suddenly I think I understand. It isn't about the number of her words, it is about something inside of her ready to give that *kindness*.

"I remember one time I was talking about a *book* I *read* to him and was telling him about how much I liked the *author*. He found out about a *book signing* and moved mountains, rearranging his entire *work schedule* to be able to take me to that *book signing*. It was also on the *weekend* and as a child, I didn't realize it earlier, but he was exhausted from working all week and still took the time to *drive* me there. He often told me he was *proud* of me and..." her voice breaks as her eyes softens even more.

"...I had done nothing worthy, yet he was *proud* of me. He gave anything and everything just to make me happy."

I don't get it. If this man is her seed bearer, it makes no logical sense that he that he would do those things. The males of my species work harder to keep their own lives and provide for themselves rather than keep around something as useless as an offspring.

Perhaps the reason her species is so weak is because they spend too much time on useless things.

She seems to have gotten everything she wanted from this *padre* of hers. That's the only thing I can understand from her relentless rambling.

If that is the case, then to get her *kind hands* I need to give her anything she wants.

It doesn't seem like that's all there is to it, though.

And I can't accept that, anyway. There might be some other possibility to the give and take thing, like an acceptable amount of taking something and the limits of taking too much.

Like how she should really use her grasper to touch me instead of flailing them around and talking about stupid things.

"Back on my home *planet, parents* had to *discipline* their *children,* or they were seen as bad *parents.* My *padre* didn't do it so much, but that female was intent on trying to look like a strict *parent* since my *padre* was not. They usually argued when it came to me, but more so when it came to my interests. I remember getting into *horror novels* and they got into a huge fight since *padre* was willing to let me *buy gory novels* and she would refuse lest people *judged* her in public. I was really into *horror novels* then even though I couldn't stand *horror movies...*"

She's going on again about something I can't understand.

Her people seem so complex despite being so weak. They have a curiosity for the world around them that isn't natural and I assume must share their findings in conversations with one another.

If I find a stable place to hunt and live, I will guard that place with my life. A *companion* is not a need of mine, but for her species, it seems to be one. Which means I need to provide that for her.

It makes my stomach roil.

I am not familiar with thinking so deeply. Until being captured and meeting this female, I had limited curiosity for the world. Well, now that I have been plucked out of my favorite hunting spot, I suppose I have a great deal of curiosity and rage toward the ones who did it.

And now I need to figure out this female.

I am going to stop thinking so deeply about it for now. It hurts my brain and confuses my body.

The simple life of just swimming around and hunting doesn't seem so bad compared to endlessly thinking and talking about unspecified things for hours. Instead of that, I'm going to do what I want to do.

Luckily I stop myself in time. "*Kind hands?*"

She stops talking, then holds her arms out.

Finally.

I surge up to the bank and drag myself closer to her, wrapping my tentacles around her. Sure, she says I cannot take what I want forcibly, but I have listened to enough of her drivel. The warmth and elasticity of her body overwhelming me, causing a feeling I don't have a word for. It is much better than the feeling I got relaxing in my old favorite resting spot after a full day of hunting.

"Wroahk! What are you doing? I told you that you can't just do that. Alright, fine. I see the miscommunication. I said yes."

She tries to shake me off, but it feels like mere tickles to me. I can listen to whatever she says for hours as long as she's also using her *kind hands.*

I hold her tight in the grip of my tentacles, but don't use my graspers and keep my mating tentacles firmly tucked under me.

She can talk and touch at the same time.

"I listened to you talk like an insane person for a long time."

"How *rude*," she huffs.

I find the harmless gesture comforting.

She continues berating me, but I remain in the same position. She squirms a few times in her position, trying to make herself comfortable and somehow brushing against the tentacles I tried so hard to tuck away from her.

She mumbles some words under her breath and goes silent for a while, staying very still. I can't tell why, but I savor the silence.

In her moment of silence, I can appreciate my position. The feel of her wrapped up tight isn't quite as thrilling as her *hands* on me, but it comes with its own pleasure.

She growls out a breath. "Fine."

She moves her grasper and starts touching the parts of my graspers and tentacles she can reach. Each touch feels like I'm in a riptide, and she seems to learn where to touch from the way my body reacts.

Perhaps the curiosity of her species is useful after all.

"I swear, it won't hurt for you to be a *gentleman*. I understand being the strong and silent type, but you won't do yourself any *favors* if you keep being so *rude*. Don't your people learn some form of *respect*? Do you even have the concept of *etiquette*? No, I doubt you would. After all, you're a *brute* who..."

My listening drums have become numb from listening to her as they tune out her words. Her graspers never stop moving, which is impressive. Her fingers move along the ridges of my suckers, finding sensitive spots I don't even know I have.

She's very skilled, I can tell, but I don't feel like saying it. Talking will be interpreted as engaging in conversation and I don't want that.

"It's such an interesting feeling. I wonder if this is why some people want to keep an *octopus* as a *pet*. Would it work as a *pet*? I've eaten one before, but I don't know much about them. Would they be a close *relative* of yours by chance? Of course not. You're not even from the same *planet*."

Her graspers move further below, and the sensations travel with them. My mating tentacles want to burst out of their hiding place, but I contain my urges.

They are urges I shouldn't even be having, but somehow, this female manages to bring out the best and worst in me. It is an unfair comparison if I place her against the other females I have met because there are none I can compare her to.

　　None can touch me as *kindly* as she does.

29

Eli

Even though he's an alien, he has the same glossed-over look in his eyes my exes had when they were listening to me rant, though I should praise him for staying perfectly still while listening to me.

I can't tell if I've just dated men with undiagnosed ADHD or I'm just a parrot because it was quite regular for them to stand up and walk around, some avoiding a conversation all together. I have once heard the phrase *pretty girls shouldn't talk* before.

Sadly, while the misogyny in the statement I reject, I can't deny that my running mouth is a problem.

Still, the words spill out like water bursting from a reservoir. It doesn't help that my brain is constantly working overtime to churn out more thoughts and my anxiety heightens the more he touches me.

I can vividly feel every move he makes and the slightly rough suckers on his tentacles. I don't know if he's doing this intentionally.

No. I doubt he is. This is completely foreign territory for him.

My body is shivering from the inside out. There's an instinct, a desire bursting from deep inside my body beneath my blubbering foolishness, waiting to break out of my skin. I can feel it in every touch, every caress.

"W-Wroahk?" I ask, surprised by how light my voice is.

I feel his chest rumble, deeper than any man's I've ever rested on. He's speaking again.

"What is it?" he clicks back, his tone surprisingly soft.

"I... never mind."

"You do not hesitate to speak your mind, but now you pause?"

"Well, it's... I can't explain it. I feel strange."

"Do you hurt?"

I hesitate to reply. My breath is caught in my throat and the sensations build.

Heat pools to the lower part of my body as I try to form a coherent thought. He's right. Normally, it's hard to render me speechless. And it's not like I haven't felt desire before, but he is not the least bit human. And an asshole.

"I... don't."

"Your body is becoming warmer. Why?"

"I don't know, not really."

"Do you only know useless things?"

That one hurts.

My *padre* used to praise me as smart, but maybe all those years of mediocrity have eroded it all. Here I am. Stranded on an alien planet, and I feel horny as hell. It's so ridiculous, I would laugh if I could get rid of the lump in my throat.

"I guess I don't know a lot, at least not much that helps when I'm here."

"I see. Do you keep speaking because you wish to know more?"

He surprises me, again. He is so alien, not understanding my culture at all, but somehow still insightful. I twirl around and stare at him. He stares back, unafraid, unabashed.

"Yes. My mind is always wanting to know more. I'm on a different planet! Right now, aside from wondering how to *freaking* escape, my mind is burning to know just how this planet moves. Do the same laws of gravity apply? I mean, they must, I suppose. But what more about this planet do we need to know to survive? To thrive?"

"You know so many words and ask so many questions, yet you have no answers. Your curiosity is never sated. Why?"

I smile up at him and caress his face. His skin feels strange under my palm, but it doesn't irk me anymore. His eyes are clear, but if I look deeper, there's just a hint of curiosity. An octo-shark-dolphin-man with more power in one tentacle to crush me to mush is curious about... me.

"Wroahk, why don't we move beyond the lake? Explore?"

His clear eyes darken almost immediately.

"No."

Well, it was worth a shot. There's not that much curiosity in his eyes, it seems.

"That's fine."

I can always convince him later.

He slinks off my body and drags a trail back out to the lake, which he does frequently so he won't dry out. He seems amphibian, maybe, but the feel of his skin is closer to a marine animal. I wonder what else makes him different from me.

Now that I know I'm safe with him, I don't like when he leaves me alone.

I follow his trail and find him floating along the surface of the river. He is splashing around, like his tentacles were lubricating. I'm wondering if he stores water in his tentacles to stay longer on land. I'm also wondering why he's doing all this to stay by my side.

I sit by the shore and watch him. Not all the rocks are sharp, though it is hard finding a good spot at first, but I find it. He sees me as I sit and draws closer, staring at me from the edge of the water. I watch his tentacles move, entranced by their floatation. I'm tempted to ask, but I just watch.

A sight that speaks many words. I understand it now.

"Why are you watching me?"

He barely ever initiates conversation. Perhaps he's changing.

"I'm wondering how the water feels."

I'm not. I'm more curious about what he'll say.

"You can come in."

He's inviting me into the water. His voice is loud enough for me to hear over the waves and the crying giant birds, but not harsh on my ears. It sounds like he's projecting, like echolocation. What a splendid evolutionary trait. I don't quite sound like that when I speak.

I mean, he obviously understands me, but I'm missing something that gives my voice the same resonance. I want to be able to do that too, although everyone will tire of my yapping even faster if I did.

"I can't swim very well."

"You won't drown."

I look back at his tentacles as he speaks. They seem sturdy enough to hold me above water, so I choose to trust him. I stand on the rocks and tread carefully, mindful of my poorly protected feet. This black suit is great and all, but the 'shoes' leave something to be desired.

I get to the edge of the water, and he stretches a tentacle out, wrapping it around me. I feel weightless as he lifts me up and gently brings me into the water.

It feels warm upon contact, but colder as my body moves below the surface. He holds onto me carefully as he swims, swirling the water as we move. He doesn't say anything as we just float on the water.

"Do you need the water to live?"

"Yes. I don't like it."

"Really? But you need it."

"I don't have to like it."

He seems irritated, yet his hold remains gentle.

"It tastes disgusting, and it feels disgusting."

"I'm sorry."

I don't know what to say, though I can certainly relate.

Instead, I reach out a hand waiting for him to move into it, and comfort him, running my hands along his upper arms as he tentatively asks and then mimics my gentle shoulder strokes.

Each touch making both of us breath a little heavier.

We stay like that for a while before we get out and head back to the cove. It seemed like I was right about him retaining water in his skin to be able to last longer on land, although it looks very uncomfortable with some of his suckers swollen.

I find sustenance for myself and sit by the tree, finishing the fruit I collected. I will worry about finding proper food for later. He sits right next to me, his tentacle wrapped around my waist. He still hadn't let go of me since we left the water. For some reason, I offer him a piece one of the fruit.

He gives me a look of disgust, or I assume so based on context so far, tossing it away with his free tentacle. I chuckle and continue eating, pausing mid chew as an idea forms in my head.

"Why don't you try tasting it? You said the fish tastes disgusting, so I was wondering if you might want to eat something else."

"Don't want."

He's so obstinate.

The look on his face is comical in how mulish it is and suddenly the ever-present arousal flares. When did his grumpiness become... cute?

"Would you like a kiss, Wroahk?" I ask, surprising myself. "It's like kind hands, but better."

"Better? What is it?"

"It's not something I can explain. It's just something I'll have to show you if you let me."

I've lost my mind. Maybe it's the loneliness getting to me, but I cannot believe I'm about to kiss an alien who would've preferred to eat me just a few days ago.

I bite into a fruit and rise to my feet so that I'm facing him. I lean in and kiss his lips, if I can call them that. They look like lips and slightly feel like them, too. It's just a gentle peck, but his whole body trembles.

Luckily he doesn't taste or smell like anything he eats.

I smile and lean back to look at him. "Do you like it?

He stares back silently, like his thoughts are racing. I can see the gears turning in his head.

I chew and swallow the bit of fruit in my mouth and wait for him to answer. It's rare to find a man who hasn't been kissed, but even stranger to find out aliens don't have a concept of kissing.

It's a bit sad.

"You... what did you do?"

He's stuttering. How delicious.

"Like I said, it's called a kiss."

I hear his clicks but can't decipher them, like he's mumbling to himself. I wait patiently, mostly because I'm amused. It's not everyday I can catch him off guard. I do wonder what would happen if we...

He stops muttering and gets his usual intense predator stare back. "I want more."

A zing of pleasure surges. "Open your mouth."

He cracks his mouth open really wide, just like if he planned to devour prey, and it sends a shiver down my spine that starts as fear, and then transitions to something else.

"Do you clean your teeth?" I ask, instantly killing the mood.

"Of course I do," he clicks out, annoyed with me again. "Do you?"

"Yes," I drawl, not sure that sticks quite count, but ever since I got here my mouth has stayed clean regardless of what I eat. "You don't need it open that much. That's good. Now follow the movement of my lips and tongue."

I decide to ignore the issue for now. I can always abort if he tastes like fish or Many Teeth.

Seeing him with his lips lightly parted and his eyes filled with anticipation makes my body throb with excitement.

I lean in again and brush my lips against him, my tongue darting out and rubbing along the edge of his thin layer of lip.

He responds, and it's clumsy, like kissing a virgin with sharp teeth, but still pleasant. He tastes a bit acidic, but in a nice sort of way.

"Again," he growls out.

I move my face closer, and this time he responds, scraping my tongue against his teeth as I struggle a bit against the rising amount of force he's using.

"Be gentle, Wroahk. It's not a fight."

He grunts but does exactly as I say.

We try again and this time, it's no longer distracting. There's no hint of a fishy taste I would've expected from an alien who feeds predominantly on aquatic animals, but it's more similar to the acidic taste you get from eating an unripe fruit.

Good thing I always liked sour candy.

I pull back and lick my lips, staring at him breathlessly.

Another tentacle wraps around me and pulls me closer, running along my body. His suckers cling to skin, one of them latching onto my breast, the thin fabric of the suit doing little to dampen the erotic pull.

His eyes are blank, his chest heaving.

I pull back, staring at him breathlessly. I didn't expect to feel this need spiraling within me. My body shivers as I wait, craving his soft exploration of my body.

"Wroahk, are you okay?"

My head is close to his chest, making his reply almost achingly loud.

"Strange... I feel very strange."

I laugh, laying against him. I don't know if aliens have the concept of virginity, but he's acting like a prepubescent boy who just kissed his crush. I'm honored to be a crush more than anything, but humanity's first exploration of an alien race can't be sexual in nature.

Can it?

His hand reaches down and pushes my face up to his, eyes swarming with desire. I grin, offering him the other half of the fruit, trying to put some space between us while I get my body under control.

"I have more to show you if you'll just eat this."

His eyes clear a bit, and his lips turn in annoyance. He snatches it from my hands and tosses it into his mouth, swallowing it without chewing. For a giant alien, it probably is just a snack. I wait patiently for his feedback.

"Don't want."

Well, it was worth a shot. I don't know if I was waiting for a miracle, but maybe it's a human thing to be vegetarian. Expecting that from another life form is being ridiculously delusional.

Maybe that's what I'm best at.

"More," he demands.

He eagerly swoops down and waits for me to claim his lips again. His eyes are closed, like he is savoring the taste. His arms wrap around my waist and his tentacles wrap around the rest of my body, from my upper torso down to my legs. His suckers fasten to my breasts and nipples, kneading them unconsciously as they move.

I can't help but moan, cutting my lip on one of his sharp teeth. I pull back and see him lick the blood off his teeth, staring down at my chest.

"Do you hurt?"

"No! It feels... good. Don't stop."

It honestly felt amazing. Even as I answer him, I'm fighting back the urge to moan senselessly. Heat pools to my groin as every part of my body is being stimulated at the same time.

"Fuck! That feels... Wroahk..."

At the call of his name, he kisses me again. I feel something different from the tentacles, much harder, pressed against my legs. I pull from the kiss and look down to see two different looking tentacles that I haven't seen before. If I'm right, those are... but where would they even fit?

"This is going to pose a slight problem," I say to myself out loud.

The strange-looking tentacles keep pressing against my leg as I wonder about another thing.

Why do my ribs hurt?

30

Wroahk

A kiss.

A strange action initiated by this female that fills me with a desire beyond my comprehension. Her tongue dances with a strange fervor and as I imitate it, my body fills with heat that makes my mating tentacles rage even more. They long to burst out from where I hide them and plunge into this female, and at some point, I lose at least part of the battle to keep them contained.

But she is not like any female I've ever seen. I don't even know where to start. We are so different yet the desires of our bodies yearn for freedom. She holds on to me, squirming like prey but more enticingly. The taste of her blood only makes me crave her more. I don't want to eat her anymore, but I want to taste her.

"Wroahk... please..."

I don't know why she's begging me in such a soft voice, but I know she doesn't want me to let go. It's confusing, but I look at her and find that she's different from the time she was trying to tie sticks to her grasper.

This time, she's experiencing what I did when she first showed me that *kiss*.

Unfortunately, I must go back into the water. My skin is drying, and I don't think I can hold on to her. I release her and place her on the ground, writhing back into the water. I hear her call for me behind me, but I don't stop until I'm moist again. I float around, filling my stomach that has surprisingly become empty.

When I go back, the sky is dark, and she's back to how she normally is. She's tossing something around, flapping her other limbs with grunts of annoyance. Her eyes light up when she sees me and she flounders toward me.

"You're back. I thought you were disgusted with me and left."

"No."

She makes a strange noise with her mouth, but her face no longer has any tension. She goes back to sit down, scratching at her torso as she does.

"Come sit with me, Wroahk."

I don't know why she keeps calling me that, but I'm even more disappointed in myself for listening. I sit by her, seeing scattered traces of the food she ate. I don't know why she even calls it food. It's hardly enough to keep her weak limbs alive.

"So, how was it?"

I look down at her, wondering what she means.

"I'm talking about this afternoon. Did you like the *kiss*? And be honest."

I'm tempted to not talk to her about it with the look she has on her face. I should learn that she is going to talk, regardless.

"You don't have to be so *stoic* about it. It's only just us two here. Do you want another one? I don't know how it'll work with your... two, uh, things, but that doesn't stop us from *kissing*."

The fervor in her eyes is back, and it frightens even me. She leans back and casually laughs. She reaches for my tentacle and touches it softly.

"*Sorry*. I was being too forward."

"You cannot harm me," I say but it seems like I'm talking more to myself. She cocks her head to the side and her eyes light up with a spark.

"Are you sure about... *ouch*!"

She immediately reaches for her side and scratches at it violently. I grab her grasper and stop her, catching her gaze.

"It just hurts too much."

I frown and touch her side. It doesn't feel too different from the last time I touched it, but this female is strange so I can't tell. She sighs and leans on me.

"I'm tIred."

She doesn't say anything aside from that and stares up at the sky. We stay in silence for a while before she speaks again.

"On my *planet*, people relied on the stars for many things. *Navigation, predictions* of *behaviors,* and telling when the best time to conceive was. Ridiculous, right?"

I don't get it. The stars are just things out of reach you can't eat. Why rely on them for anything?

"I'll sleep now," she says, yawning.

In just a short time, her breathing becomes even as she falls into slumber. I keep looking at the sky, wondering if I need to rely on them to find the enemy.

I need to rip those things that stole me from my home apart, then I'll be able to keep her.

"*Kind... ly...*" I say in a low rush of wind.

She says I can't take anything just because I want it, especially not her. For now, I just have to endure until I get my chance.

I look back up. If they lead me to that, then I suppose the stars aren't so bad even if they aren't edible.

31

Eli

The first thing I notice when I wake up the next morning is the itching. I felt like taking my skin off and the area felt weird. However, the next thing I feel is hunger. My stomach growls for attention and I reply to it.

"Alright, alright, I'm going."

The thing with maintaining a plant-based diet on another planet is nutrition needs to be obtained by a constant and regulated food schedule. My stomach serves as an alarm.

It's been a few days, so I know how to find my way around the cove. I have the usual scavenging point and some to put aside to see if they're poisonous or not. Edible plants wasn't a particular hobby of mine back on Earth. I know how to do it, of course, but what limited knowledge I had about what's safe to eat and what's not is useless on another planet.

"Time to eat meat? Nah..."

I continue scavenging, and by the end of the hour, I have enough to eat and keep. The giant birds above don't swoop down to disturb me, so keeping the fruit under a branch will do. The giant tentacled man also serves as a deterrent to food thieves.

Speaking of the tentacled man, I think I'm delusional. It's dawned on me again. Kissing an alien? What has gotten into me? I can't even believe I was willing to go even further.

I've lost the plot. Completely lost it.

I turn my gaze to the sky and sigh. It's early morning and the sky still isn't blue. I never thought I'd miss the blue skies but here I am. All that air, all the normal elements I'm used to, all of it is gone. Now, I don't look the least bit like I used to. Who did this to me? Why?

More than that, I need shelter, appropriate shelter. Staying under a gigantic tree or just sleeping on my back is bound to catch up with me soon, even though my body somehow heals all physical wounds.

The daily discomfort and the mental dissonance are things that this strange healing doesn't help with. Sooner or later, my mind will break.

All I've got now is an alien, my perpetual horniness, and my never-ending urge to speak.

Isn't life just wonderful?

I contemplate calling out for him as soon as I wake up, but I decide against it. He's out there and will come around when he's ready.

I know it's useless, but I stare up at the sky, looking for signs of spaceships. There aren't even streaks across the sky to suggest there is air travel. I'm not sure if alien vessels employ carbon-based energy sources, anyway. Probably use nuclear or something I've never even heard of.

Where's your handy-dandy Geiger counter when you need it?

I'm not well versed in astronomy or space exploration but if I can get dumped on another planet and survive, then I bet humans have already found life beyond Earth and were just keeping it a secret.

All those theories and conspiracies I used to roll my eyes at, but a few dozen feet away from me, a giant tentacled man is swimming around in a lake.

I would have preferred to read about it or watch a damn show.

The more I move around the cove, the increasingly itchy my sides become. It feels like it's coming from inside my skin, like something is trying to force its way out. My mind races as many possibilities come to my mind, most of them involving me being a host for a parasitic race of insectoid creatures living on this strange planet.

This makes me stop behind a tree and check my sides, my clothes disappearing. My eyes widen as I see what has been bothering me the entire time.

The scream escapes my throat before I can stop it.

32

Wroahk

The night is silent and long, but the morning brings chaos. The sound of her screams bring me to shore and right into the cove. I find her reaching for her sides, screaming unreservedly.

"Wroahk!"

"Silence!" I click back stridently.

Her screams disorient me, making it hard for me to navigate. She stops, but her eyes are still wide with fear, and I realize that she is showing more of her skin again.

She points to her sides, and I see that they're different. She now has bumps on the side of her bare chest. They looked somehow like...

I look down at my torso, feeling the same bumps on my side. Only, they aren't bumps. They're gills. My gills that I use to breathe in water.

"What happened?"

"My ribs were itching from inside my skin, like the bones were pulsing all night long. I finally managed to go to sleep with that incessant itching and just as I'm finishing up breakfast, I notice these bumps!"

"They're not bumps," I say, frowning.

"What are they then?" she asks impatiently.

"Gills."

"Gills? I have gills, Wroahk! I'm a fish? No, no, no. This is... This is..."

"You don't look quite as weak anymore."

"Seriously, Wroahk? Seriously?"

I don't really see why she's panicking. It is strange that she woke up with an extra body part, but she's a strange thing. Nothing surprises me about her anymore.

She falls to the ground and scratches at it, yellow eyes red and puffy. I sit by her, feeling a new emotion rise from my gut. I have

no word for it, I just know I am feeling it toward her. It is not...
unpleasant.

She suddenly screams again but this time, she runs behind the
large tree in an instant. My tentacles reach around the tree and
bring her back out, dangling her upside down by her limbs. She
looks disgruntled but I wait for her to speak.

"I was *naked*, you *dolt*!"

I don't understand her words, but I hear the rage behind them.

"Put me down right now, Wroahk!"

I release her and she falls to the ground. She yelps as she falls
and glares distastefully at me as she rises back to her feet.

"How very *rude* of you! I should... oh, never mind! I forget you're
an alien sometimes. *Men* are all the same!"

"I am not the same as you."

She grunts and dusts herself, still glaring at me.

I reach out for her again and pull her closer, tracing my grasper
over the bumps on the side of her chest, now hidden under her
black layer of extra skin.

I prefer it when it is brown. The bumps feel rough and irregular
against her, but familiar to me.

First, she stole my voice. Now, she's stealing parts of me.

"How can you steal my body?"

"Do you think I want this? I am now breathing through my torso,
which last time I checked, isn't exactly *human*."

"And you are... *human*?" I ask skeptically.

"Yes, I am... I was... I don't know anymore!"

She screams again, wriggles out, and starts moving around me
and mumbling.

"Oh, my *gosh*, how will I ever be able to go back to *Earth* now?! In
a *magical world* where they rescue me, I'll be poked and prodded
by the *government*. I'll be turned into a *lab rat*. A *lab rat*, Wroahk!"

"You sound concerned about that."

"Isn't it concerning?"

I have never seen emotions expressed so freely in a living being
as I've seen in her. Her eyes, her nose, her mouth, and her entire
body move with her change in emotion.

It's fascinating.

"I know you're not *human*, but I swear, you're just like a *man*
who looms over a *woman* when she's changing a *tire*, telling her
it's wrong but not offering to do anything. That stupid *seniority
complex* that doesn't benefit anybody!"

"What's a *seniority complex*?"

"It's you, right now, assuming you're just better than me."

I cock my head to the side and look at her. The fragile skin that holds her frame together would easily be punctured with a graze of my teeth. Her limbs I could snap with negligible force.

"But I am better than you."

She glares at me again and huffs, turning to the side. There are scattered plants by the tree, but she doesn't offer me some like the last time. She finishes it off, reminding me that I haven't had anything to eat yet.

She scratches at her side, twisting uncomfortably on the spot.

"This is madness."

"What?" I ask, still staring at her side.

"It feels like I'm... suffocating."

"Why?"

"It's these gills. It's the equivalent of covering my nose for no reason. But I don't know how to control these *so-called clothes*. If I think about breathing, then..."

The covering on her body disappears, casting her bare. She curls in on herself, covering her body. She sighs.

"It's hard to make them come back and I don't even know what to do to breathe. Isn't that concerning enough?"

I stare at her, not sure of what to say. Like most things with her, I don't understand it, but for some reason, she's hurt.

So I must stop it.

"You need to go into the water. You can't breathe on land for too long or you will dry out internally."

"What? I'm not like you. If I go in, I'll drown!"

"You won't drown," I say, staring at her gills.

"How can you say that?"

"I've had them since birth and I've never drowned before."

"Well, *whales* have gills, too. Wait. They don't, but I don't remember what it's called. They have to come up for air and die by drowning, eventually. What am I even saying? Basically, semi-aquatic *mammals* can still drown, even though they have the organs to technically float in water. Guess what? I'm not a semi-aquatic *mammal*! I'm just a plain old *mammal* and I don't want to die on this strange *planet*, where my body can't even be found because I drowned!"

"You will not drown," I repeat.

"Well, how would you know that? I'm not like you."

"You stole my voice and can speak my tongue. You stole my body this time. You can swim."

She looks at me and I stretch a tentacle toward her, excitement rising inside. I was alone in the water since she wasn't capable of swimming. Now, I'll be able to have her by my side at all times, on water or on land.

"Come into the water."

She looks at me from the corner of her eyes. "You're like a *siren*, tempting me to jump into the water so you can drown me and feast on my flesh."

"I already said I won't eat you."

She's a different kind of delicious. I would rather savor her for a long time. For the rest of my life.

"Right. And I'm supposed to take your word for it. Perfect."

The sky crackles and she jumps again. We both look up to see dark clouds promising a destructive storm. She moves close to me, clinging to my arm. The skies darken, taking on a dark purple hue.

The clouds rumble and she squeals again, clinging tighter.

"You're afraid. Why?"

"Why wouldn't I be?! For all I know, the sky's about to split open!"

"Why would the sky split open? It is simply a storm."

"*Gaaah*! Why are you so frustrating?"

The sky flashes again, sending a boom down to the ground. She jumps on me this time, holding tightly to my sides like quivering prey. My tentacles wrap around her this time, holding her close.

"Will you come with me into the water?" I ask again, even though she's secure in my arms.

I can't just take her. I have to have *consent*.

"Are you sure? I'm afraid of deep water."

I don't bother trying to make sense of something so stupid, though it occurs to me that she must fear water like I fear the open air.

She'll have to let it go if she plans to keep stealing parts of me.

"I'll be beside you. What could frighten you when you're with me? I'm going to keep holding on to you."

And I'll never let go. Her *kind* touch will always be mine.

33

Eli

Wroahk's rough and unkind, but at least he solved the mystery of the new bumps and long flaps. Every single move I make, I feel myself gasping for air through my sides.

We move toward the water, the storm building around us, and my panic rises.

How does this make sense? How can I just grow gills? I wake on an alien planet looking so strange and now this?

I'm now more alien than the giant tentacle monster. Alright, fine, that's hyperbole, but it's not like I could blend in anymore if I get back home.

Maybe it's the plants I ate. I only mutated after eating them, after all. Oh, I knew there had to be a catch. I mean, I've been ingesting alien lifeforms for a few days. It was bound to catch up to me.

But what is it? What exactly is this mutation?

Maybe it's something in the air. The only reason I'll ever need gills is to breathe. I groan. It burns so bad, each breath making it worse. It's like I'm trying to smell through my clothes.

If I make the suit recede and don't picture what I want correctly, I might be naked in front of him again. It's already strange enough that I tried to jump his bones yesterday.

Not that he seems to have many of those.

"Are you hurt?" he asks me.

There's concern at the corner of his eyes. Why? Why does he care? Because I touch him kindly? Because I'm the only other intelligent being here? Why does he want to keep me alive?

"Yes, it hurts," I grumble out. "I didn't want your stupid gills."

"You look less pathetic this way. Less pathetic means you're less likely to be abandoned," he responds, his voice cold.

"Abandoned?"

He looks me in the eye, his words unflinching.

"The weak and useless are always cast away, including those who cannot breathe underwater when they are born."

"What? You just abandon your young?"

"It's better for the survival of all of us if only the strong ones grow to adulthood," he responds.

"You can't just do that."

Damn, his species is brutal. That's eugenics. If we cherry-picked and plotted out the survival of the fittest, I highly doubt the human race would have survived.

The wind is picking up now, and we are nearing the edge of the water.

"Your species is clearly intelligent, you have a language, but as far as I can tell, you have a sparse population, don't you?"

"I can't know that," he replies, trying to tug me into the water.

I'm not ready yet, so I let me mind analyze as the wind whips around us.

"Right. I guess not. Your lack of unity must mean you're still a primitive species yet to develop the concept of tribes. I don't know if that's a good thing or a bad thing, given how violent and driven you are. You are strong, Wroahk, and with that strength might come leadership. You have to develop the concept of community first."

"Why? What's that? Wait. It doesn't matter, let's get in the water."

"No. Community is something important. Something very important, and I think you already know it is. It's probably the reason you haven't killed me. It's something every species eventually figures out. The strength that comes from being around others. Community."

"But I am not like you. Why would I need it?"

He pulls on me with his tentacles, but I resist, digging my feet into the sand. I know from the growing wind speed that I'll need to give this conversation up, but there is time yet.

"Think about it, Wroahk. Even plants are rarely alone. For most species to breed, they need a multiple of two. Community is a basic need of every living thing, even if their culture tries to resist it. Sentient beings seek out things like them. If you don't develop this concept as a species, your kind will die out, Wroahk, no matter how many offspring you have."

He just stares at me, silent, like he's computing the words I just said.

I'm not even sure why I'm lecturing him, I just know it's really important that he understands this concept.

Plus, I can't stand the thought of abandoning kids. Humans continue to survive because they choose to care for our young and elderly. Most animals don't abandon their offspring, and I need him to be better than that.

It's crucial.

The pain in my sides worsens, and I start to get dizzy, like I'm suffocating. I tell him this and he urges me to come with him inside the water.

I just shake my head, every human instinct telling me deep water is death.

But the weather doesn't give me much of a choice a few minutes later. The sky rumbles and the earth shakes with lighting strikes. The skies adopt a deeper shade of purple, looking like the Earth's skies before rain.

From the pressure in the wind, it's going to be more than just rain, though.

Just as he wraps his tentacles around me, there's a giant crack of lightning, and a rumble shakes the ground. From behind, I hear something falling. Turning around, my eyes widen as I see one of the giant trees slowly bending, then with a groan, it breaks.

Wroahk stops asking and instead drags us both into the water. My head is still turned to the cove, so when the next rumble hits, I see another tree fall.

I know I can't stay out here, but when I whip my head back to the lake, the image of the Many Teeth trying to kill me pulls up a scream.

We reach the edge of the water and he pulls me in without hesitation. It's cold, and it hits me dead in the face. I gasp, my human instincts kicking in immediately. I scream at Wroahk, kicking and flailing in the water.

Trying desperately to stay in the shallow water.

"I'm going to drown, Wroahk!"

"You are not," his clicks are deeper, echoing in my head. "Believe that you will not drown."

In theory, I have gills so I should be able to breathe underwater. But what if they're not functional? What if this is how I die?

He doesn't give me time to think and just pulls me under. Air escapes me in bubbles and the suffocating feeling is back. I float, suspended in the water, with Wroahk's tentacles still around me. He's still looking at me, waiting for something.

"You are not used to breathing through them, so you'll have to use a different method to breathe down here."

Well, no shit.

I glare at him, surprised I can even understand him.

The itchiness and burning are gone, but they're replaced by a new sensation. I look down and see a pocket of air by them, similar to the one coming from my nose. They're functional but they're being restricted by the black suit.

He makes a click that sounds closer to annoyance and drags me down. I continue to kick out my rage, since I can't scream down here. Above us, I can vaguely see raindrops pelt the water like little javelins. I can't even imagine being out in that. The trees didn't survive it, so how can I?

We reach the bottom of the lake and Wroahk shoves me to a spot and stares at me. The burning feeling of suffocation is still intact.

"Breathe."

I just glare at him because I can't respond.

"If you refuse to breathe, you'll drown."

I point frantically up to the surface as my vision starts to blur at the edges.

He holds me tighter and refuses to move. "Breathe or die."

What the fuck?

The urge to struggle is strong, but I resist it. I'll only run out of air faster that way.

I focus on the clothes. They seem to appear and disappear at will, but there's a pattern. It's just my theory, but if I try to call out what I want in my mind, then...

The sides of the suits open and the ridges on my sides are visible. The feeling of suffocation gradually fades, and air bubbles rise from my side. I don't know how it's working, but one thing's for certain now.

I'm no longer drowning. No thanks to him.

I glare at him again. He can click underwater, but he's not speaking, more like projecting. I've "stolen his voice" before. Let's just see if I can do it again and give this alien a piece of my mind.

I try, but fail, bubbles only communicating my anger, but not the specifics. I thought he was different than my stepfather, but I was wrong.

I let out a breath. No, that isn't fair. They aren't the same. People like my stepfather are cruel because they hate themselves and want to tear you down with them. Wroahk is the most confident person I have ever met.

He's definitely violent. His whole culture is that way, but I don't think he is cruel.

Stupid, arrogant, and a complete asshole, but I don't think he was trying to hurt me. It won't stop me from raking him over red hot freaking coals as soon as I'm able, though.

34

Wroahk

The skies roar with impatience above us.

She feels lighter in my hold under the waves, like the weight of her life is as light as the gentle pull of the water. Her struggle in my arms reminds me that she's indeed alive and fighting to stay alive.

She hasn't realized it yet, but she's not drowning.

She really shouldn't keep her gills covered like she did. My kind has always displayed their gills proudly, a challenge to the creatures of the oceans. We have defeated every uncanny thing so far.

I don't like how small she is in my hold, like she can slip away at any moment, so I hold on tighter.

I have thought often about bringing her down here with me. The water is terrible, but staying down here is better than up there. I don't know how she can breathe underwater, but I don't need an explanation, especially not from her.

It would probably last all day and she would end with as many questions as she tried to answer.

After she finally relents and decides to live, I move us into an underwater cave.

The cave is even darker than normal, though the luminous snails cast a dull light, the skies dark with the violent storm. I can still hear the thundering from above, but it doesn't seem like she can. She was jumping with each booming sound of it before we came into the water.

Even less equipped to survive down here than I initially thought. It has ceased to surprise me.

She's still angry, likely knowing I would've let her drown if she didn't figure out how to use the gills she stole.

How else would she know if she could use them?

"See? You're alive."

Her eyes say so much. It's such a relief that her mouth does not.

She scuttles deeper into the corner of the cave and doesn't look at me. I can still see her clearly, but I know she can barely see me. All that's similar about us are the gills.

I reach out a tentacle to tap at her feet, pleased when she jumps. She can't complain, so she just grumbles, like she wants to kill me with just her eyes. I decide to leave her alone and wait for the skies to clear.

It takes a while, so I venture out to find something to eat. Most creatures safely hide during a storm and are alert. The ones who can't are left in a panic and are easier to catch. I take some of those first and keep searching around the nearby ridge to find more.

It's an easy hunt and I come back to the cave soon after.

She's still by the corner in the cave, but she looks curious. I reach a tentacle around her waist and bring her out, swimming around the underwater ridgeline with her in tow.

I don't know why I'm doing it. She could just as easily wait out the storm in the cave, but I want her with me. Want her to see more. Maybe it will make her want to come here more often.

Where she can't speak.

I swim for quite some time, whacking away Many Teeth who try to investigate her long, yellow weeds. For some unexplained reason, I even show her how to chase a school of fish out of their hiding place.

As if she could hunt without me.

Eventually, I bring her up close to the surface and watch the last of the storm clouds move away. She points at the shore, death in her eyes. I let her go and she swims to the surface like she's fleeing from me.

She can't flee from me.

I follow her, and she climbs up among the rocks, coughing. She glares back down at me and her lips part.

"What the *hell* is wrong with you? You were seriously going to leave me to drown in there, weren't you?"

"You didn't."

"Oh, because I have gills? What is the difference between tossing me into *shark*-infested waters and what you just did? And that stupid, *smug* look on your face! You're so infuriating!"

I float close to her, noticing she isn't going back to the cove. When she's talking, she seems to focus on delivering her message more than anything else. If she tries to leave, she'll stop talking and I'll follow her.

"Why are you angry?"

Her expression changes again.

"You don't know? You seriously don't know? *Wow*! I can't believe I'm wasting my time trying to explain basic *decency* to someone like you."

She's saying things I can't understand again and waving her graspers frantically.

I'm not sure why I feel the need to explain, but I do. "It is the way I was taught. It's the way we were all taught."

"Right. Semi-aquatic *mammal*. Wait, you didn't hatch from an egg, did you?"

I decide not to answer that. She huffs and squats until she's right in front of me again. I want to *kiss* her and feel the warmth of her mouth again.

I want her, but it is very clear she does not want me.

There is a pain in my chest I cannot explain when I think that.

"You're not even listening! I swear. You... I shouldn't bother with you."

She rubs at her face, then continues. "That thing you did underwater, the echoing thing. Teach me how to do it."

I stare at her, the thought of her speaking to me under the water seeming more and more like torture.

"No."

"No? What do you mean, no? Why won't you teach me?"

"I will not."

"Excuse me, *mister*! You can't just tell me no with no reason! That's *discrimination*!"

I decide I like it. The expressive range of emotion that crosses her face.

It's always changing, never dull. She's always full of life, always bubbling like sea foam. She's just as weak, of course, but I am finding that it matters to me less and less.

I especially like it when her face contorts in anger, and she yells at me. Raising your voice and exerting your presence is the way of a predator.

She's doing well now.

"You're not listening again! *Arrrghh*! I give up!"

She sits by the shore and folds into herself. I raise a tentacle and poke her, but I get no reaction. She's dull now. I want to see her expressions again. I poke her harder and this time, her head snaps up.

"What do you want?"

"Touch," I say, holding my tentacle out.

She looks at me with sharp eyes and says...

"No."

She fighting back. It's rare that prey fights back. I raise a tentacle and wrap around her waist again, intending to bring her into the water.

"Wroahk, don't you *fucking* dare..."

There is a menace in her voice now, and it thrills me. She doesn't have to touch me with *kind hands*, but I need her near me.

She's back in the water again, her head above the water, though I would like to dive deep, and my tentacles are wrapped around her. I hold her face with my grasper, relishing in how soft it is.

"What are you doing?"

"*Kiss,*" I urge, knowing I can't take it, but hoping she will offer.

"I'm not going to *kiss* you after what you just did."

"I helped you. Saved you from the storm. You didn't drown."

Recognition flares in her eyes, and she doesn't look pleased.

I pull her closer, my hunger for her growing stronger. I want more, but then I remember how empty it is when I take.

It's hard, but I manage to stop, letting her loose in the water. "Touch?" I ask again.

She moves her limbs in the water, staring at me, thinking.

"Wroahk..." she whispers, then swims toward me, her face still above the water. "Yes."

She leans in first and places her lips on mine, initiating a *kiss*. My mating tentacles fight for dominance against my other ones, threatening to burst out and caress her like the others do.

Her formerly sharp, angry eyes are now clouded over, her graspers roaming over my tentacles.

She moves her mouth to my neck, and I resist the urge to break her before she can do any damage. Then I feel her weak teeth dig into my flesh. I'm taken aback when she clamps down, her teeth feeling almost as abrasive as mine.

Then she hisses out her rage, clearly still angry with me. The next moment, my tentacles flail wildly.

It feels so strange and so good. Then her soft tongue glides over my neck before she bites me again, then sucks hard and I wonder if there is something else about her that is similar to me after all.

A gurgle escapes my throat, and I hear her laugh.

"I didn't think it would work on an *alien*. Guess I'm very good at it."

"What are you doing?" I question her.

"I'm giving you a *hickey*. I guess in your words, it's probably something like marking your territory."

"I am not a territory," I reply fiercely.

She shows me her teeth, while running her finger up and down my torso.

"Of course you are. Another *kiss*, Wroahk?"

I can't say no.

It feels... amazing. Her graspers hold on to my tentacles, wandering below like she's searching for something. I touch her body like she touches mine, following all her dips and curves.

While my tentacles spread from my torso, she only has two thin limbs. In between those limbs, there is a greater heat, and I can taste a difference in the water near there. I move in my grasper and feel around like she did to me when she showed me what *kind* touch was.

She gasps, arching in my hold, but not trying to get away. She looks down and seems to be shocked by what she sees. She looks back at me, her eyes clearing up.

"Touch?" I ask her.

"Yes."

She furrows her face and reaches down herself, the black covering disappearing from her body.

"*Fuck*. I'm really wet."

"You're inside the water," I point out.

"Not that, *dummy*. *Dios*. We've barely *kissed* but I'm..."

"Should I check?" I offer, worried that she might be hurt.

"There's really no need to—" she gasps again as I turn her over to look at it, spinning her so her face is down in the water and her legs are spread open before my face.

It looks unusual with its fold, and it seems too small. Is this really her mating organ? It doesn't look like I'll fit. And what's this small thing here?

My grasper darts out, but I stop myself just in time, annoyed with once again clamping down on simply doing what I want.

"*Kind* touch here?"

She moves her head up and down, her mute signal of agreement.

I touch it and her body trembles.

I flip her over to make sure she is not in pain. She has a dazed look in her eyes and I can sense the heat radiating from the place that I touched.

"Is that good? Do you want more?"

"Yes. I'll hit you if I want you to stop, or we could just stay above the water and—"

I flip her back over, confident that I will know her signals of *consent*, then touch her again.

She holds on to my tentacles, air bubbles floating up to me since she can't speak now that she's upside down in the water. I double check to make sure her gills are uncovered, then go back to my task.

I ignore them since she isn't hitting me, and decide to explore, keeping an unoccupied sucker on the place that made her react while I explored the rest of her mating organ with my grasper.

After a few moments I realize that while it might be small, it can stretch.

I pull it apart with my fingers, feeling some resistance. Fluid pours out of it, but it's not water. I lower my tongue and taste it, finding it just a little sweet. I move my tongue further in, exploring her mating organ and the depths of her channel.

The more I do, the more her body shivers. The air bubbles become more frequent and her hold on my tentacles become tighter. Soon enough, more of the fluid gushes from inside her and fills my mouth. I swallow it, licking it up until there was nothing left. I decide to flip her back up, putting her face back above the water.

She trembles, doesn't say anything for the longest time, just takes in long breaths. I watch her, still holding my tentacles to her body.

"That... that was..."

"Your mating organs are small," I say before she completes her statement.

She scrunches her face again and points her finger.

"First of all, that sounds *rude*. It's not supposed to be big. You're the one who's big! Second of all, you're the one who suddenly decided to eat me out without warning. I'm beginning to think you're actually planning to eat me."

"You taste good," I say, not understanding what her point is.

She clearly liked it and hasn't told me to stop.

"That was *consent*? Was I wrong?" I ask.

"It was *consent*. You did well; I am just *teasing* you now. In fact, I want more."

A thrill runs through me.

I pull her back and part my tentacles, showing her my mating organs. She stares at them, eyes wide, like she cannot believe what I'm showing her.

"I know people abuse this line, but those are not going to fit."

Compared to hers, mine are much, much bigger. I know that both of them won't fit in one hole. However, I don't let it bother me.

It's the first time I've ever done this without the threat of losing my head. My mouth already knows how good it feels inside her. Now, it's time for them to feel it.

"Yeah, no, we're not doing that. I'm not ready for double penetration."

"Double?" I ask, cocking my head.

"I've always thought about it, *yeah* but who ever knew I would meet one *man*... person with two... *humongous* things. I don't even think it'll go in the back. I might just die."

"You will not die. Do you have another mating organ?"

She slaps a grasper over her mouth and shakes her head.

"Do you want me to stop?"

She lets out a long groan. "No, I don't. I—"

That sounds like plenty of invitation.

I pull her down with me to the cave where she will stop saying all her confusing words, and *kiss* her, careful to make sure she always has a limb free to hit me with. I check for her other opening with my graspers, ready for her to tell me no, but she doesn't, so I keep checking.

It's not far from the first one and it's much tighter. Slipping a finger in is hard at first, but I'm able to move my finger in her and the more it stays in there, the more the opening widens, like it will accommodate whatever I plan to give it.

I look back to her face, and she has a dazed look in her eyes, but rouses when I move closer to press my lips against hers

She holds on to me, air bubbles escaping her as she gasps. I remove my finger and use a tentacle and a grasper to hold her as I push my mating organ inside her tighter hole, holding her still with my other grasper and a *kiss* as I seek out the other entry.

It isn't as tight, and she lets out a long groan as I move into her, the inner walls stretching around me in a surprisingly violent hold, but with a slickness that excites me.

I struggle to fit in for only a moment before I feel her stretching to take me in. She bites my lips as my mating tentacles twitch inside her, the force of her hold increasing. It can't hurt me, but I can feel her shuddering movement as she adjusts.

It's better than anything I ever thought I would feel, being here with her without trying to dodge her teeth or keep too many limbs from being ripped off.

35

Eli

I've never quite been given head so meticulously and thoroughly that I felt like I was actually being eaten. He made me cum twice. He kept an always-twitching sucker on my clitoris, driving me absolutely mad with his ministrations.

Then dragged me down here and barely put it in, but I felt stuffed immediately.

Now he's continuing to stretch me. My vision blurs for a moment, no, I think I actually blacked out, because when I come to he is fully seated and moving. He doesn't stop, pushing in the front and back doors while grunting, his hold on my body and jaw firm.

My body is shifting to accommodate him and it's blowing my fucking mind. How else can I explain him fitting those giant things inside me?

They look similar to his other tentacles, except shorter, and with a pointed, ribbed end, which is currently rubbing up against my cervix and making my eyes want to cross.

There are suckers rubbing against the walls of my pussy, and the apparently even more sensitive walls of my ass, the thin walls between both points of penetration making the sensation like nothing I could have ever dreamed.

The fullness of both make each one of his movements almost overwhelming, and as I realize there's no pain from the back door entry, I relax, instead enjoying how he's set up a rhythm where he is pulling one out and pushing one in.

There's a building tightness in my core as he drives me wild.

I almost tell him, then realize I can't. No dirty talk in the water.

Then I realize there's another feeling building, one I've never had before, similar to what's growing in my core, but deeper, farther back.

It distracts me as I try to figure it out, but only get so far as narrowing it to the contact between his two tentacles.

Now that I know I can take him, I don't want him to stop.

He starts talking in his underwater echo voice. "It can't go all the way in, but it still feels..."

There's excitement and something else in his eyes. All I can do is hold on and go on the very bumpy, glorious ride. His mating tentacles are moving back and forth smoothly inside me, and then they start to piston in and out.

Judging by the tingling heat and that he can continually glide into me, I assume he must be secreting something. It's adding to the sensations, making an orgasm build low in my belly that just keeps getting bigger and bigger instead of throbbing through me.

Finally, it explodes.

My moans float up with the air bubbles, but I think it's adequate to say he's fucking my brains out. After that, he finds his rhythm, teeth bared, and I can barely find a coherent thought with those things inside me.

They're hitting every single nerve ending at once, stimulating my already sensitive core. He might drive me mad.

Then the other sensation that's been building in the skin between his tentacles bursts over me and suddenly it's a whole stream of bubbles as I try to scream out, which just continues until he places one of those glorious suckers on my clit and does a hard pull.

When I come to again, I can feel the after effects of three different types of orgasms.

His teeth graze my neck, laying soft bites and kisses along it. He's an incredibly fast learner. He holds me to him with a tentacle around each shoulder, laying his suckers against my nipples, so my entire body is being stimulated at the same time.

More than just my body is floating as he glides in and out of me, picking up speed. I climax again, another long buildup finally breaking like a burst dam as all my neurons fire and bubbles burst from my mouth to dance along the ceiling of the cave.

Then I feel his giant organs contracting at the same time and dumping a huge double load inside me.

Shortly after that, I lose that tentative hold on my consciousness as whatever he pumps into me sends lighting bolts of pleasure on contact.

The next time I open my eyes, I'm floating near the shore. Wroahk is still with me, his eyes filled with concern.

To think the alien is actually concerned if he killed me with coitus after all he did makes me snort out a laugh. I sigh and reach for the shore. That's when I discover that we're still attached.

Suddenly, it's all too much. Too strange, even if it was the singular most pleasurable moment of my life. I feel like I'm losing myself, like he's suddenly taken over every last possible part of me.

I don't know if that thrills me, or terrifies me. Both, possibly. Either way, it's a lot.

"Wroahk, what the hell? Just pull them out for now."

"Are you hurt?" he says, feeling me all over.

"No, I feel fine, actually. It doesn't hurt," I say, looking down. "Can you pull out?"

"I'm not ready to..." he looks like he wants to say something, but he doesn't.

Instead, he does what I ask. He sinks below and I have to deal with another problem. The moment he pulled out, his cum spills out, like a small ocean stuffed inside me.

Can I get pregnant by an alien? We have two different anatomies, so surely, it's impossible. But... the gills? Can I really know for sure?

What we just did was reckless beyond belief. Not just because of some small chance of an alien-human baby, but because it just... shouldn't have been possible.

I take a deep breath, realize I'm being ridiculous. "This is your new normal, Eli," I mutter.

Now that I'm over my little freak out I can appreciate how that wouldn't have been possible without these crazy changes to my body.

Without them I wouldn't have just had the most intense sexual experience of my life. By multiple factors of ten.

My head buzzes with thoughts as I clean myself up, trying to wash away the fluid inside and around me, but it doesn't seem to want to come off. It still shocks me that I can breathe in the water, but it's very convenient.

When I'm done cleaning myself up as best as I can, I try to retreat to the cove, but my leg is caught by a tentacle.

"Stay."

The memory of the fallen giant trees comes to mind. I raise my hand in surrender and find a dull rock to sit on, but then think better of it.

"Right. Double penetration."

I grimace, but figure I need to find out the damage at some point. I sit down gingerly, but no pain comes.

Huh.

I can't go back to the cove just yet, since the sky still looks angry. It's not like I can just sit around on a rock forever. The last thing to do is... well, enter the water.

I look at it and sigh. It's not cold or anything, and I know he won't let anything hurt me, but that isn't why I want to stay out. I just crossed a line.

The alien wasn't willing to let me go before.

And now I let him fuck me.

What the hell, Eli? Am I really that desperate for attention?

Will he let me back out again if he feels he now has a claim? Except I'm feeling increasingly thirsty the more I stand by the shore.

"I'm going to regret this," I mumble to myself before lowering myself into the depths.

He's waiting there, just staring at me. I raise my head above the water just to tell him why I was there and for him not to get any ideas.

"I think you broke my back. It's not obvious because of my incredibly fast healing, but there's no way I just did all that without damage. Even if I haven't found it yet. Plus, there's this feeling of thirst I can't just get rid of. That's why I'm here."

"You are hurt?"

"Uh, possibly. Yes. No. I don't know."

He's silent and doesn't hold me, but hovers around. I decide to simply float along the surface so I can still speak.

I take a breath, but then realize how nice it feels. I now see why people do it. It's incredibly peaceful. I feel his tentacle wrap around my ankle to stop me from straying far. His face is above water, too, staring back at me.

I look up at the sky. We really went at it all morning like beasts. It's already moving into afternoon and my stomach is reminding me to feed it. The rumbling alerts Wroahk, who draws closer to me.

"I need to go in there," I say as he approaches, pointing in the direction of the cove.

"No. It is not safe."

"I know it's not, but I need to forage for food, and I can only get it in there."

"Eat here."

"I don't know how best to explain this to you, but I can't eat fish. I'm vegetarian. I can only eat plants."

"How could that be enough?" he asks, taking on the dismissive tone I'm familiar with.

"It is enough," I respond forcefully, but it sounds more like I'm trying to convince myself. He looks at me like he doesn't believe me, but doesn't say anything more.

I climb out of the water, and he follows behind, his gaze sharp.

Making it to the cove, I can now see the true situation of everything. My normal forage path is blocked off by fallen trees and most of the fruit have fallen, now being feasted upon by insects. There won't be much for me to gather, I see.

Still, I'm not discouraged. I keep pressing onward.

Foraging is also soothing, and it doesn't take long to gather enough.

"I've gotten what I need. We can go now," I say to get his attention.

He looks at my armful again, with the same look of disbelief but doesn't say anything.

He follows me back to the rocky shore and slips into the water as I eat. It doesn't taste great, but at least it's edible. I finish up and throw the remnants far into the lake. It doesn't take long for it to disappear. My stomach churns for a bit, but it's okay. I look at my reflection in the lake and find something strange.

"Please, no, no, no. No more surprises."

Yet, there it was. Something moving just behind my head, tossing with my every moment. Something lurking just behind my field of vision. It's there, blending in with my bright yellow hair.

"I already look like a badly produced neon sign! Please lord, don't let that be a tentacle."

I raise a hand and feel the soft glide of flesh in with the hair, complete with suckers.

It's a fucking tentacle.

I focus on the idea of making it move and feel... muscles on my skull. The shifting in a place that has never felt the contraction of muscles makes my stomach heave.

I look back at the water. There are easily a dozen of them floating around my head like I'm some sort of demented, yellow Medusa.

They're miniature, compared to what he has, and they are bright yellow just like my hair, but they look just like his.

They weren't there yesterday.

"Wroahk!"

His head pokes out of the water almost immediately and he looks directly at me. I point to my head.

"What is this?"

"I do not know."

"What do you mean you don't know? Except for the color, they look just like yours! What is this?"

"It is the same as last time. You stole my voice, now you are stealing my body."

"That does not count as an explanation, damn it!"

There is so much he doesn't know, so much that makes me anxious. I can't just be growing gills and tentacles out of nowhere.

"*Basta. ¡Qué rabia!*"

I just keep muttering every Spanish phrase my father ever taught me like it might somehow anchor my reality.

Then more I never learned start tumbling out, but I stop myself. They aren't special, not like the ones he taught me.

And I'm pissed off that there are whatever Spanish words I want to say ready to be spoken, like the ones I learned from him are now cheap somehow.

Nothing has made sense since I got to this place, and I can't just chuck it up to a mutation. No, something more serious is going on and I just can't tell what it is.

"How did this even happen?"

A tentacle reaches out of the water and pokes me. I glare at him but he just stares back in return. He reaches out the tentacle to me, like a hand. I give him a deadpan stare, but he doesn't desist. The tentacle is still raised to me, like a gesture. He's trying to tell me something.

"Look at it. It is harmless."

The tentacle dances in front of me, like a rope.

I suppose right now it is harmless. It has held me safely, though it has also broken creatures in half.

Still, I let out a huff of breath. He's right.

Regardless of my feelings on the matter, the tentacles on my head are part of me now. Like Wroahk, they won't harm me.

So, I don't need to panic, I tell my heart.

Just think about what he's saying. My forehead wrinkles. It is surprisingly thoughtful of him, especially since there is no clear connection to any agreement we have made.

"Thank you."

This alien is calm and straightforward. Maybe I need to be more like him.

"Calm down, Eli," I say to soothe myself. "They're just tentacles, your tentacles. They can't hurt you."

"Yes," he agrees. "They are natural."

Natural. That's a funny word. Not a word I would use to describe being stranded on an alien planet and fucking an alien but here we are. Plus, I'm feeling queasy. Did the fruit go bad?

"Wroahk?"

"Yes?"

"I used to be human, a different species. I don't look like I used to anymore but inside me, I'm still human. Eli the human who used to work so many jobs to make a living."

I scoff at myself. Is that really what I want to be known for? In a whole new place, with a whole new body?

I tried so hard to scrape by and for what? To end up stranded here looking like something I'm not. It's just the plot of a horror movie.

Thankfully, I'm not a carrier host for a pod of parasitic insects. My skin prickles. *Dios*, I hope not.

I pull over my cape of sunshine and pull up a memory to distract me.

"One day at work, we were offloading a huge shipment and I thought I was a big, strong girl who could do anything. I tried to lift one of the boxes and ended up dropping its contents all over me," I snicker remembering the look of horror on Adrian's face.

"You see the thing with those stupid uniforms is that they're all low quality and they have low porosity. Basically, I stank like fish for weeks. That's one of the main reasons I'm a vegetarian now."

"What a waste," he says.

"Yeah, you say that about the food but what about poor old me? Imagine trying to weave through a crowd during morning rush hour smelling like fish? Well, as I found out, You don't have to weave. The crowd just clears itself."

He looks at me, obviously with no idea what the hell I'm talking about.

"You missed my joke, didn't you?"

It's the same blank-eyed stare he gives me. He doesn't understand me. If he were human, he would've gotten it.

No worries. I'll teach him to appreciate my jokes in time. We're stuck together, after all.

I blink at that thought and how it no longer makes me upset. Just feels good, actually.

"*¡Qué rabia!* Anyway..."

All that time stealing moments away to study a new creature, never nearly enough time, but still fun. Seeking vicarious adventures from reptiles and spiders. What did I even think adventure looked like? Definitely not out in the stars, enduring pain, frustration, and... well, I guess pleasure, too.

Weird.

The feeling of dryness and thirst in my throat returns. I look back at Wroahk. He's completely adapted to being in the water.

He doesn't leave it unless he must. The question is, do I have to as well?

I'm not ready to give up the land.

36

Wroahk

She finally lowers herself into the water, her complexion changing as it soaks into her skin. Good, maybe she will cease her constant scratching.

She moves the water with her graspers, keeping her eyes on me until she approaches me. The midday sun is now high in the sky and the temperature has risen.

"I don't think I said it earlier but it's like a whole beautiful ridge down there. Surprisingly colorful and so unique. Untouched by *technology*, I was *pissed off* at you, but it was fun."

There is nothing in the water but creatures and predators, but she thinks it's fun. How careless can one person truly be?

Then I remember my own impulse to show it to her and wonder if her carelessness is infecting me.

"Don't you think it's fun, Wroahk?"

I consider it. There is nothing that can threaten me in these waters. It's not very amusing to hunt something that can't move very fast or just tastes plain disgusting. I don't think it's fun, but she seems to be set on her perspectives, so I decide not to answer.

"You don't think it's fun, do you?"

I don't think I'll ever understand this creature. So fickle, so annoying... yet, it feels so good and warm inside her. And I can't deny that she has made me think. Made me curious to know more things.

It makes my head ache, but I can't deny I like the challenge. It's like a hunt for a completely new type of prey.

Like how I have had to learn new ways to hunt her. *Gentle, kind, careful*, ways.

"Why are you looking at me like that?"

I feel the urge to enter her again, but I fear her body might be injured. I noticed her flinch back near that rock, which means there's something wrong with her that she's not telling me.

I can't simply guess what's wrong with her other than the fact that her mouth is like a never-ending stream. I assume she will tell me, but for now I will keep my touch *careful*.

"Man, it feels lonely with just us two here. Maybe that's why we did it."

Did what, I wonder? She keeps talking and I don't ask.

"If there were other people here, I wouldn't feel so lonely. It's not quiet, but it is at the same time. The water stretches out so far and there's a cove with resources. We can start a little *community* with our own *rules*. Like a *space exploration movie* where they build *colonies* on a *different planet*. I don't have the *technology* for it, I guess, but there has to be some trace of what brought me here."

For me, there's more than enough living beings around us. For her, it doesn't seem to be enough. How many will she need to not hurt?

My skin twitches with an unpleasant sensation thinking of having more people around like her.

Never.

She wants to talk to someone, and she wants that person to talk back to her. I still don't agree with the advantage of having more people around us.

She thinks we have enough resources to feed someone else? When all her species eats is plants? Ridiculous.

"You don't seem to like the idea of someone else being here. I bet a predator like you doesn't like the idea of *distribution* of resources. You don't want it, but the fact is you're a *social* animal. You already proved it by *sparing* me. Plus, I drive you mad with my incessant talking. Imagine if you had someone else here that didn't talk as much as I did? You'll be getting social benefits as well as having someone else to gather *resources*."

"No."

"*Community* is important, Wroahk. We need to go out there and find out if there are others. What about the rest of your kind? You say the water is disgusting, so I already know this isn't your domain. You have language and you have customs, even though you don't teach your young. You strive for survival and victory. This is my only proof that you are a *social* species. You need interaction or you'll die."

"I will not die."

She is wrong. I don't need others. I don't need her. I don't want to share with others. I don't want to share her with others. She's weak, and she needs others. I do not.

"You believe you won't. But I believe you will. One day, you'll get tired of me *yapping* off your *ear*. You'll want time away from me. Who will you be with then?"

No, I would not miss her incessant droning, but the idea of her not being with me is unacceptable. I need to stop her from saying such uncomfortable things.

I pull her closer and *kiss* her, hoping to silence her. She doesn't resist, kissing me back. It's silent now and my desire is rising. I pull back, remembering she was hurt.

Her face looks like she just ended a successful hunt. "You find me tedious, but you know I'm right."

She is tedious. I put her back on shore as my instincts to hunt and kill something arises before my frustrations overcome my control. She watches me as I plunge into the depths, leaving me with parting words.

"Don't get lost out there."

It isn't possible to get lost, so I don't understand the meaning behind her words. I know the water better than her, just as I know myself better than she does.

All these things she's saying, it sounds more like it applies to her than it does to me. She's the one who needs someone constantly by her, listening to her never-ending words. She's the one afraid of no one else being there.

Why? Why is she so afraid? Because she's weak? It might be. Before she gained the gills to swim underwater, protecting her was even harder. I had to switch from land to water, risking drying my skin out. My body constantly felt sluggish and my tentacles felt like rocks I was dragging around.

Is that how she feels? No wonder she needs others.

Now that I can bring her into the water, it's much easier.

Except she might be a creature who cannot be left alone and the idea of never finding solace to let my mind rest sounds... terrible.

There are many like that who roam the oceans, many who die without the attention of another one in their species. Sure, their overwhelming numbers ensure their survival and accelerated breeding ensures they won't die out but separate one from the group and it dies.

She must be one of those, though I never thought a species capable of speech and reasoning would be among their number. It makes sense that she would develop such an obsession with this idea of *community*, though.

Separated from her kind, she craves to fill a missing presence in her existence with my presence. She constantly talks to me, even though I can't understand most of what she's saying. She's doing everything with reckless abandon just because I'm the only one she sees.

She won't let go of me because I'm the only one. Her idea of *community* does not matter to me, but to her, it is essential for her survival. What that all comes down to, in the end, is that her survival is dependent on me, and not just to hunt for her.

How did I get myself into this position?

I swim up as the sun sinks down on the horizon, finding its way out of the sky. As the dark approaches, I find her still by the corner of the shore, her gaze directed up. I push my tentacle in her direction to signal that I am back, and she turns in my direction.

"Did you have a good swim?"

She always asks such completely useless questions.

"It was good," I answer, surprising myself.

It was, actually, despite the fact I couldn't stray far or she might be in danger of a Many Teeth moving past my constantly established territory. It was quiet, just like I needed, but eventually I felt that pull back to her.

"That's nice. My skin feels like it's on fire. I've been itching since you left. I don't like this feeling, Wroahk."

I swim closer to her and see that she's scratching at her limbs ferociously. I hold her grasper to stop her and notice something else on her arm. I look in her eyes and see another emotion in them. Despair.

"When did this happen?" I point to the fins on her arm.

"I don't know. I didn't even feel it. I just looked down at the water and saw it. My body's been itching so much."

Her voice is trembling again. I wrap my tentacle around her and bring her down into the water, holding her close to me.

She clings to me, silently resting on my torso. She's quiet, which is just strange. She's almost never quiet.

"Are you hurt?" I ask quietly.

"... yes."

She doesn't say anything more, unnerving me. I thought I wouldn't miss the chatter, but I do. Her silence is unnatural, signaling pain that she is not allowed to feel. I don't want to admit that she's right, though, so I say nothing.

"I don't want to stay in the water tonight, Wroahk."

"Does your skin still itch in the water?"

"... no."

"You must stay here so you won't dry out."

"Why would I dry out, Wroahk? I'm a *terrestrial* species. I don't belong in the water. Why... why is this happening to me? Of all the *billions* of *humans* on the *planet*, why me?"

She is constantly making me feel like I know nothing. And there is... fear. Yes, she makes me afraid.

I have not felt this since I was in my nursery group, and I should have never felt it again. Only anger. Rage.

I try to bring those up, but they don't come. I can't control what is making her afraid, and she is infecting me with her emotion. How is that possible? She makes me question my reality.

"I have to go," she says.

I want to crush her to me and pull her down, but this emotion is in me now. Will she leave me if I pull her down into the water again? No, I will never let her.

There are different types of leaving, though. I thought I would like when she stopped speaking, but it caused this fear in me just now. There is no storm to blame.

She slips out of the water and pushes herself up on the rocks, stumbling as she does, then turns back to look at me, her eyes like dark chasms, and runs toward her cove.

I sink back into the water, various thoughts now filling my head. I'm not one for thoughts or emotions. She made me like this. She changed me, yet she's changing too. My changes are on the inside and hers, on the outside. I revile my changes, and she does too.

We are not so different after all.

I lift myself up after absorbing enough water and follow her up to the cove. Normally I can hear her from any distance, but she quietly hid herself. In the trees, I see a familiar looking fluid, one that I often use to move around on land, using my tentacles. I follow these traces of her and find that she climbed up to some of those trees, finding shelter there.

Her breathing is almost imperceptible, but it's there. I can feel her. I focus my senses a bit more and see that she's trembling up in the trees, barely making noise, which is just so strange. As I turn my back to leave her be for a while, I feel something.

My instincts scream at me, telling me something is there. My water reserves are drying out so I don't have much time on land. I'm also not faster here so whatever is coming, if it's a threat, I'll need to deal with it as silently as possible so they don't hurt the female.

I move toward the water, spreading my senses out. I suppose I should be glad that it is not going after the female but wandering at the edges of my territory.

After a quick swim to the shore, the one that surrounds the yellow female's island, I make it to the rocky shore and spot something just by the edge. Keeping my eyes on it as I remain just under the surface of the water, the thing draws closer.

It's the first time I'm seeing a living being that looks like her. It has different color head weeds is on the back of a huge orange beast with a long tail.

I look back up to the purple haired one. There is no doubt about it. That thing is also female.

Seeing her, what my yellow female said comes to mind. She wanted to see other people and live with them. She wants to be with them, talk to them and stay with them.

I know she can't survive if she doesn't have this.

The despair in her eyes makes me... uncomfortable. So unsettled, in fact, that I'm about to do something inconceivable.

I move silently in the water, drawing closer to the creatures. They're scanning the area below as well, the beast sniffing out everything in the surrounding area. The beast's rider, that female, her eyes are alert and she doesn't have tentacles in her hair like my female.

Only their builds are the same.

They draw closer and closer to where I am, like they are searching for something or someone. Could it be my female? Why do they want her? Do they want to take her away from me?

No. Never.

The thought of not having her *kind hands* frightens me. The tentacle reaching out of the water to alert them withdraws immediately and I growl at them, even though they can't hear me.

How dare they try to take my female from me?

My anger rises and I dive into the water, heading straight for the nest of the many teeth I had passed so many times while hunting. Since I established dominance in the water, they instinctively flee when they hear me coming. They scatter the moment they sense me near their nest, but I manage to grab a big one, dragging it up to the surface with me.

I want to throw it at them, punish them for trying to take away my female. However, they're not there when I come up. As I release the Many Teeth, I stare at the cliffs, a new emotion rising inside me.

I don't know its name, but I want it to leave my body. I know what I just did is something she won't like and I feel... something. Like I should have made a different choice and now I can't admit it to her.

I hate it, whatever this ache is called.

37

Eli

I need to start facing things instead of yammering away about whatever flits through my mind. As if gills and tentacles aren't enough, I have fins. One on each side, resembling the green shark fin Wroahk has on his blue arms. Or I'm back to hallucination.

No such luck. Wroahk sees the changes, too.

Well, if he is real.

I'm being ridiculous. He's more real than any person I have ever met. So sure of himself, it makes me jealous.

I could tell he was surprised to see my new changes, but he just accepted them and moved on. I could learn something from him. Well, lots of things, while teaching him some as well.

I clamp down on my mind trying to wiggle out of this by thinking about the ways he is wrong.

Of course he isn't concerned, though, it isn't his body constantly changing, it's mine. Morphing every single day into some mold for him...

Stop it, I chide myself. *Face it.*

I ran away because I don't want to keep changing to be more like him. Will I eventually lose my sense of empathy completely? Be the same killer he is if I stay near him?

I'm feeling unsteady now, dizzy. It might be best for me to get out of this tree, but then the image of Wroahk using his tentacles for everything comes to my mind. My own are small, so I don't know if they'll work, but I decide to try.

Just thinking about it, my tentacles stretch up and cling fast to a branch, holding me securely, though the pressure on my skull is so weird. Who thinks they'll ever say something like *my tentacles*?

My thoughts are still running unchecked, and it disgusts me. I can't just keep longing for things I don't have. So, I'm turning into a freaking kraken or some shit. I need to just deal with it.

I make myself focus on the reality of it, on the plus side.

Alright, well, Wroahk is probably the strongest, most self-assured person I have ever met. He doesn't have that self-loathing I've developed a fine-tuned radar for, the sense that makes me run away from a person with it as fast as possible.

I know not all the people like that are abusers, but I won't take the risk. He doesn't have that issue. In fact, he is becoming noticeably softer with me, though it hasn't diminished his strength.

I can be more like Wroahk, just with less cultural violence. I glance at the yellow tentacles holding me in place, my long hair tangled up in them. They are strange, yes, but also beautiful, and obviously useful.

Then there are my gills, which are currently burning, urging me back into the water. Alright, so there is a downside, but how many people have dreamed of having them? I mean, I never did, but still.

I feel acceptance building, and it feels... good, so I see if I can transfer that feeling over to my childhood.

That's much harder, and my mind swirls in circles of memory, the same ones that I've never been able to make sense logically.

It doesn't matter how many times I tell myself that people like my stepfather can't be understood. That its a good thing I can't understand him, since it means I'm not an abuser.

My mind wants to make sense of it, figure out a way to avoid it.

The last thought makes my heart skip a beat. He can't reach me here. I don't need to try to figure him out, or guess what he might be doing, or be constantly scanning my surroundings and every social event to look for more like him.

Not only do they obviously not exist here, but I am certain that Wroahk would break them in two the moment I showed any fear.

The realization makes me want to go back to him, to feel his tentacles holding me close.

I try to climb down from the tree, but my tentacles feel weak, brittle almost.

Shit. I only meant to have a moment to myself, not turn myself into smoked calamari.

My skin feels like paper. It hurts and cracks every time it touches the bark, but I can't stop climbing down in the middle unless I want to be easy pickings. The feeling of thirst at the back of my throat has become more intense than ever.

I'm drying out, just like he told me I would, and it's not that I didn't believe him. I just didn't really know what that meant.

Of all curses throughout history and all the torments, why did I have to turn into a fish?

Climbing back down is a struggle. I hear rustling and look over to see the giant, tentacled man staring back at me. He watches me with even more intensity than usual, like he's waiting for something.

I'm partway down, but it hurts like hell.

"Help me down!" I yell at him.

He doesn't respond to me, just stares at me from afar.

"Can you not hear me? I'm stuck here."

He can hear me. I know he can. His unflinching stare panics me. I don't like his silence.

"Wroahk, *hijo de puta.*"

He doesn't respond, but I know he knows I'm swearing at him. I don't understand why he's being like this. He's helped me in a difficult situation before and I didn't even have to ask him.

I'm the one who has to suffer the pain of changing into a new species. I'm the one who's stuck on a tree I stupidly decided to climb because I was feeling emotionally imbalanced.

Dammit.

I just want to get down where it's safe, and skin that stupid alien alive.

I turn to face the tree, my biggest obstacle. I know I can heal a broken bone, but I don't know if I can heal a broken neck.

"Come on, Eli. You can do this. You have to stay calm. You have to stay—agghhhh!"

My foot slips and I dig my fingers into the branch, breathing heavily. I keep on moving down, then across the cove. It's a long and hard journey. The back of my throat keeps burning and my vision blurs as I slowly, painfully, make my way toward him.

I can still feel his intense gaze, following my every movement. Is he waiting for me to fail and fall?

He hates weak prey.

Will my last moments be spent between the teeth of the monster refusing to help me?

I thought he was reasonable and because I talked to him, I thought he was gentle and kind. I deluded myself into thinking he's just like me, just like a human being with empathy and emotions.

Everything has gone wrong since I met him.

Stupid, stupid, stupid. Why did I think I could rely on him?

My feet finally touch the shore. I sigh in relief, staggering as I get to the end of my journey.

His gaze is even more intense, his tentacles rising from the water like they want to hold me.

Why doesn't he, then? I clearly need him.

38

Wroahk

Watching her slow progress is even more of a torture than hearing her endless talking.

My tentacles reach out, my body screaming at me to help her. I want to; I so desperately want to, but I can't.

She has beached herself. A person's survival cannot depend on anyone else. She must overcome this by herself.

With her tentacles, her gills, and her fins, and clearly her skin now, she is like me. Although I do not know how, I must carry on my duty and turn her into an independent hunter. I never planned to take on a nursery group. I'm not old enough for it, and she isn't young enough, but that is the only similar situation I can think of.

You don't help another being by saving them from being beached. You only extend their lives long enough to do something equally painful.

However, the thought of her not being by my side brings me discomfort. There is no one else who can touch me as *kindly* as she does. There is none as foolish as her to get so close to a predator like me.

I move closer to the shore, despite myself.

Although she trembles like prey, she is very bold. She keeps climbing down, her anger and her desperate wish to survive aiding her every move.

Maybe there is a strength in her, not just *kindness*.

Her limbs touch the ground, and she stumbles toward the water. The desire in her eyes to live burns strong, bringing her closer and closer to me. She makes it to the bank, her breath shallow.

She is still too far away. Her fierce gaze fixes on me like she wants to say something, but I immediately pull her in, disregarding all rules.

"Let me go!" she says but I ignore her just as I ignored the rules.

She doesn't understand the significance of what I've done, and she likely never will. I couldn't take the risk anymore, couldn't stand the idea of her falling short of safety or being permanently harmed.

I told myself nothing could harm her, even herself, and yet I made her climb down. At the same time, no one should be helped if they are beached. I don't know which one is more important anymore.

I feel like the easy assurance of my life has been ripped apart. No rules are clear anymore and I want to scream out my rage. Instead, I feel her *gentleness* creeping over me, and something... fills my chest. Something buoyant and big, directly related to having her safe in my limbs.

"You did well," I tell her, in a voice I don't even recognize as my own.

There is still anger in her eyes, but anger is good. The anger of a hunter is a great motivation toward victory, just as she has shown today.

Then I'm distracted as I defend her against the creatures attracted by the smell and taste of the blood from her wounds spreading in the water. Many Teeth surround us on all sides. I hold her to me with my graspers, and fling out my tentacles, batting some of them away, grabbing on to others.

Once I have all of them accounted for, I grab the smallest one, darting two tentacles over to it to break it apart. Another Many Teeth takes advantage of the opening that makes for it to bite into another of my limbs, clamping down, but most of the others start a frenzy feeding.

I move us down farther into the water, including the Many Teeth grinding its teeth painfully into me. I try to pry open its jaws, but realize I'm wasting time. Instead, I wrap a tentacle around its jaw and help it bite me, the added pressure detaching my tentacle. Then I fling the Many Teeth away as it snaps frantically at it's prize.

That one will smell like me for many days, making it easy to locate and break every bone it its body for thinking it won. For now, it enjoys its meal and I swim down to the cave with my own prize.

It is easy to defend, and after a quick sweep of my remaining tentacles to ensure nothing is inside, I let her float in the middle of it, my back to the entrance and tentacles ready to flick any threat away.

I let her soak in the water, and after a moment see a layer of her body peel away. She's still maintaining a distance from me, her eyes angry, so I have to remain *patient* if I want to ask her anything.

Looking at her now, I think I can understand some things she has been saying. Deep inside me, gurgling up as an urge, there's something that pushes me to *care* for her. I want to remove her despair, not be the cause of it.

The only thing I can make of that is that I'm slowly going insane.

I watch her closely, waiting for any sign. Her eyes are on the exit, and I can feel that she wants to go back up, though isn't reckless enough to go out to where the Many Teeth are.

She isn't used to her changes yet.

I don't want to imagine how life on the surface feels like, constantly staying there daily without a dip in the water. This lake feels disgusting, but I can't imagine surviving without it. I don't understand why she wants to go back when it's better down here. She even said she likes the underwater ridge.

That should be enough motivation to stay down here.

She moves farther back into the small cave, and it's clear she's not used to swimming. She's barely using her fins and if she didn't have gills, she would've drowned straight away. I'm amused by how much she struggles when she cannot escape me.

There's defiance in her eyes and it just draws me in.

The silence is wonderful as we wait for the Many Teeth to disperse, but I must admit I am curious to know what she is thinking.

Insanity really must be creeping in, because I pull her to me and move her back up. The Many Teeth have had their fill, and once the frenzy passes, my echoes remind them this isn't a place they are safe.

I loosen my hold on her and she clumsily swims to the surface. It's more like thrashing and it draws the attention of one of the Many Teeth who thought it could hide from me. I watch it investigate her and slowly emerge from its hole. I move behind it as it stalks her, waiting for the perfect time to snap out my limbs.

I make sure it's silent when I snap its bones and drop it back down into the depths so I can keep following her, making a bold statement to the creatures who watch.

When I resurface, she's waiting for me by the shore, fury burning in her eyes.

"What have you done to me?" she demands, like I have an answer.

"Get back in the water, you'll dry up."

She takes her eyes off me for a moment, focusing on something behind me.

"Was something following me?"

"You swim like you are injured and weak. Of course, there was something following you."

"I don't care for your quips, Wroahk! I don't care if you think of me as weak or useless. What I will not stand is you stripping away my *humanity*!"

"I can assure you there is nothing you have for me to take."

"Oh, really? So I'm just really crazy and yelling at you for no reason, then. Typical *man*!"

I don't know why she thinks I am doing this. She was the one who stole my body and my voice.

She is also bravely shouting, despite there being an abundance of predators around. Maybe she really is becoming like me.

I like it.

"Just come back inside the water."

"No! I'm going to find something to eat! And don't you dare follow me."

I slink behind her, ready to pull her back at the first sign of desiccation. If I broke that rule, I might as well just keep breaking it.

She finds more of her plants, and they make me shudder. If she really is stealing part of me, then they'll weaken her quicker than drying out.

"I swear you're the worst kind of *stalker*. Why are you hiding behind the trees?"

"I am not hiding. I'm staying closer to the water so I can hydrate quicker. You should do the same."

"No, *thank you*," she responds with venom in her voice.

It makes that odd feeling stir in my chest again. To think how despite having no actual venom, she has become more intimidating.

I watch her eat her leaves, waiting for some kind of reaction. I don't have to wait long because the leaves don't stay long in her body before she retches. When she raises her head, all I can see in her eyes is panic.

"No, no, no, no, no, this can't be happening. Please, this can't..."

She falls to her knees, eyes to the sky. She whips her head back down, reaches down like a ravenous beast, and throws the leaves into her mouth, crushing them between her teeth. Not long after, she retches again.

She spends so much time pushing against nature.

I reach my limit at this point and move closer to intervene before she grabs more.

"What are you doing?"

"Let me go, *diablo*! You ruined my life!"

"I will not allow you to hurt yourself."

"See if I *fucking* care! I have had it with your attitude and your desire to own me! How would my poor *padre* in *heaven* feel when he sees his *daughter* turning into a monster?"

She thinks she is a monster?

I look closer at her, noting that I no longer think of her as disgusting, not even the parts of her that aren't from me.

"What is your word for something that you want to keep looking at? Something that makes you feel pleased to have your eyes on it?" I ask her.

She stills, some of the anger leaving her. "*Beautiful.*"

"You are *beautiful.*"

Her mouth drops open, then closes, then opens again. She looks like a fish.

A sound like she makes when she is pleased escapes my throat. A rising and falling cry that surprises me, but also feels good.

Maybe I am the one taking her voice now.

I wrap my tentacles around her, squeezing her tightly. She stares back in defiance, but doesn't fight against my hold.

All of this because she can no longer eat her nasty plants? What's wrong with eating food like me?

"You aren't allowed to hurt yourself. Those plants are hurting you."

"*Screw* the *damn deal*! It was made under the assumption that I'm *human*. Do I look *human* to you, Wroahk?"

"I do not know what that is supposed to look like."

"Of course you don't. If this is really a dream, I would love to wake up right now."

Her voice softens at the end. I stop squeezing and gently place her down.

I watch her skin closely, worried she will dry out. Seeing the cracks on her skin, I reach out again and carry her with me, taking extra *care* and take her inside the water. Submerged, all she can do is release air bubbles, but it doesn't look like she wants to talk, anyway.

I take her down to the cave and wrap myself around her.

I have never felt like this before, but I feel a need to say something to her to make her feel her. I search my head for words, but I can't find any.

I've always lived alone, and I thought I would remain like that until I died. Skills like that were always useless.

Now, I have her. The *human* with the *kind* touch. I don't want the warmth of her skin to disappear.

After a moment, she returns my embrace, her limbs holding me tightly and her new yellow tentacles wrapping around my chest as she trembles.

"You are weak and confused. I do not know how you feel, but I have seen prey lose their minds because of these emotions. You doubt yourself because you are used to being weak, but you must understand that you have gained strength. You cannot be strong with the head of weak prey. You must accept your own strength and keep living."

I will not let go of her *kindness*.

She looks up at me. She isn't angry anymore and I can see what was hiding behind it now. Fear.

The best way to avoid that is to feel strong.

"You should get used to hunting. I can show you how."

She shakes her head vigorously. I move closer, pausing to give her time to say no, and then move to give her a *kiss*.

She responds with violence, but not to hit me to tell me to stop. Her teeth almost puncture the skin near my teeth, her arms wrap around me, and she pulls me close with her graspers. With this *kiss*, I feel...

The best feeling ever, though there is no name for it.

She fights for dominance with her tongue and squeezes me with her weak arms. Her lower limbs attack my tentacles, but I have no trouble against them. I want her to struggle more. I want her to fight me more.

I want to taste the fury in her blood.

She moves her lower limbs so they squeeze me tight, *kissing* me and nipping at me with her teeth, then pushes me away, her grasper rubbing at her lip where it is already healing from where she caught it on one of my teeth.

Her rage tastes even better than I hoped.

"You will make a fine hunter, female. You already possess the madness for it."

She raises a single finger at me without turning and moves to the corner. I feel proud of what I have accomplished and turn around to guard her and think... so much thinking.

She isn't quite ready yet to make her first kill, but she shows early signs of the needed violence.

39

Eli

"You survived. You are not as weak as you used to be," he calls back as I see his tentacles disappear.

Is that really supposed to be some sort of consolation? I really want to strangle this alien, but he just fought through an entire horde to save my life.

And it was freaking hot as hell. Dammit.

The least I can do is just let him say what he wants. I'm tired, too tired to say anything to him, even if I could.

For now, all I really want to do is just... breathe.

The cave looks much more inviting than it did before. It isn't as dark, and this time I get to take a closer look at the blue-glowing snails, just as curious as always about their differences. It seems shell patterns might be universal. Interesting.

They are eating the green and red algae coating the walls of the cave, which is just big enough for me to move around a bit, even with Wroahk's massive body set up at the entrance.

Probably there to block me getting out as much as to block anything getting in. I lift a lip and snarl at him. He doesn't look impressed, then he moves away from the cave opening.

My stomach grumbles, but I'm not even sure what to feed it anymore.

The world has gone mad. No, I have gone mad. Every single day I wake up, I find that I have been stripped of everything that made me the woman I used to be.

I really thought that since Wroahk is an intelligent creature, it would mean that I can still eat whatever I want and not indiscriminately kill like he does. Clearly, the change was physiological, even down to what I can freaking eat.

I can no longer maintain a vegetarian diet. Everything I thought I knew about myself, gone in the span of a few days. This transition is not just stealing my body, it is stealing my life.

It doesn't matter how much food I shove into my mouth. It won't stay down, no matter how hard-headed I want to be.

He's watching me again, even though I thought he left. He can probably see forever in the water, the bastard. I feel his eyes on me, never changing, never moving.

It's infuriating. I can't understand why it has to be him. He's the monster that threatened to eat me the first time he saw me. Now, I don't even understand what he wants.

Except I know that what I want is him.

Diablos.

This isn't helping.

Calm down, Eli. Breathe.

Breathe through what exactly? My nose? My lungs? My gills? I've been using all three of them completely normally, like it's how I was born.

It's too quick, too fast, too weird.

The tentacles in my hair, dammit. I don't actively see them, but I know they're there. It's like this thing where you are constantly looking at your nose, but your brain won't let you see it unless you focus on it. In this case, if I instruct them to move... they stretch out and touch along the cave rock behind me.

I shudder. It's like having eight more arms, except with different ways they interpret sensation.

I shiver, then feel a slight change in temperature. Are they temperature regulators? That's just a guess. I don't know much about this body and Wroahk doesn't seem to be curious about the mechanics of his.

I doubt his species has any interest in biology.

I'm not the judgmental type, but I have my limits. If I accept the tentacles and the gills and the fins, what else will I have to accept? Being oviparous and laying eggs like a cephalopod?

I retch.

He has tentacles, so that's the closest biological earth group I can place him in.

My stomach grumbles, reminding me that I'm still unfed. Wroahk has gone off somewhere and I'm still at the bottom of the lake. I'm not curious enough to venture out, not with Many Teeth out there.

No need to become fish food.

I look around, my eyes resting on the kelp-looking things at the bottom, wondering if I can eat them instead, but I stop myself.

My little fit up on the land was stupid, and I'll forgive myself a lot, considering how much stress this has been, but not that.

Stupid means dead here, and as much as I've tried to keep myself alive, I'm terrible at it. I would have been dead a dozen times over without him.

No sense in making his job harder. I won't survive without him.

Dammit, that sounds like something he would say. I refuse to be the weak thing he thinks I am, though I suppose I can't do much about my physical strength.

That doesn't mean I should keep ignoring my most important one, as I have a very unhelpful existential freaking crisis. This is my new reality, and I am way smarter than this. It's time to stop letting my emotions run wild.

Wroahk comes back as I steel my resolve. He studies my face for a bit and holds out something that resembles a cuttlefish. He seems to war with himself for a moment, but then pushes it toward me.

I push it back and shake my head.

"You have not eaten yet."

I haven't been feeling well these past few days, but my pride is all I have left. Eating the poor, defenseless animal he hunted for my survival is the one thing I'm not going to do. I refuse him staunchly.

"You have to eat it, or you will starve."

His tone has become more forceful, and he is more demanding. I turn my head away, but he isn't lenient.

He wraps his tentacles around me in an instant, drawing me closer to him. For some reason, he is very considerate about not covering my gills, even though he is holding me against my will.

I feel my anger rising, and then remind myself that not two minutes ago I decided to not be stupid. I need to eat the fish.

He lets out an echoing growl as I hold my arms up.

He stops, and I gesture for the fish. He holds it out and before I can overthink it, I cram it into my mouth, somehow swallowing it before it can sit on my tongue, the taste of the water already vile enough as it is.

Since when can I gulp down entire fish? I retch

He looks pleased with himself when I look back, and it makes my eye twitch. I push past him, out of the cave, and after spinning around to look for Many Teeth, I try to make my way to the surface without looking like prey.

I don't get very far before a tentacle wraps around my leg and yanks me back, then I'm wrapped securely with tentacles writhing around me.

"Not without me," he clicks out.

I glare at him and point at the surface of the water, shocked when he takes me there.

The moment we break above it, I give him a piece of my mind. "That was disgusting. I hate this."

"You seem to want death. Is being like me really so repulsive?"

I struggle to give him an answer because I'm supposed to be the nonjudgmental one. I've prided myself on it.

The reason I don't eat animals in the first place is because I want to be impartial to all living beings and I don't like discrimination against species. I didn't want to put myself on a pedestal with the little power I have.

I don't want to be like that monster, my stepfather. Asserting my control, just because I can.

I let out a breath through my nose, clearing it of water.

This isn't the same. I can't survive on plants anymore. I didn't terrorize that poor fish, I just did what I had to do to live. Just like it probably did when it ate something smaller than it.

I look at him and think of it from his point of view. His whole life is about survival, and now I am this burden he never wanted, but can't seem to give up.

He wants me to live, as crazy as that seems based on our first interactions.

He cocks his head, still staring at me. There's nothing in his eyes but his curiosity.

I've been pissed off, but it isn't logical that he's the cause of what is happening to me. He tells me exactly what he thinks, even if I hate it.

He genuinely doesn't know what is happening and is just trying to help me.

That said, the man needs to work on his empathy.

"Wroahk, what would happen if you were to suddenly lose your gills?"

"Why would that happen?"

"Just... imagine. I grew gills, so it is possible for you to lose them. What would happen then?"

"I would not be able to breathe inside the water, so I would need to leave it. Then I would likely dry up and die."

"Yes. You need to exist inside the water, or you will die. Now, what if you lost your fins and your tentacles?"

His expression changes and I see confusion intermingling with disgust. I watch him slowly reach a conclusion.

"I would become weak, useless, and die."

"Yes, you finally get it. I didn't die, but it feels like I am. If I took everything that made you, well, you, it would take away your identity and everything you have learned, everything you became, all the time you've lived, everything would disappear. Part of you would die."

"...are you dead?" he asks, his voice oddly quiet.

"I am dying, in a way, Wroahk. Everything that makes me who I am is going away and I'm going to become something I don't recognize. I don't want that. It's why I am resisting, even though I know I can't."

"You are still in front of me. Not dead. I cannot let you die, but I see now what you mean that a part of you already has."

He is becoming more emotional, and ironically, more human.

The detachedness he used to have is gone. I don't think even he realizes he has changed. I have changed as well. Not just physically, but I'm changing from within. I don't want to accept it. I don't want to be someone else.

I'm becoming more forceful. Violent even. Earth Eli would have had a panic attack just thinking about making him mad, but instead, I am fighting him any chance I can get.

It should terrify me, it has since I was a teen, but not anymore. It feels good. I feel more powerful than I ever have.

Which is crazy, since he's the most vicious person I have ever met. He could kill me with just the tip of one tentacle.

Except he won't. I know it. There is this surety with him I haven't felt since I was safe with my *padre*. That I could do or say anything, and he will just stay here with me.

Even if he doesn't understand why he stays, he will never leave.

It's funny because after my *padre* died, I used to think about death and reincarnation a lot. I spent a lot of time staring into people's eyes, wishing I could see a glimmer of the pure soul that filled everything.

I used to think he'd become a dog or a cat and would continue to watch over me like that. They were just rambling thoughts of a hurt child.

Except now I'm staring into the shark eyes in front of me, looking for that glimmer of soul.

Wroahk suddenly raises his hand and puts it to my face, pulling me to him gently, wrapping me with as many limbs as he can until only my face and gills are uncovered.

"You are still warm. You are still alive. I will not let you die."

That is the last piece of gentleness I am spared before he grabs me and shoves another cuttlefish looking thing toward my face. I smack him hard, and he changes tact, shoving it into my hand.

He backs off, then makes another move toward me, like he really wants to cram it in my mouth, cover it, and make me swallow it like someone trying to get a pill down a dog's throat.

He doesn't, and leaves me the choice to eat it, which I do after a hunger pang hits my stomach again, but I'm still pissed.

"You don't need to shove things at me, Wroahk! You hold it out and I choose to grab it or not."

"Your life belonged to me from the moment I decided not to eat you. I will not let you harm or kill yourself. I can hear your hunger."

"Is that supposed to sound romantic? It's really fucking not, you asshole. I curse the day I met you."

Dammit. I can already feel my strength returning from the fish and my stomach is finally settled down after days of griping. I don't want to admit it.

"*Consent* applies to what I eat, too, Wroahk."

His face falls as he makes the connection. "I will not forget. Do you want more?"

This time, all he does is hold one out to me.

How sad is it that it feels like progress that he isn't whipping his tentacles waving food in my face?

He learns, at least. I'll give him that.

Even if he's just as stubborn to admit it as I am. Just as willing to say words that don't match his actions.

"I thought you said you wouldn't hunt for me."

"As long as you are alive, I will do what I must."

I'm still pissed off, but part of me has to admit that, for him, that's saying a lot.

It doesn't sway me, though. Okay, maybe a little, but it shouldn't. He's an alien and I'm slowly becoming one myself. I need to distract my mind.

"What's it like? Being you, I mean?" I ask, wondering if he'll prefer to answer me this time instead of being perpetually silent.

He's not forthcoming with answers. Rather, he's looking around, searching for something. I hope he doesn't notice that I'm still hungry. I have to find a way to slip away from him. His hold is tight but if I can distract him again...

My stomach growls at that exact moment. My eyes widen as his gaze meets mine and I can see the gears turning in his head.

"Don't you dare," I warn him.

He doesn't, though I can see his limbs twitching with his desire to feed me.

It's going to take some patience as I let myself adapt. Nothing good ever comes out of rushing or trying to deny reality. There's been plenty of loss before this. I just have to focus on my goals, just like always.

I don't have to panic or try to overthink everything... just calm down and breathe and simply accept that I have another way of doing that now.

In and out. Gently, slowly. Better still, I don't have to imagine that I'm floating because I truly am threading along gently in the water, being pulled by a tentacled man who is intent on keeping me alive.

It could be worse, really, even if we are going to have to come to terms with how freaking bossy he is.

After I calm down, I turn to swim toward the cave, his tentacles in the water all around me, barely leaving room for my body to move.

I can see the outline of the cave now. There's some kind of smeared marking on the edge. I focus on it, and then understand why it's there. It's a marking from him. That's why none of those crocodile-looking things ever approach the cave.

There are more things I can learn if I just lean in, observe, and ask.

I don't know if I should hold hope that I can somehow become human again. Being human on this planet seems dangerous. I'll have to survive and learn to be like him, whatever species he is.

He's being smothering now, but like the time I was climbing down the tree, he won't always help me. I have to learn to survive on my own.

With quick movements, he pulls us into the cave.

He's wrapped around me now, keeping me down, probably assuming I'll bolt at the first sign of freedom, and he's probably right.

How do I copy how he speaks under the water? Reflect the sounds through the water? Or perhaps its refraction. I can't really tell.

I open my mouth and think of what I want to say. There's plenty of thoughts running rampant through my head, but I can't say them all at once. I just have to send a specific thought through the water.

"Hello."

It doesn't work. I can't hear my own voice outside my own head and all that comes out is air bubbles. I have to try again.

"Hello."

An echo. A whisper sent through the water, like a forgotten voice. It's a strange feeling, like I'm speaking through a microphone and a speaker at the same time. My vocal cords feel like they're expanding. Still, I don't know if I've succeeded because he isn't responding.

"Can you hear me, Wroahk?"

He still doesn't respond. I can't tell if he's ignoring me, or I really can't reach him. My voice might as well be an echo scattered through the water, reaching everything else but him.

I try several more times, but eventually grow too tired. My eyelids slowly grow heavy, and I slip into slumber.

40

Wroahk

Overwhelmed.

That's how I feel right now. I shouldn't feel anything, I shouldn't think so much, but I do. For the first time, my... head is... opened?

Not the one on my shoulders, exactly, but the one currently swirling around like I'm riding an ocean current.

I don't like it.

I've only ever needed my head for hunting. Observing prey, watching it, calculating when I need to make my next move, and enjoying the chase. I never needed to understand how the prey felt, never have I ever needed to make the prey feel better.

This is not my way.

'What would happen if you lost your gills?' she asked.

What else? I am a hunter who has lived his entire life in the water.

She hates the changes. She almost screams every time she sees her reflection in the water.

Every day, she changes into a new creature. She is frightened, and she is confused. Those emotions are common in prey. But... she isn't prey to me.

I want to keep her.

Her question still makes my head hurt. What will I be without what makes me myself? What would I do if I find myself stranded on land with just two lower limbs like her, no gills and no fins?

Would I still cling to the water, even if I could no longer have it?

I look at her tentacles, her fins and her gills and wonder if I would fight as much for my survival if I were to change like her.

I thought she was stealing from me, and I hated her for it.

If it was intentional, I don't think she would be this scared. She looks like she's genuinely suffering, even though she has no pain in her body physically.

Not when she is under the water, at least.

I have never held something so tightly in my tentacles as I do right now without the goal of killing it. All the things I've crushed and all the things I've destroyed, all of them do not feel as heavy a burden as what I grip right now.

She feels like a weight that extends far beyond her slight form.

All this creature does is talk and talk. The very sound of her voice annoys me and once her lips open, I want to shut them. Yet, I don't. I let her be.

I don't understand it, but this is what she has made me into.

Kind touch. It came with changes I never imagined. Both of us are becoming something we never thought possible.

The warmth of her emotions when she imprints on my body makes it worth it to me, and soon she will understand the worth in her own changes.

There's something different about her again. I felt it when I put her grasper on my face, but I didn't tell her. I should've but I didn't. When I saw the panic in those eyes, I wanted nothing more but to *calm* her, to protect her, to keep her safe from those very emotions she so vividly projects.

It must be her eyes. It's like they're reaching out into my head and swirling it around, putting on pressure that her graspers otherwise cannot. When she screams in pain, somehow, I can feel that pain, too.

I don't like it.

Those eyes of hers, those vivid reminders of her life, they're closing now. I know from her breathing that she's just falling asleep, but it makes me feel... fear again. What if she doesn't open her eyes anymore? What if the warmth of her body disappears?

What do I do then?

Since the first moment I had it, I've endlessly craved her touch. As time goes on, I only want it more, want her more.

I cannot stand being separated from her, even in slumber.

I put my head on her chest and listen. I can hear her heart. It thumps on in her chest, steadily and quietly. It's nothing like I've ever heard before. I'm used to tracking heartbeats when I'm hunting, but this one is unique.

When I hear it, I don't think about stopping it. I think about letting it beat, making it stronger.

Letting her swim, even though she's clumsy. Feeding her, even though her teeth are blunt. Holding her, even though all she does is fight back.

Even now, I want to keep her no matter what I must do, or what I must kill.

I hold her close, wrapping my limbs around her now. I don't know what this is. I've never done this before.

I'm sure she would have a name for this action. She always has a name for everything. She called our lips touching a *kiss*, so what would she call our bodies continually touching?

She made everything so... different.

My head is still on her chest and I'm counting the beats and numbering the intervals. It is useless energy to number a life, but I am afraid of it stopping.

All she's doing is sleeping and all I'm doing is worrying about her. Why do I worry? Why have I changed so much? I never wanted to change. I was fine the way I was. It was cold and... well, I was fine.

Was I really? I haven't lived a long life, but I've lived long enough to know that not all her words are lies.

I can survive on my own, but do I really want to?

I have before. I wandered the great oceans, rode currents, and hunted more monstrosities than her puny mind could comprehend.

Of all the places in this new world, why did I end up with her? Why her? Why did I get the rambling, never-stopping female stupid enough to offer me her touch? Teach me about a *kiss*, from which there is no escape from wanting more.

As has become my reality, there are questions and there are no answers. No matter how many times I ask the same ones.

It looks different, but her skin feels just like mine now. She hasn't realized it yet, but I hope that when she wakes up, she likes it.

Hope. I never do that. I never hope for anything. It has always been something for the weak.

I don't know what to make of this new experience. Thinking of her constantly may dull my teeth as a hunter. I will no longer hear other heartbeats like I used to before because I will always search for hers.

I will no longer spend hours patiently waiting in the dark to catch masterful prey because I want to get back to her. I'll be stuck with easy kills.

"Mhmmm..."

Her sudden groaning startles me. I know she is still asleep because her heartbeat remains unchanged. I look at her and caress her skin. Her skin is now my skin. Her body is now my body.

What would happen if the females of my species were more like her? If they didn't want to bite the male's head off? If they stayed together after mating?

Is that the start to this *community* she won't stop talking about?

Through her endless words, I understand that her species depends on one another to survive. Do I need to depend on her now? But she is weak and her ability to provide for herself is... terrible.

Depending on her seems unwise.

It is much better for her to depend on me. That, I can accept.

Yes. It is just that simple. I don't know why it took so long to occur to me. All she has to do is continue to depend on me and she will always give me her *kind hands*.

In return, I will protect and provide for her. I understand her point now. It isn't a *deal*, it is... something else I don't have a word for.

This is why thinking is so exhausting, but now that I've started, I cannot stop.

The best thing to do right now is control it.

The night is long and while my eyes grow weary of watching, I cannot bring myself to sleep. Not while she still resists her changes. I don't want to wake up and find that she's no longer in my limbs.

The morning comes and my eyes are still open. I wait for her to awaken and for the pain in her eyes to no longer remain.

She looks disoriented when she wakes but doesn't struggle against my hold. Just lays there and looks at me. She can talk underwater, but I don't want to acknowledge it.

I have food ready for her, but I know better than to force her.

She doesn't resist and feeds herself, and my limbs relax. She is watching me, too, more than she has. She wants to know something, but she doesn't speak, and neither do I.

I release her from my hold, but she doesn't swim away immediately. She looks at me, surveys the cave and keeps moving around. Her limbs are more streamlined and she's moving more smoothly in the water.

She's learning now, instead of resisting.

She has yet to notice her skin, so I don't tell her. The only thing that hasn't changed is her teeth and that desire in her yellow eyes to express her thoughts faster than should ever be possible.

"You can hear me, can't you, Wroahk?"

I don't reply, but she doesn't stop talking this time.

"You can pretend not to be listening, but that doesn't mean I'll stop talking. You should give me more *credit*. I'm not stupid."

I refuse to respond. She can't know I can hear her. It will only make it worse.

"Oh, do be prepared, my tentacled *alien man*. I have many questions to ask you."

There's now rage burning behind those eyes. I have seen her rage before, but this one is unlike the others. It's controlled and channeled. She's focused now, just like she should be if she wants to be a hunter.

I approve.

My mating tentacles stir as the desire to touch her and give her pleasure surges. Higher than anything I have ever experienced. I want her fingers to dig into my flesh as I taste her. I need to feel her again.

"Don't look at me like that, Wroahk. It was easy to figure out. I always know when you're listening and when you're not. You probably don't realize it, but you have a *tell*."

She is clever.

Our nights are going to be even longer now. I hope my mind will survive intact.

41

Eli

He finally lets me go and I swim up to the surface to feel the sun on my skin. I rub along it like I'm bathing, and that's when I feel it.

Something is different about my skin. It doesn't look like it's changed much, but on closer inspection, I see there's a hint of blue around the fins at the back of my arm, and my skin feels just like his now. I sigh and float along the water, spotting him at the corner of my eyes.

I want to start yelling, but what's the point?

It's already changed. All I can do now is live with it. I don't have much of a choice, really.

He brings me breakfast. He seems to vacillate between letting me feed myself and some irrational fear that I won't takes over him and I can tell he's battling his desire to stuff food in my mouth.

I drift along, trying not to think of anything. The cliffs look fine after the storm the other day. It took down trees, but I guess the rocks were indestructible. I let my mind wonder what they're made of, thinking of all mythical metals stronger than diamond.

My eyes fly back up there and I notice something, just for a moment. I feel like my eyes are playing tricks on me and I almost shoot out of the water. His tentacles recoil like a rope, pulling me back in. I just knew he wouldn't let me go so easily, not like this.

"You cannot leave."

Of course I can't. I can't beat him or even fight him at all. But I do have the right to find out if what I saw was really real and not the sun of an alien planet playing tricks on me because I cannot afford tricks right now.

"I need to check, Wroahk."

"Check what?" he asks, eyeing me nervously. I wonder why he's the one who's nervous when he's the one who has me trapped in his tentacles.

"I saw something over there," I tell him, pointing to the cliff. He and I both turn to the look at the same time and the shadow I thought I saw was no longer there. I hear him speak.

"There is nothing there."

"There was something just a moment ago. If you let me go check..."

"Too unstable. You cannot leave the water yet. You will..."

He doesn't complete the statement, but I realize that he believes that if I leave the water, I will die. I mean, there is some truth to it, but I can't accept that there aren't windows of time that I can be out of the water.

I swear, he might be more scared of me dying than I am.

But that's the thing with fears. You have to take them one day at a time or they will overwhelm you. You need to let them go just as fast as you can.

I draw closer to him, putting my head back down to face him. As I thought, his face is becoming more expressive and human like. I don't know if this is a good thing, but I'm glad for the ability to understand his emotions.

"Wroahk, are you absolutely sure there's no one else here?"

"There is no one else here."

"You haven't seen a creature that looks like me, well, looks like how I used to? Are you sure I'm the only one of my kind here?"

He hesitates. My heart starts beating faster, watching him. He's hiding something from me and I assume trying to figure out the concept of telling an elaborate lie to cover an initial lie.

"The thing is, Wroahk, people of my kind are rarely solitary. We seek out and protect each other. We move as a pack.. a, uh, school of fish that relies on its numbers and its close-knit relationships to survive. We are the apex predators on my world because of it. I need other people. Am I the only one of my kind you have seen?"

I look at him, begging him not to lie to me.

He turns away and swims down instead of answering. For the first time, I follow him willingly, wanting answers. He swims directly inside the cave and folds on himself, seemingly about to sleep. I remember him being wide awake when I woke up, and I realize that he probably hasn't slept yet.

"You can't sleep! We have to go out and check if there are others."

"...no."

It's the first time he's responded to me underwater. I smile, loitering around him, trying to get him to answer me again.

"You can be dull on any other day of your life, but not today. We have to find out if there are others. I need to know if I was part of a crew who crash landed here and lost her memories. That's a fairly good guess, isn't it? I mean, that means I had a whole second life out among the stars, but... forget it. Let's just go."

It still doesn't move him. He looks like he's going to sleep, no matter what I say. It just so happens that I know the exact right words to say to stop him.

"If you don't help me, I'll stop touching you *kindly*, Wroahk."

He finally turns to me and I see exhaustion in his eyes.

"There is nothing out there."

"How do you know that? We've only been living in one part of this lake for as long as I've known. You swim over there, but I'm sure you don't go too far. Come on! We have to satisfy our curiosity."

"I am not curious."

I frown and cross my arms. He rolls his eyes and then closes them. Yet another human expression.

"I can't live like this, Wroahk. I'm going to go out there by myself."

"You are living just fine, and you will go nowhere without me."

I move closer to the mouth of the cave, stretching out my tentacles.

"Is that a promise? Because I can tell you now that if I continue to stay with you, I'll become sad and lose the energy to be kind to you. It's called depression, the mental death of any social species. We still have a good deal, Wroahk. Let's just go out there and see what we can find. It's a whole world. We would be crazy not to explore it."

Saying it like that is a gross oversimplification, but he won't do anything to harm me, mentally or physically. I have to take advantage of it or we will stay in this stupid bubble like octo-cavemen.

He's become softer, I know it. Why else would he follow me out to the deep, even though he could've just left me wrapped me up like he always does? He cares for my well-being. He's serious about keeping me alive.

It feels... good, actually.

It's a reckless idea to explore, I know that much. But if there is another out there like me, I really need to know. Is there a way off this planet?

He moves to wrap around me, but I shake my head. Sure, it's a nice and protective gesture, but I would prefer not to be treated like a child.

Or a safety hazard... even though I am one. I prefer to have my dignity still intact. I hold out my hand to him instead. He studies it, most likely wondering what he's going to do with it. All that and he doesn't take it. It makes me embarrassed. It's like trying to hold hands with a boy in middle school all over again.

"Just take my hand and hold it instead of dragging me along. You can't swim properly if you're dragging me along, right?"

"I can swim just fine," he huffs.

"Still, I don't want to be dragged around. Let's just swim."

"You cannot swim properly," he points out.

"I have to learn somehow. Now, just hold my hand and let's go."

He grumbles but he does what I ask.

He wastes no time now that he's decided, and I realize just how fast he has been going the whole time as we move across the rocky structures of the lake.

"Slow down! I can't swim that fast!"

He doesn't slow down. He just drags to a halt, almost throwing me into a spin. I feel something pop and just pray that it's not my shoulder that got dislocated. I flex it and it doesn't seem broken. After confirming that, I glare at him.

"What the hell is wrong with you?"

"You asked me to hold your hand."

"Yeah, and you almost broke it. Would it kill you to go steady? Did you learn how to swim by going as fast as you can?"

He doesn't reply but I can tell he isn't pleased. Lack of sleep can make people grumpy, I know that, but I also need to know if there's more out there. This might be my only chance to find out, and I'm not going to waste it.

"Remember the way I taught you to. Be gentle. Be kind. Just lead me along and don't drag me along."

He stares at me for the longest time. I thought he would insist on returning to the cave, but he just holds out his hand again.

"I will be... kind."

His effort surprises me. I give him my hand and we try again.

This time, he goes slow and steady. I try to copy his swimming but it's hard since he has many legs, and I have just two. The only thing we have in common is that he keeps them together to go slow. I do the same, moving my body the way he does.

After a while, I realize the fins make it easier to copy the fish and I remember the times of my youth pretending I was a mermaid.

I look down at the rocks and fish and marvel. It's beautiful. Many of the fish blend into the rocks as they duck and hide from us, while others have surprisingly bright coloring for a lake. It's incredible.

There are thousands and thousands of the blue snails lighting up the lake bed, illuminating the outline and contours as I get close enough. The water isn't murky, which makes me wonder if it is a glacial lake. Except there is a current, so maybe it is more like one of the Great Lakes.

Such a mystery.

"How big is this lake?"

"Small."

My brow furrows. "Not compared to an ocean," I tell him. "How much more of it is there than what we've seen?"

"From the taste and the currents, where we are in just one small part."

"And you didn't explore?"

"Why would I?" he retorts. "There is no salt, so all I will find is more terrible-tasting prey."

I let out a huff of bubbles. "It's beautiful, Wroahk. I can't believe you didn't want to see more of it."

"It's just water. There's nothing to see."

I laugh, ignoring his cynicism. I try to pull him down with me, intending to touch the rocks. He pulls me back, a frown on his face.

Well, that's new. Human expressions look odd on him, but I like what it says about his inner changes.

"What are you doing?"

"I want to see it up close. It's not everyday you get to explore an unpolluted lake."

"You do not know what is hiding down there. Why do you want to see it?"

"There's just fish around here. I think we'll be fine."

He doesn't believe me, but doesn't argue anymore.

I'm starting to think he has a daily quota of words.

I dive closer to the rocky bottom where multiple schools of fish all swimming around between gently swaying plants of green and purple.

There's even something gleaming white staring back at me. I look closer at it, trying to figure out what kind of fish it is, compared to fishes I've seen on earth. Wroahk's still attached to me as I move closer, and I can hear his grumbling as I press on.

I ignore him and move forward, still curious.

The white goes away, and I frown in disappointment. Instead, I see something flicker, like an eye. I'm still curious, but I move away slowly.

As I back away, I hear low growling.

As Wroahk pulls me away and flings his tentacles out to snap out at the suddenly stirring creatures, I realize it was multiple

Many Teeth, who had covered themselves in silt. Now blinking up at me and snapping their teeth.

Yikes.

"I do not know why you tried to get closer to their nest."

"You didn't say it was their nest."

"I didn't think you would be reckless enough to go look at it."

"And I assumed you would point out if I was heading toward them."

He wraps around me with his tentacles, but this time I don't disapprove. I can't out swim them, only he can. I watch safely from inside my new cocoon as he roars back an echo to intimidate them, making them stop their lazy float in our direction.

His clicking becomes violent as he searches for a way to escape. He sees a route and immediately goes for it, the Many Teeth following.

Wroahk speeds up, and I shut my eyes. The resistance around us is increasing and the water feels different. I feel his hand around me as the familiar feeling of his suckers disappears. It seems like our trip has come to an end.

"Did we lose them?" I ask, looking around.

"Yes. They did not follow us here. I do not want to know why."

The creatures not following us could mean a bigger predator and that is much worse than being chased by a group of crocodile-looking creatures.

The scenery around us has changed. I can no longer see snails and I was right in saying the pressure has changed. There's something different about this part of the water, something sinister. I don't like it at all.

"Let's swim up. We shouldn't stay here too long," I say, looking at him. He holds my hand and begins to drag us up. We are still pretty deep in the water, and I can tell he hasn't had anything to eat all day. Maybe the bigger predator in the water is him. I certainly don't want to be breakfast today.

As we move up, something in the water catches my eye. It is moving toward us, well, not exactly to us but in our general direction. It looks like it's sinking, being dragged down by the water's pressure. If it wasn't for Wroahk, I don't think I'd be able to swim against this water's pressure.

"What's that?" I point at it.

"Please do not bring us danger again."

"But it's getting closer. Shouldn't we check what it is at least?"

"No," he refuses firmly. I huff out a breath but don't argue with him. Eventually, we are going to pass it and I'll be able to see what it is. Hopefully, it's not a corpse or something. If it is...

We pass by it, and I can see it properly. My eyes widen as I see the gray-green creature with huge black eyes sinking down toward the depths. It doesn't look like anything I've ever seen before, and it scares me.

I swim toward the surface, pushing myself to go faster until my head resurfaces near the shore.

42

Wroahk

We should have stayed in the cave.

When has knowing more done anyone any good? It certainly hasn't done her any good. All she does is talk, want to know, want to seek, want to learn, even if what she learns isn't what she wants.

There's nothing but danger deep in the water and I try to tell her that, but she doesn't listen to me. It's like she feels like now that she can swim underwater, that she is capable of anything.

I'm ashamed to admit it, but it is that thought that propels me forward. I am feeling... excited. It's not the usual excitement I get from hunting, but a different kind, the kind I only get when I'm around her.

The satisfaction that she needs me to protect her.

Then she catches sight of one of the gray-green males I drowned.

I have never told her about them, so I'm not pleased to see one drifting right at us. She swims faster than I've ever seen her swim and scrambles onto the shore.

I follow her.

"What the *hell* was that?!" she exclaims, her eyes wide.

"I do not know."

"You've stayed in this lake the longest. Don't tell me you don't know what they are."

"I do not know what they are. All they do is lurk around the lake and I don't like it, so I pull them in and drown them."

"What do you mean, you drown them? What if they're my way out of here?"

Out of where? Is she planning to leave me by using these creatures? What is she talking about? They don't even look anything like her.

"Can you at least bring it back up?"

"No."

I'm not carrying that thing back up with me. They taste terrible. I have no interest in eating them, so I just let them sink.

"Please, Wroahk. I need to see what it is. I can't catch a live one since you'll just kill it."

"... I don't kill them all."

She cocks her head to the side, her eyebrows furrowing as she looks at me.

She doesn't believe me, but she's not the only one I've spared. There are just some of these creatures I cannot bring myself to kill. Instead, I throw the nearest Many Teeth at them and they run away. It takes much less effort to deal with them, but I prefer not dealing with them at all.

"Oh. That's surprising."

She doesn't say anything for a while and just keeps staring into the water where the thing drowned. I don't know if she'll keep convincing me to try to bring it back up for her, but I won't do it.

"Why don't you eat them?" she suddenly asks.

"Why do you ask?"

"Well, I've seen you eat the Many Teeth before, even though you don't make it a habit. You eat almost everything inside the water, and you've threatened to eat me before, too. So, why do you not eat these things? Are they native to this *planet*? Do you make it a habit to not eat other intelligent beings?"

She seems to think it's an important question but there's a simple reason I don't eat these creatures or make it a habit to eat the Many Yeeth.

"They are vile, but you are sweet. I have preferences, you know."

"So... what you're saying is I look delicious to predators?"

"It is not only how you look. The way you smell, the taste of your blood and the warmth of your body are all things predators track to you, and it makes you an interesting prey. Most things in this water want to hunt you."

She squeals and clutches her legs to herself, keeping her body out of the water. How is she just now realizing this? I have told her repeatedly.

She should've known since the first time the Many Teeth attacked her.

"I should have never asked, even though I knew the answer already. So, if it's not worth it to eat them or kill them, have you ever tried talking to them? I have a feeling they're not just a *primitive* species. I think I saw a *backpack* on that one down there."

I decide not to respond to her, though I have heard those things speak. It doesn't sound anything like the way I speak. She is the only one I can communicate with, the only one to steal my voice.

"Look, can we at the very least get the backpack? Just swim down and pull it off the body? I'll stop talking about it for the rest of the day if we do."

"Stop talking completely?"

She looks like she wants to kill me. "For today I won't talk about you killing aliens."

I flick a tentacle in annoyance, then turn to go get it.

"No, I want to come, too."

Her words don't make sense considering her response to finding out what hunts her, but I'm weary. Instead of continuing these useless words, I grab her, and move toward the sinking creature at speed.

I follow its vile taste in the water; the pressure increasing as we keep diving lower and lower. She makes a groaning sound, holding her graspers to the side of her face, but doesn't tell me to stop, so I keep moving.

Suddenly, all of my suckers are sending me signals to retreat. Hers must be as well because when I glance at her, she's pointing frantically back up.

I waste no time in reversing direction, whipping my tentacles in a swirling frenzy, my heart racing with rare fear. When she starts screaming out bubbles, looking behind us, I don't look, just urge my body to move faster.

Her screams stop well before we reach the surface, but I don't slow down, moving my limbs in powerful strokes until we explode onto the lake shore. She's shaking, her tentacles wrapping so tight around me now that they won't impede my swimming that she's blocking most of my airflow.

I try to shift her, but her grip is surprisingly strong. "What did you see?"

"I-I don't know. All I saw was a giant row of long teeth sticking in all different directions in a really wide mouth. Not like the Many Teeth, much, much bigger. It was gaining on us, but then it just stopped chasing."

My limbs relax hearing that last part. "It's a creature of the deep, then. It won't come up past certain pressure levels."

"Are you sure?"

She's still trembling and I pull her closer, running my graspers through her yellow weeds. "Yes, I am certain of it. We simply need to stay out of this part of the lake."

"But that blocks exploration to find out what's out there," she mutters.

I decide not to mention the other opposite way around the island. I explored all sides of it when I established my territory, though I didn't stray far.

"Yes, no need to explore. Let's go back. We have seen enough."

"No, we haven't. We've only just got here."

I wrap a tentacle around her waist and pull her inside the lake. She squeals again when she hits the water, and I feel her graspers pounding on my torso.

"I need to stay here in case more of the aliens come back. I have so many questions."

"They are not like you. We have to leave."

"No, we do not. Don't you get it, Wroahk? This is our opportunity. We might actually have the chance to leave this place and find better water for us! I mean, I just got your skin and even I know something about this water isn't right. We can't stay here forever."

"There is nothing wrong with staying here."

There is no need for anything to change. I have no desire to leave or be separated from her. I don't know why she has so much hope that nothing terrible would happen if she speaks with the grey-green creatures, but I can sense the danger when I see them.

"We can't leave this spot, Wroahk. I don't know when there'll be another opportunity. I don't want to stay another day with those Many Teeth. What if those creatures you've kept drowning decide to form an *extermination force* and use whatever type of weapon they have to hunt you down? You can deal with one or two of them, but can you really deal with a whole population of them?"

"That is why we need to go back. They're not anywhere around the island."

"If they have the *technology* for *backpacks*, what makes you think they don't have the *technology* for *diving suits* or simple *harpoons* or flying? Think, Wroahk."

"I do not want to think! I have never had so many thoughts in my life, and it only started because I met you. What good has thinking done for you and me? We can just hide under the water for as long as we need."

"That is not sustainable. I don't know why you have such a strong aversion to change, but you have to get over it. I've already changed more than I would have ever chosen. I need you to do some of it for me. There's nothing left to risk than the one thing I have left, my life. I am prepared to risk it to understand what is happening to me and how to get out of here."

Why? Why does her gaze focus only on what is above and not what is below? All my life, I've only ever focused on what is below.

Why does this yellow woman want what is above us? Why is she always talking about leaving me?

"... we... we can come back tomorrow," I tell her, my heart constricting.

It hurts something inside of me to see her expression change to happiness. This pain does not come from a physical injury, but it is all-encompassing. I do not understand it, much like I do not understand her.

All I know is it's from her. She might look more like me now, but she is nothing like me inside.

I take her back through the more shallow water on the one side of the island, avoiding catching the attention of the Many Teeth. We make it back to the cave and she settles in the corner, silent. I leave her there and go hunting, wishing to clear my mind of such heavy thoughts.

I have never felt the need to do such a thing, but that is before I met someone so... impossible.

The water is calm and silent, unlike my thoughts. The fish have come out of their hiding spot, all swimming around the alcoves. I return to the cave after finding an appropriate catch and a part of me thinks I won't find her in the cave. However, when I come back, she's where I left her.

She has a stone in her grasper, and she's dragging it across the wall of the cave. I place my kill in the back of the cave so it doesn't float away and swim up to her, curious. She notices my presence and turns around to briefly acknowledge me before continuing.

"Why are you destroying the cave? Is this how you express your dissatisfaction?"

"No," she replies, like my question is stupid and places down the stone. "I've gone *prehistoric*."

"... what?"

"When my species was still developing, they used to convey their history and their stories through carving on the wall. I can't send a *text* or draw a big *SOS* sign in the cove, those trees are blocking everything. I'm just practicing for the rocks out there."

I decide I don't need to know.

"Eat," I tell her

She turns to check where I usually keep what I bring back. "I'm not hungry. You can have my share."

I study what she's carving, but cannot understand anything and I don't know why I even tried.

She explains, regardless of my lack of interest. "I'm *writing* in my language. If anyone who knows my language sees it, they'll be able to know where I am. This is my first step to freedom."

My tentacles clench with my desire to pull the rocks apart.

43

Eli

It's dark.

I'm stumbling and can't see or feel anything. I'm just wandering aimlessly, unable to find my way and don't understand what to do. Somebody, please...

I can hear a sound. It's a low growl. It's coming after me, I know it. I'm always hearing it. It's hunting me. I don't want to get devoured.

It has endless rows of large teeth. I'll be gone in a bite. Someone, please just let me go. Just let me... arrghhh!

***

My eyes fly open, and I regret doing it immediately as the water rushes in. I curse immediately as I try to get the water out of my eyes. I don't know why I keep agreeing to sleep underwater, but I'm regretting it already. Some parts of my body have changed, but the others are still as human as they come.

Wait. Are they? After my initial instinctual reaction I realize the water doesn't sting my eyes anymore.

Oh, hell no. Shark eyes?

I open my mouth to ask Wroahk what he sees but realize I am alone in the cave. Wroahk usually tells me when he's leaving, but I must've been too tired to hear him. I don't like being alone.

My thoughts spiral out of control and my anxiety spikes.

Staying in the water is too unsafe for me. I swim out carefully, extending my senses. My tentacles come in handy here, splayed out to their maximum length to sense for predators. I apologize to them for thinking they were practically useless. He explained to me last night how diversified the application for them is.

I make it past the shallow point and I'm heading for the surface. My senses suddenly pick up on something and I turn around to check, but there's nothing as far as my eyes can see.

Determined not to stay there for too long, I push my head out of the water and drag the rest of my body with it, moving to the cove.

As I walk through the grass, the feeling that I'm being watched doesn't fade away. I know he's not Wroahk because my senses can recognize his one-minded stare. This one is different, more unsettling.

I feel like I'm being hunted, and I've had my damn fill of that feeling.

There are a few discarded branches around.

Huh, I wonder if I could spear a fish?

I instantly retch. If it were up to me to provide for us, we wouldn't make it past the first day. I pick weapons up and sit by the tree, holding some sticks of suitable length.

I have truly come a long way. It's taken some adapting, but I have somewhat embraced this lifestyle. Everyone needs a routine so they can stay focused and keep their sanity. Mine just happens to be as unhinged as the planet I'm on.

Yes, I'm about to sharpen a stick like a cave woman.

If I look on the bright side, I can say every day is an adventure.

As I sharpen it, I hear a low growl. Whatever it is, must be nearby. I can't see it yet, but it's hoping to catch me when I'm off guard. Sorry, whatever you are, but I'm not as weak and hopeless as I first was when I arrived on this planet.

Climbing the tree is my fastest way out, but not just yet. I don't want to repeat that terrible experience.

I hold up my stick and keep my body below the grass. It provides a suitable camouflage for me as I slink forward. I already feel the burn of thirst behind my throat, but I can't just jump into the water now.

My sharpened sticks won't work and I'll be exposed. Even worse, I still don't know where Wroahk is.

"Please come back soon, Wroahk," I plead earnestly, moving toward the cove entrance.

The growl follows behind me, getting closer. Whatever it is, it can see or sense me. All I have to do is keep making slow progress with no sudden movement and maybe I can hide properly in a cave without this thing jumping at me.

Of course, all of that is blind hope. I hear a roar behind me and I take off sprinting. I feel slower and heavier on land then before.

Great.

Fortunately, I know the area well and I can dodge and weave through all of it, keeping a suitable distance between me and this monster. From the repeated growls, I can already guess it's a Many Teeth, though I haven't seen them on land since one tried to kill me.

I never thought I'd run into one after what Wroahk did to mark his territory. This one seems to have been stalking me for a while. It's huge, too, huge enough to ignore Wroahk's warning.

I can't deal with this thing with mere sticks. And I also can't stay out of the water anymore.

Dammit.

I run straight for the shore, watching my footing over the rocks. If I create a trail of blood, it's only going to attract more of them. Once I reach the shore, I dive straight into the water, heading for the cave.

There is a large splash behind me, and I know it has entered the water. I swim faster, trying to keep my body streamlined and my head straight as the pursuit intensifies.

I really want to look back, but I can't afford the time.

Then I feel Wroahk's tentacles grab me. Finally, my dark knight has arrived.

"Where the hell have you been?"

He drags us into our cave, then puts his finger to his lips, shushing me. I'm more than ready to speak my mind, but his gaze is on the Many Teeth. There's excitement in his eyes, like a man getting prepared for a long hunt.

I've only seen him like this a few times and the result has always been a bloodbath.

"Don't tell me you want to hunt that thing?"

"It's been hunting you. Why not?"

I sigh, giving up. There's no stopping a man from indulging in his hobby.

"Just don't come back covered in blood again. And wash out your teeth. I don't like tasting blood, unlike you."

"Why wouldn't I wash out my teeth?"

I pull him in for a kiss, taking away the trepidation I've felt since waking up until now. He draws me in closer, holds me by my waist and kisses me back even as the alien reptile threatens to smash down the walls of our cave.

"I'll be back."

My fists clench as I watch him swim off. That thing is bigger than him, but he doesn't relent as he smashes into it. He manages to draw it away from the cave, leading it deeper into the lake. If he goes too far, he'll get surrounded by a nest, but I don't think I'll have to worry about that.

Wroahk

The beast has been tracking her for some time, though it slipped away each time I pursued it. More intelligent than most, so I had to set a trap for it.

I will not allow something ominous following us around and I certainly am not capable of holding my temper enough for it to continue. So, I decided to do something drastic. I used her to draw it out. I assume the reason it hasn't shown itself yet is because I'm always around her and I'm always watching.

I am closing in on it, and as I get closer I recognize it. It was the same one whose nest she disturbed yesterday.

I catch up to it, slamming into it and push it farther away from the cave. It manages to strike me with its large tail and gain some distance from me, turning to growl.

I easily move out of the way, taunting it, trying to move it farther away from her. The farther we are, the better. I doubt I will fail, but it is large enough that I would rather give her time to escape if it is needed.

After I move it far enough away, I make a dive for its tail and grab on to it with my tentacles, using my body weight to detach it. My attack is successful, though at the cost of half a tentacle to its tearing teeth. Its roars of pain shake the entire lake, but I know it won't draw the other many teeth here.

They are likely finding a hole to hide in, no interest in challenging the largest creatures of the lake.

I extend the pleasure of the fight, pulling chunks and bites from it here and there. Unfortunately, all too soon, it loses too much blood and lies limp in the water. Staying here is worth it for her *kind hands*, but it's at the cost of another part of me.

There is no thrill here. No challenge.

I cleanse my body and teeth and take up the fish I already hunted for breakfast.

Eli

While he's gone, I return to the shore. Now that there's no threat to my life, I can safely gather the things I need to start a fire.

For now, I'll start a pit, then all I have to do is supply it with some sticks, and find out a way to start a spark.

I'm in the middle of setting up when Wroahk returns and slaps two fish by me before splashing back into the water. I don't say a word and go back to moving stones.

"Are you injured?" I ask him.

From what I can tell, the man can grow back parts of himself. I wonder if he passed on that little upgrade.

"Nothing much."

Of course. Of all the predators in this lake, he's the most dangerous one, well, minus whatever is in the deep.

I shudder, but push it out of my mind.

Then I realize I've completely forgotten about my eyes. "What do my eyes look like, Wroahk?"

"Like you stole them," he clicks back.

"From you?"

"Yes."

I expect some sort of pouting rant about how I'm taking parts of him, but instead, he just looks... pleased?

I can't say that dark, soulless shark eyes make me feel that way, but I've reached my limit on the angst.

They don't sting in the water and it's not like the yellow was better. I shrug, dip into the water to rehydrate, and then get back to work.

Once I'm done setting up the pit, I move back to the water. I can see him properly now and he's done as I asked. He doesn't reek of blood, and his teeth are free from gore.

"Thank you for saving my life... again."

"This time, it was intentional," he quips, eyeing me up and down like I am tastier than the meal he brought. "Where's my reward?"

I lean down to kiss him. I see something far off, like a spreading puddle of blood on the surface, but I decide not to focus on it, ignoring my tentacles trying to tell me about it.

We are safe and that is all that matters.

He stops kissing me, then pulls me under the water, moving lower. Once he starts kissing my thighs, I know I've got to slow down this train.

"I want a cooked meal for once."

He doesn't stop kissing me, moving closer to the juncture of my legs.

"I don't know what that is, but it can wait. I'll taste you now and then I'll devour you once we are done eating."

I shiver, deciding I like this plan.

"And then we are going back to find others?"

He doesn't answer, but he also doesn't say no, so I figure a bit more delay isn't going to make much difference. With a start, I realize that the raging lust I used to have each time I saw him is gone. It's more of a gentle thrumming now.

Tied to what we've done and who he is.

It didn't feel natural before, but this does, and not because I'm desperate for attention. I'm stronger than that.

I just... want him.

"Taste me, Wroahk."

46

Wroahk

I can't explain it, but there is something deeply comforting about watching her doing whatever human thing she's doing now, especially now that I know it is connected to something I brought her.

It's a deep connection I can't explain in words. So, I explain it using her body.

Her little gasps and moans fill my ears as she grasps on to my head tightly. My last fight only made my hunger more voracious, and I can't stop myself from trying to devour her.

"Wroahk, please..."

With just a flick of my tongue, I find where she's weakest and make her essence come quicker. Her body jerks as she orgasms, pouring out the warm liquid on my tongue and straight down my throat.

It's better than the blood of any hunt I've ever tasted.

"You're mean," she mumbles as I thoroughly clean her up without leaving a drop, though the way she holds me makes me question her words.

She walks back to the pile of rocks shakily, going back to some mysterious task.

I surprise myself by speaking. "I have something to tell you."

"Mhm. That's new. What? Did you find something exciting to hunt?"

"No. It was not an exciting hunt. This morning, I..."

I wonder how she'll feel if I tell her the truth. Would she not touch me *kindly* anymore? Would I have to find a new way to get her to pay attention to me? I don't know. I just have to do this.

I don't even know why.

"This morning, I used you as bait."

She goes rigid almost immediately. I can't read the expression in her eyes, so I can't tell if she's angry or sad. Maybe she's both. Maybe she's disappointed.

I don't even know if I want to know.

"Wroahk..." she starts, taking a deep breath. "I already know that. I'm not stupid, you know. I would just prefer to be told, and not have to guess."

"Yes."

"Good," she says, her eyes still narrowed at me.

I can't resist the urge to *kiss* her. She responds, letting me pull her back into the water, even though she seemed very intent on her task.

She feels good.

I feel something else for her. Something deep and meaningful. I don't yet know how to describe this feeling, but I know now that she is more valuable to me now than anything. Even the most thrilling hunt.

Our *kiss* becomes more exciting as my tentacles spread her legs open. I know the perfect spots to touch her now and make her body easy to control in my arms.

With the prodding of each, she becomes a wave of moans, holding on tightly to me like she'll be swept away in a tidal wave.

Her body now takes me in quite easily. It's like it's waiting for my shape, ready to accommodate me anytime. Her body is mine to play with, a new type of hunt, and a far more pleasurable one.

She is tight around me, her muscles contracting with each of my movements, her graspers digging into my skin to show her pleasure.

With each thrust, I can feel the strange emotion from earlier rising in my chest. I want our bodies to become one, our breathing to become one, and I want her to be mine forever. I still sense reluctance in her. She gives me her body but not yet her mind... her *kind hands* are still reluctant.

Her eyes often skim the horizon, and she's constantly searching for something along the trees. I know how much she values her freedom, and I know how far I'll be willing to go to keep it from her.

She's made me like this, and she must bear the consequences. She isn't allowed to leave.

"Ohh, Wroahk, that's too... much... *fuck*."

I know better than to increase my speed, so I just make my mating tentacles wider and more sensitive. I know it feels good for her since it's touching all the right places for her and by how much she's screaming my name, begging me to never stop.

There is an answering warmth building in my abdomen, and thrumming along each limb as they wriggle inside of her and I feel my seed build up.

Whatever else she planned to say is cut off by one of my limbs in her mouth, the slow exploration of her tongue and the sides of her mouth increasing my pleasure.

Three more hard thrusts and I release inside her, watching her body shudder as the liquid seeps in, bringing another wave of our pleasure.

Her chest heaves and there's a tired smile on her face.

She's covered in traces of me. She's marked as my territory.

"What's... that... look on... your face?" she asks in between deep pants.

"Nothing."

She will not enjoy my thoughts, so I don't share them.

"All this is hot, but my body isn't indestructible, you know," she complains, but her face says something different than her words.

I reach down to *kiss* her near her yellow tentacles.

"You take me so well, though."

Her face instantly turns another shade, and she turns her head to the side. Is it an attempt to hide? I've never seen worse skin concealment.

"I do, don't I? It's weird as *fuck*, but I like it."

"Your body has learned my shape. It is like you were made for me."

Her face becomes yet another shade as she refuses to show me her expression.

"I didn't think you were capable of *flirting. Damn.*"

"I don't think I'm doing such a thing."

Seeing the hunger in her eyes makes my mating tentacles rouse inside her once more. She feels them come to life and hits my chest hard.

"*Fuck.* You really are a wild animal. I *love* it."

I dismiss her comments and claim her lips. She wraps her grasper around my neck, pulling her body to mine. The fleshy organs on her chest always feel nice to rest on, and touching them pulls out such lovely sounds.

I lower a grasper to touch them, using the other one to keep her graspers pinned above her head so she won't let them get in the way again.

Then I roam every limb I can over her, increasing both of our pleasure.

She moans, her body responding to my every touch.

With every thrust, I claim ownership of her body. She'll always be mine. It's fine if she doesn't know it yet.

47

Wroahk

She's asleep again and I am watching her. She told me what she was called once. What was it?

'Eli. You can call me that and I'll call you Wroahk.'

That is what she said. Eli. That is her name. I have never referred to her by her name before, but I've always known it.

I rejected the idea of using it before. Why?

I would be acknowledging her.

I would be acknowledging these feelings and would be acknowledging her as equal to me. It was an impossible ask at the time because I knew just how weak she was. She is still weak, and I still have to protect her.

Except she needs more from me than that if I want to keep her from seeking her freedom and that means acknowledging her.

"E...Eli..." I murmur, trying to get the sound out of my throat.

I don't even know what it means, and I don't know if I'm pronouncing it correctly. However, I know its significance.

"Eli," I try again, trying to imprint it on my tongue.

She stirs unexpectedly, like she hears me calling her, and I let out a breath when she doesn't wake up. I don't know if I can call her by her name just yet. It still feels like my tongue can't quite manage the shape of it.

The sound of her name, her quiet breaths, and the subtle air bubbles that follow her every exhale, the tiny jerks of her limbs and the warmth of her body keep me up as I watch her.

She wakes up and wiggles out of my hold, staring intently at me. She likes looking at my face, like she's reading for information.

Sometimes, it's unnerving how accurate she can be.

"How long have you been staring at me? Nevermind, can we go look for others now?"

I suddenly feel exhausted.

"Eat first."

I push my body to hunt for her, gathering as many of the bottom feeders as I can before barely stopping myself before pushing them down her throat. She only struggles when she's feeding, but she doesn't do much after that. I know she longs for the surface, but she cannot go there. There is no place for her there anymore.

I feel even more exhausted. I have gone many days without sleeping on a hunt before, so I know my exhaustion is not physical. It is because of all the thinking I'm doing? But even that isn't quite right.

I've been thinking hard since the moment I met her. It doesn't explain this heaviness in my limbs. This lethargy.

My mind shifts back to figuring out ways to delay her, then remember she was making something on the shore. I take her back to it, relieved when it works and she goes back to whatever odd thing she is making.

48

Eli

I can feel him staring at me like I've grown two heads again. In his defense, I have grown tentacles, fins, and gills, so it might not be impossible. It's much harder to stay on land these days, but I am training myself not to forget the essence of being human.

When I reach my hands forward, I notice the new webbing between them and it feels like I just cursed myself.

Dammit.

I take a deep breath, and just let it go. At least I'll swim better now.

"That is long enough. Come back inside the water, Eli."

I jump when he says my name, then whirl back around, searching his face to see what earth-shattering thing must have changed. He's never said it. I figured he never would.

Only his torso is above water and he's wearing the same annoyed expression as always. He floats closer to the surface, his tentacles rising slightly above the water when he moves. I move closer to the water, sitting by the shore and dipping my leg in.

He's saying my name.

He has changed, that much I can tell. That initial coldness and penchant for murder has all but disappeared. Well, it's still there. He's very ruthless against those who try to intrude on his territory. I assume the sinking stacks of Many Teeth is piling up at the bottom of the lake.

I move into the water, trying to puzzle out what has shifted in him.

"There's no need to worry. Just us two here," I reply, caressing his face.

I wrap my legs around him, staring deep into his eyes. All I do is touch him, and the desire in my body flares like a storm. The urge is uncontrollable, and the desire is reflected his eyes. It surges even more when he snakes his hand around my waist.

"Be gentle," I whisper to him as he bends to claim my lips.

He's rough without meaning to be, and far too gentle in other ways, but he's figuring it out.

He's learning to avoid scraping my lips with his teeth, although I know he enjoys the taste of my blood. His long green tongue makes kissing an adventure, wide, thick, slightly bumpy, and a massive overstimulation of the senses.

I pull away first. He lets me go as I dive back into the water, hydrating myself. He releases me, letting me catch my breath, the predator in his gaze as he roams his eyes over me.

A tentacle pulls me close, one of them flicking between my legs, more at each breast.

He pulls me in close, his face near my ear as he whispers. "I can taste how much you want me."

He has no reason to tell me he can sense my lust. I know he's doing this just to rile me up.

It is most definitely working.

His arm rubs on mine, softly, slowly, like he's trying to lather me up.

"*Basta.* You can be rougher. I won't break."

He moves behind me. "Kind hands."

Right. He is entirely dedicated to making sure he treats me as gently as I treat him. He mirrors so well that I'm scared of the changes I've seen. He's still cold and abrasive, but during these moments, he's as gentle as the lake current, sweeping me off my feet even though I'm resisting.

My heart is stuttering. I have to admit I'm moved. If this situation wasn't so weird, I would've already leaned into it, with more than just my body, at least.

I turn around to face him, leaning in to kiss him again. He doesn't refuse and our breaths blend as we steal each other's air, my tongue moving meekly under his overbearing tongue.

Kissing is his one exception to being rough.

It's hardly sweet, but goodness does it make the butterflies in my stomach frenzy.

His hands move from my waist to my chest. He seems drawn to them, like they're completely new. He traces his fingers from the nipple down to the base, sending shivers down my spine at how intentionally he's teasing me.

His teeth scrapes against my neck, his tongue teasing my collarbone.

"Can I taste you?"

I know I asked him to ask but this is just embarrassing. I barely nod my head before I'm flipped over and I feel the warmth of his face against my lower lips. His long tongue wraps around my clit, licking and tasting me thoroughly.

I can't get used to this pleasure coursing through me like lava. "Wroahk..."

"Be patient," he echoes back, returning to driving me against a wall.

I feel my first orgasm build and with one last caress of his flattened tongue, my body almost evaporates as I reach my peak. His tongue brushing against my clit as he licks me clean, elongates it and all I can do is latch on to him and let the feeling overwhelm me.

I don't think it's possible to have normal sex after something like this. There isn't a man in the galaxy who can satisfy me more.

My stomach grumbling stops him from going any further, his eyes already searching for a meal while I'm wishing he didn't stop. However, he cares more about my well-being before anything else.

"Whatever you catch, I'm not eating it raw anymore."

I can deal with being a pescatarian. It's a move up from being vegetarian, but since I need it to survive, I can make the change.

However, eating things raw is gross.

While he dives in the water to find us some edible fish, I scrounge around to find something to make a fire.

I go back up to the cove, making a run for it so I don't dry up. The leaves and branches are still where I left them and are dry by now. I pick them up, dragging them back to the shore. I look around the rocks and find the perfect rock formation to use as a fire pit. As I'm setting up, I hear him emerge from the lake behind me, putting his catch right beside me.

It's a huge fish, bigger than my torso. I don't know where he found it and I have nothing to compare it to. Thankfully, it doesn't have scales, so preparing it won't be hard. Now I just have to convince him to gut it since he can't start the fire himself.

"All you have to do is cut the fish open, pull out its guts before we can eat it. Come, I'll show you."

I've seen plenty of fish cleaned, since my *padre* liked to take me fishing. I prefer not to hurt living things, but the fish is already dead.

All I can do is thank it for its sacrifice and cook it well.

I slice into it with a hard rock, point to what needs to come out, and let him take over.

He might grumble at me for all the new things I introduce him to and the thinking he would prefer not to be doing, but he always watches intently.

I go back to trying to start a fire. I gathered every different type of rock I could find, and I just have to hope some combination of them will make a spark.

When I glance back he is already done and is washing the fish and himself in the lake.

Using bits of leaves here and sticks there, my fire pit has come together. Because of the sheer size of the fish, I might have to use it as a stove rather than roast it. I pick up two broken rocks and start striking them against each other.

The first strike sets off Wroahk because he writhes over immediately, demanding to know what I am doing, snatching rocks out of my hands.

I explain it to him, and he calms down, and eventually stops grabbing the rocks back out of my hands after I curse him out for three solid minutes.

He's calm now, but looks angry when I catch him glancing over in my direction. It makes my lips twitch, as I continue to try new combinations.

It's a reddish rock against a greenish one that finally does it, which explains why it took so long. Neither color is something I associate with strikers.

I position myself near the sticks and leaves, and strike them together again until one lands exactly where I want it.

I blow on it excitedly, but patiently until it catches, then continue to feed it kindling until it is strong.

When I look over at him in triumph, his face displays his discomfort.

"You are too close, Eli."

I open my mouth to argue, but then I realize he's right. My skin really hates me right now.

It's a challenge to take continual dips into the water while also feeding a fire without dousing it. Eventually the coals are big enough for what I plan to do and I bring a suitable sized rock slab to place over my fire pit to cook my fish.

We laze in the water for a while as the rock heats. Then I place the large fish on it before heading back to the water.

He surprises me by sitting by me on the shore. He leans over to kiss me, holding my chin in his hands. I smile as I stare at his lips.

"That will take a while. Want to—"

I don't get to finish before he takes me down into deeper water.

His normal tentacles spread me open, teasing me with their slight brushes. He keeps his lips on mine, distracting me. His distraction works as I almost don't notice him entering me. However, his sheer size makes it impossible for me to ignore for very long. I gasp as his other mating tentacle goes in, filling me up even more.

He stays there for a bit with both holes filled, probably trying to give me a moment to get used to it. This gentleness doesn't suit him, but I'll take it. Even without moving, his mating tentacles are enough to rouse me to another orgasm.

"You... can move," I say.

He returns with a surprising kiss on my forehead, waiting for me to signal that I am ready for more.

Maybe this new body isn't so bad if we can do this...

I nod my head, letting him know I'm ready.

He thrusts almost immediately, and it feels like all the air is taken out of my gills. I feel him hitting the deepest parts of me without remorse, taking away all my inhibitions.

All I can do is gasp for air as he plays me like a drum, bringing me closer and closer to a crescendo.

Not long after, he releases whatever the fuck he has in his semen that makes me feel like I'm on fire, bringing multiple shudders from me.

He holds me close to him, cocooned, with his suckers thrumming all over my body.

Then I remember the fish. My eyes open wide and I try to get his attention.

"We have to go back. It'll burn."

"No," he says, kissing my forehead again.

I kick out at him, and he eventually relents and brings us up to the surface.

I sprint toward the fire pit. Thankfully, we got there just in time and only one side's a bit burned. I flip it to the other side with a stake and just wait until I can pull it out. I use multiple leaves as a plate and hand over a slice to him.

I feel like a wife serving her husband some parody of a dinner. Fuck. Life sure does get weird sometimes.

He picks it up and sniffs it, staring at it suspiciously. I ignore him and blow on mine to cool it off, eager to taste it. I catch myself salivating and remind myself that I need to eat this meal with reverence and not hunger, even though I'm starving.

The moment I take a bite, he throws the whole thing down his throat, still somewhat hot. I stare at him with wide eyes while he sits there in silence.

"That was hot. Are you okay?" I ask.

Without a single response, he turns his back and dives into the lake. I watch for a few minutes before I see him resurface and come back to me.

"I was drying out."

"Okay."

I don't press further because he seems embarrassed. He doesn't eat more but watches me finish the one on my plate carefully. I wait for the other slices to cool before handing it to him.

"Don't worry. These won't burn your throat."

He reluctantly takes them. A glance back over and I know he's enjoying the meal.

It didn't taste as good as the grilled fish my *padre* would make, but it was still very edible.

Not bad for his first cooked meal. From the way he looks at the fire like it might jump out and attack him, it's likely his species is in its early stages of development.

Although, I suppose they may never reach that point. It's weird to think of cooked food and the warmth from a fire as only a human necessity.

"Did you like it?" I ask him.

His tentacles twitch, his shark eyes look away. "It was strange, but not unpleasant."

Wow. For him, he might as well have started dancing and whooping in excitement, but I would have liked some more enthusiasm.

I roll my eyes and change the subject. "Let's go to the other side of the lake now."

From the look on his face, it's the very last thing he wants to do, and his black eyes are darting from side to side, likely thinking of a way to distract me.

"Stop delaying it, Wroahk. Just take me there. This time you can just swim me over so we don't waste time and I don't stir up any more Many Teeth."

His body slumps, but he doesn't argue.

He swims slowly at first, but after a prod him with a sharp finger and narrow my eyes, he moves so fast I get dizzy.

I'm still trying to get my bearings when we stop abruptly. I decide to ask him some questions while my heart catches up.

"So you have only seen the weird green guys? No one who looks like me?"

It takes me a long moment to realize he hasn't answered, and when I look at him, he won't return my gaze.

What the fuck. He has seen someone like me.

I break the surface of the water, then give him a piece of my mind. "All of this time telling you what I needed and you just—"

I'm interrupted momentarily as he pulls me back down and I have to switch over to projecting echoes deeper in my chest.

I let out a long string of curses, which sound really weird as a mix of English, Spanish, and whale echoes, and then I get myself back under control again.

He's moved us around so I can see his face, though he's holding both of my hands with his tentacles so I stop trying to scratch him to pieces.

My chest heaves for a moment, and he looks excited by my anger. It makes me want to scratch the smug look right off his face.

"Was it a male?"

He keeps my gaze. Nope.

"A female?"

He looks away. He saw someone and didn't tell me.

I'm going to fucking kill him.

Eli

I stop thrashing and whipping Wroahk with my hair tentacles when I hear someone speaking in a gravely voice. A frisson of excitement threads through my chest when I can understand them.

"I know I heard someone speaking, my Ree."

I wriggle around toward where the voice is coming from and see a distorted image of what looks like a black figure riding a giant orange cat. There's no time to puzzle that out before I'm spinning through the water.

He let me go, which means he's about to attack.

Fuck.

It takes me a moment to get oriented and then I swim quickly to the surface. I hear a gasp from behind me, realize I'm facing the wrong way, and use my newly webbed hands to reorient myself.

I only catch a glimpse of what is clearly another woman, though an odd one, before Wroahk shoots up onto the shore, his green tentacles writhing. He snatches the woman off her cat mount. The cat roars in outrage, but she screams at him in the same gravelly language I heard before as Wroahk drags her into the water.

"Wait!" she yells out.

The mount's roar transitions to speech in response. "No."

My mind stutters for a precious moment and then I'm screaming, too. But at Wroahk. "Stop! I'll never touch you with kind hands ever again if you don't stop."

The effect is instantaneous, and he releases the woman in the shallows. The cat had already been diving in for her and it only takes it a moment to pull her back up onto the shore and a short few moments after that for it to have her halfway up a tree.

Wroahk's tentacles are around me and I'm right back to yelling at him in my whale voice as he drags back, the water coming up in waves around me and muffling every few words. "Let me go, you bloodthirsty idiot of a man."

He doesn't let go. "¡*Basta*! ¡*Diablos*! Just let me talk to them!"

He finally stops, but I can tell by his grip on me he is angry. I can't see his face or I might be punching it right now, so that makes two of us.

"Do. Not. Take me away," I tell him in a voice that brooks no argument.

From the way his grip ever so slightly loosens, I can tell he has conceded. "Good. Now I won't have to beat at your stupid skull with my 'endless words' until it rattles."

The shiver that passes through him at the threat makes me grin. I turn back to the woman and cat person in the tree, sloughing off my anger so I can embrace the veritable geyser of excitement wanting to pour out of me.

I can barely see her. I can only make out hints of her black suit. She's clinging to the cat person. Mostly I just see a giant amount of fur, most of it orange, but some light green swirling through it. It is puffed out like an electrocuted lion, except it's far too large and alien to be one.

Not to mention the colors are wrong. And, you know, it speaks.

I push the thought aside. I am far more interested in the woman.

I hear her speak again, her voice muffled. "It's alright, Thivoll. I'm alright. Can you take us down again so I can talk?"

"You can talk from here," comes the hissing reply.

The woman grunts in annoyance. I'm pretty sure her cat friend is male, judging by the depth of his voice.

My throat hurts and then I'm no longer making whale calls, but instead sound like I've been smoking for a few decades.

"Hello! Are you human? Sorry, that sounds rude. I don't exactly look human anymore either. Ack! I'm sorry. Let me start over. I'm so excited to see another person! I'm Eli, who are you?"

"Seriously, Fluff Brain. I want to at least see her. Move."

I can already tell I'm going to like this woman. The cat man... Thivoll doesn't come down from the tree, but he does reposition them on the trunk so she can peek out from over his fluffy shoulder.

Her eyes don't have any white left, just like mine, except hers are a beautiful blue. She's crying, clearly excited.

"Hello, Eli. I only knew you as Citrine, and it is so good to see you again."

"Again?

She shakes her head, like she's trying to clear her thoughts. "Yes, sorry, I'm not making much sense. I'm just as excited as you are."

My smile is hurting my face by this point. "That's alright."

"My name's Ree. You were with me on a spaceship, but you were in a cryogenic chamber that kept you in stasis. We were abducted by the genali, pretty much gray blobs with elephant legs. There are other hunters here, too, lots of them, despite our efforts to kill them, like the little green men from movies."

"Oh, I just saw one of those."

Ree looks alarmed and her giant cat pulls in a deep, whistling breath.

"I don't hear or smell anything, sweet one."

I shouldn't be shocked he's speaking. He already has a few times, but I've only just gotten used to the idea of having my own alien.

"Uh. Hi! I'm Eli. It was dead. Sorry, I should have said that, too."

"Greetings Eli, my name is Thivoll. I am very glad to meet you."

I whip my head over to Ree. "Your alien is so polite! Mine just wants to kill everything."

"Oh, well, mine does too," she quips back.

When we both start cracking up, I know I've officially lost my mind on this insane planet.

Ree gets herself under control before I do. "Anyway, where was I? Oh, yes. Abducted by aliens. This is their hunting ground. They bring sapient species like these two and dump them here for trophy hunting."

I'm confused. "I can't believe anyone would pick humans for trophy hunting. As Wroahk likes to point out to me, I am pretty much defenseless."

Ree shakes her head. "No, they didn't. We were on our way to be sold as sex slaves when we crash landed here."

Well, that explains my suddenly larger breasts and flat stomach. "*Qué asco*. Really?"

"You're right. It's disgusting."

I blink, surprised. I didn't expect she would know Spanish.

She grimaces and continues. "There were ten of us. I know one died for certain. I found one, Silver, just to have her stolen by another of the prey. Hopefully she's okay. Thivoll thinks he was obsessed with her and that he'll treat her well. Kira and Drasuk are back at our cave. I have another woman, Amethyst, still in her cryo chamber tucked away with them. We met a prey alien who knew where another woman was, but he hasn't returned yet. Another is out searching for others."

That all sounds crazy, but I guess it's high time for me to adapt to this being our new normal. "Why is Amethyst still frozen?"

Her eyes roam over me. "I'm sure by now you've noticed that the more contact you have with... Wroahk was it?" I nod. "Right. It starts changes in us. Just a bit of contact with Silver to treat her wounds—the woman who was stolen I mean—and she started to change. I want Amethyst to be able to decide. It's from nanites, but I don't really understand it. We have translators, too, and heal faster, stay clean, plus other things."

I let that sink in for a moment, and then latch on to the least mind-boggling revelation. She clearly likes precious stones.

"So you named me Citrine?" I ask her with a smile.

"I did, sorry. I called myself Indigo to make up for how rude it was. I'm so happy to replace it in my mind with Eli." She starts crying again and Thivoll pulls her close to him and rearranges them again so he can start patting her butt.

I raise my eyebrow at her and she gives me a smirk that lets me know he doesn't realize ass grabbing isn't something you do in public.

My throat hurts again as I turn to where I think Wroahk's head likely is down in the water. "I want to go to shore so I can hug her."

His response is muted, but still forceful. "No. No one else touches you."

Ree makes a pained sound then starts speaking in the whale voice. "Greetings, Wroahk. I would never harm your Eli."

That brings him up out of the water, ripples of it splashing gently against my neck.

He is wearing his angry face, which is no surprise. "Why must everyone steal my voice? No."

I roll my eyes at him and Ree catches me doing it. She gives me a small smile, then she looks thoughtful.

She lets out a small hum like she just realized something. "We thought something was watching us from the water a while back. Was that you, Wroahk?

"Yes."

I whip my head over to him. "You seriously saw someone like me and you didn't tell me? I still can't believe it."

"You never asked."

"*Uy, qué care-chimba.* I specifically asked you multiple times!"

Now that I think about it, I didn't until just a few moments ago, but I'm too pissed off to admit it. He knew what I wanted.

I can't believe it's a coincidence that I haven't seen anyone else in days and suddenly they are falling from the fucking sky.

They've always been here around us, just a short swim away. He just hasn't been telling me about it. I really might strangle him, but before I get a chance, our company reminds me of their existence.

Ree starts laughing and I can tell her translator let her know I just called him a dickface. I'm too enraged to join in.

"I tell you everything! We've talked about community over and over again. Why would you not tell me?"

He is back to wearing his impenetrable mask. "No. You talked about community. I was trapped with your ceaseless words."

I might actually punch him. "You—"

"I hate to interrupt, especially since I have no idea what you are saying, but it isn't safe to keep talking out in the open like this," Thivoll rumbles at us. "There are hunters in the region now."

I keep talking in Wroahk's language. "Could you please interpret, Ree? I want to make sure Wroahk hears this and knows that if he doesn't agree to it, I will go to the bottom of the lake and waste away in misery."

I can tell by the way she raises her eyebrows that she thinks I'm being overly dramatic, but she'll figure out why I have to be like this. Or I will tell her later. Actually, there is no time like the present.

"Wroahk doesn't think in shades of gray, Ree."

From the way she raises her chin with a knowing expression and a hum, I see that she gets it. I give myself a moment to think over how to best present this to him.

"Wroahk knows how important a community is for me and my continual health."

I give her a moment to catch up with her interpretation, then speak again. "Although he has been characteristically stubborn about actually agreeing to anything, I know that once he tells me he will or will not do something he keeps his word."

He squeezes me a bit harder to let me know he doesn't like where this is headed, but I keep going. "Our island is a very nice location for a community. It is completely surrounded by water with Many Teeth creatures in it that will kill anyone else, but who are no match for Wroahk's strength and cunning."

He loosens his grip at the compliment, but I know he won't like the next thing I am going to say. "Wroahk will keep the Many Teeth away from you. Tell me you will help keep anyone I say is part of my community safe, Wroahk."

He squeezes me tight again and just stares at me. "Say. It," I bite out. "Now."

"I will help keep anyone you say is part of your community safe."

I let out a breath, relieved. "You will protect anyone in my community like they were me."

"No."

I see where I went wrong there. "You will prioritize protecting me, but will also assist our community when you can, which will include protecting our island."

He repeats it.

"Good. You will help people I have identified as being in the community cross to our island."

He agrees to that, too.

I'm surprised, but I just keep going. "Ree and Thivoll—the ones clinging to that tree right there—are part of our community. So are any and all women like me that we find. And Kira and...

"Drasuk," Ree reminds me.

"Kira and Drasuk. I will keep adding people as long as they are actually allies. Say it."

He does, but adds a caveat. "If they ever try to harm you, they are no longer community."

I nod. "Fair enough."

50

Wroahk

All the *deals* were terrible, but I know by now when she is serious enough to remove *kind* privileges. Her anger is making my mating tentacles twitch, but now is not the time.

She starts talking with the woman again in the language I don't know. She's just as ugly as Eli used to look. Maybe more so. The male with her has been looking at me with a promise of death in his eyes if I come any closer to his female

He can have her. One is more than enough.

I think about how this means there will be at least twice as many words, and I shudder. Except then I realize that I no longer have to pretend I'm listening in order to avoid threats and suddenly this all seems like a much better idea.

They will speak to each other. How have I not realized this before?

Except what if Eli likes them more than me? What if they take her from me? Despite my agreements, my tentacles start reaching toward them.

The male seems very confident, even after I so easily stole his woman. I shouldn't underestimate him. Especially since it was him I went to grab, but couldn't.

Just like I couldn't harm Eli when she fell from the sky. Except why was I able to grab the purple female?

None of it makes sense.

Eli starts using my voice again. "You will keep the Many Teeth away while they swim across to our cove. Repeat it."

I agree to yet another one of her *deals*, even though I already said I would do as much, and then pull her down so we are underneath the pair as they swim. They are even slower than Eli.

Many Teeth come to investigate, of course, not being able to resist the sounds of their flailing. I let one get close to them near the top of the water just to see what the male will do.

I have plenty of time to intervene, of course. I'm not risking *kind hands* for something so useless.

I'm not even sure what the male does. There is a blur of movement above the water and then the Many Teeth is thrashing. The male doesn't even pause in his efforts to reach the other shore. Not long after, the water behind us is murky with Many Teeth blood, except there is no killing frenzy.

The ones nearby flee with strong swipes of their thick tails.

A thrill passes through me. Finally, a worthy opponent.

Then I remember that I'm not allowed to fight with him, even if whatever prevented me from grabbing him wasn't already a barrier. And I also remember that if I die, Eli won't last more than a few minutes.

Not with such a weak body and ridiculous ideas about making everyone her *friends*.

Will she still want to touch me if they are here? There is that new feeling in my chest again. One I do not like. That ache that keeps surging up every time she talks about freedom.

I can't keep resisting giving her what she wants, but the more I think about how much better they will be able to understand her, the more that terrible feeling grows. Maybe they will be better at keeping her from being sad and she won't want me.

I think I made a terrible mistake making this *deal*.

51

Eli

I let out a relieved breath when we get to the other side mostly without incident. There were some weird sounds in the water, but as much as I tried to maneuver myself in Wroahk's grip to see, I wasn't able to.

I shrug it off once I see Ree and Thivoll rise onto the shore ahead of us, Thivoll's scaled black paws the last to rise above the shimmering distortion of the surface.

Wroahk pulls us up but doesn't take us onto the shore. His grip is still steely and if I wasn't trying to be a good host, I would already be yelling at him.

"What do you think?"

Ree slides off Thivoll's back and they both look around, then Ree turns back to me. "This seems perfect to me, Eli."

My heart does a little leap in excitement. "I'm so glad."

She grins back at me. "I'm not sure how many allies we can find among the prey, but there should be plenty of room. There are four more of us, not counting Amethyst to find. Then... Well, we've been talking about it a lot and we think we'll essentially have to go to war if we ever want to be truly safe."

I gulp, not liking the sound of that, but they would know better than I would. "I've been kept pretty isolated by Wroahk, so I'm not really sure what all is going on out there. It's a bit overwhelming to think about, actually, but I do agree that the best place to start is to make sure we have as many people safe here as possible."

Thivoll makes a humming sound, then shakes the water out of his fur. It's jarring to see someone you have categorized in your mind as a person do such a thing.

He helps reestablish his sapient status for my sluggish mind by speaking again. "I can hear and smell someone over there. I've been keeping track of them as we talked and crossed."

He points to a section of the lake far east of where we just crossed. "I'm quite certain it isn't a hunter."

Another thrill passes through me. This feels like Christmas. "Do you mind staying here and away from the shore while we go check it out?"

"Please do," Ree says, her voice letting me know she's just as excited as I am.

My throat hurts again. "Thivoll said there is someone over there." I point the same direction. "But it isn't an enemy. They could—"

I don't get to say more because he is moving us through the water at speed. I really need to figure out how use the echo voice without harming my gills at this speed. Because repeatedly pummeling him with my fists is doing nothing.

Just like I know it won't, but I still do it anyway.

Then we are moving so fast I can't easily use my fists or my gills and by the time he stops, I'm dazed. But when he releases me, which is a shock in and of itself, I kick my way to the surface.

I hear screaming as I break the top of the water. I take a moment to clear the water from my eyes and I see why. Wroahk flung a Many Teeth onto the shore and a giant purple man is running away from it. The scene doesn't make much sense at first because he is clearly large and powerful enough that even a snapping Many Teeth shouldn't be much of a threat.

When he jumps up onto a tree, still screaming, I get a hold of myself. "The purple man is part of our community."

I start moving toward the shore, yelling it several more times just in case it didn't penetrate Wroahk's thick skull the first time.

He pulls himself up out of the water at the same time I do. His face promises violence, but I know it isn't directed at me. It might be because of me, but never at me.

"Fine. But don't go near him until you have talked or I will throw another Many Teeth. Not everyone can be trusted, Eli."

I scoff. "You think no one can be trusted."

"It is safer that way."

"I won't live like that, Wroahk. It wouldn't be living, actually. It would be a slow death. You would be killing me."

I can tell I pushed him just that one step too far, but he already agreed to let the purple man have a chance, and so his rage finds an outlet in the Many Teeth currently trapped by one of his tentacles. He lifts it and violently slams it onto the ground.

I jump, then cringe when he does it again. I make myself turn away, ignoring the sounds of continued assaults on the creature.

The purple man is clinging to the tree, his row of three bright teal eyes wide and terrified. The muscles under his enormous arms are bulging with the effort to keep him up, though he didn't make it far. His shorter legs are scrambling to find purchase on the bark below him.

He's muttering incoherently, but it must be enough for my translator to work with because I feel the telltale shift and pain.

"Hello. My name is Eli."

His language feels mostly like grunting and so I'm not sure if I'm properly infusing it with a trustworthy, bright tone.

I will just have to try harder. "I am so very, very sorry Wroahk scared you. He has problems containing his anger sometimes. It's alright, though! He promised me to give you a chance to talk and won't attack you again as long as you are peaceful."

The man's three eyes shift behind me. The sounds have enough squelching mixed in that I know it must be pretty gruesome back there.

"I think it's probably best if you just focus on me. Yes, like that. Can you tell me your name?"

"R-R-Rannek."

He stutters out his name, still trying to climb the tree and clearly not designed to do so. His back feet are large and look heavily calloused, as does the one hand I can see gripping the bark in front of him. Each of his limbs end in three thick, flat digits without visible nails. The skin there is a lighter color purple but the rest of him is covered in a dark, shining coat of short purple fur.

Wroahk must have gotten it out of his system because the sounds stop. "It is so great to find you, Rannek."

He blinks several times, darts his eyes behind me and then back. "I'm sorry. What did you say your name was again?"

I let out a sigh of relief. "Eli. You can call me Eli. Did you get taken from your home planet, too?"

"Yes. And I have been running away or hiding ever since. This place is terrible. I have seen so much violence. Like nothing I knew ever existed."

He takes another look behind me and I cringe. We are not exactly looking like friendly poster children for peace and harmony right now.

"Yes, I know what you mean. Wroahk came from a place where all he knew was violence, but it wasn't like that for me. I'm still working on teaching him what it can be like to have friends."

I am so happy when that term translates and need to know if the most important one does. "He has agreed to help me build a safe community."

Bingo! I keep myself from doing a little jig. This scene is scary enough as it is, and I have no dancing skills to speak of.

"I know we probably don't look very trustworthy right now, but would you consider taking a swim across the lake and talking with some more of us?"

He looks behind me again and his fur shivers. I finally hazard a look myself. Wroahk has a chunk of the Many Teeth in his mouth, its blood flowing down his chest, and is giving Rannek a death glare with his shark eyes.

Would I say yes to going anywhere with that?

Dios. I did say yes. I am totally insane.

My throat stings and I am back to a yelling whale. "Wroahk. If you try to run away potential friends by looking like a serial killer I will not forgive you. I know what you are trying to do so just stop it."

He shifts his gaze to me and I raise my tentacles at him to let him know I mean business. "Get that out of here and clean yourself up. No sane female would ever touch a male who acted like you are acting right now."

"This is a common way for me to act, and you still touch me."

I turn back around, not acknowledging the fact he just questioned my sanity. I do that quite a lot myself, such as less than a minute ago, so I don't have a good retort.

There is a big splash I assume to be him lobbing the Many Teeth back into the water and then the smaller ones that lets me know he is going to wash himself off.

Rannek visibly relaxes a moment later. Best to not tell him that Wroahk would be up here in less than two seconds if he tries to hurt me.

It seems like we need a nice neutral topic. "What job did you do before you came here? I cleaned and helped people buy food. Uh, I helped them get food."

The word *buy* didn't translate. I really want to know more about a culture that doesn't have a word for purchasing.

He slowly slides down the couple feet he made it up the tree. The three digits on his limbs seem to work the same exact way. They are situated in a triangular shape and each one can bend in toward the oval shape between them. The only difference is the scale of his feet is larger than his hands.

"I am a builder of useful beauty. Mostly of clay, but also wood and stone."

There is no way this man is a threat. "I love that. I wish I had enough time to develop some artistic talent, but I always worked too hard."

The male is looking more and more relaxed, but he's still periodically darting his eyes to the water. "Everyone should have time for art. In my village, everyone worked hard, but there was time left for what we loved. That way, no one person was left to only do the unpleasant tasks."

I'm feeling smug now. Wroahk will hear about this one until he complains about my words rotting his brain.

I found a model community member on my first recruitment attempt.

"Would you help me build that sort of place?" I point back behind me toward where we left Ree and Thivoll. "No one violent can get past the Many Teeth creatures to get there. You would be safe."

"Even Wroahk?"

I feel bad quashing the hope I hear in his tone. "Actually, he is the reason the island is safe. I know he didn't make a very good first impression, but he won't hurt you once I tell him you are my friend."

Rannek looks back into the thick woods, and another shiver passes over him. "It might be a mistake to trust you, but I can't imagine staying out here. I have been injured many times as I ran, though I am healing faster than I should."

So he's been altered, too. Interesting. "We will keep you safe. I promise."

I turn back to the water and my throat shifts. "He is a friend, Wroahk. A very sweet soul I can't see ever hurting anyone."

He comes up from the water. Rannek takes a step back, but doesn't run away.

Wroahk doesn't look impressed. "He fled from a Many Teeth. He is not a worthwhile friend if he would retreat from such an easy fight."

I narrow my eyes at him. "*Basta.* You are being mean."

"I am stating the truth."

"You are stating a truth based on your old existence. Everyone plays a different role in a community. He is a sculptor, which means he can likely build."

Most of that didn't translate, but I don't bother rewording what I meant, since I don't think there are equivalent words. He will just have to witness what it means.

"I need you to take him back with us. Oh, and absolutely no more trying to kill people before I can say if they are part of a community or not. It was obvious you were searching for a way out of our agreement. Say it."

"I will wait to kill them until you assess them. But if they try to harm you, they die."

"Well, I like living, so yes, that sounds good. Take us back now?"

When he surges up out of the water and grabs both of us with his tentacles, I realize my error in not being clear in how I wanted us conveyed.

I can hear poor Rannek's muffled screaming the whole way back. Considering it takes a couple minutes, I'm impressed with his lung capacity. He still has air left in his lungs after Wroahk tosses him up on the shore of the cove because he lets out a shriek when he sees Thivoll and starts scrambling away backwards.

Luckily, Ree is quick to soothe him. "It's alright. He won't hurt you. He is just a giant teddy bear. Hello. My name is Ree. Your fur is beautiful. Such a similar color to mine. What is your name?"

The woman seems to have some sort of superpower when it comes to interacting with terrified people because the big purple male quickly settles for her.

"Rannek."

Thivoll joins in the conversation. "Please tell him I am sorry I frightened him."

Ree translates and then goes to sit beside Rannek. "Would it be rude if I touched you? Maybe a hug?"

Rannek shudders. "I would like that, thank you."

She puts an arm behind his back and pulls herself close to his side. She is tiny next to him. I tear up watching such a tender moment. I'm hoping it makes an impression on Wroahk, but he isn't even looking.

He is staring at me intently.

Thivoll breaks in again. "Ree would like me to go move Amethyst here right away, and get Kira and Drasuk to move some supplies. I would also feel better moving her chamber and not taking a chance that whoever stole Silver is looking for another human. Please tell your Wroahk that he might not be able to kill me, but I can kill anyone I want on this planet. If he harms my Ree, I will make sure his death is excruciatingly painful."

I clear my throat, but Ree beats me to a response, but it isn't directed at my already notoriously violent... boyfriend? That just doesn't sound right, but now's not the time to figure it out.

"We'll take care of it, Thivoll."

She turns to me. "Will you ask Wroahk to escort him? I doubt he will respond to me."

I nod. "Thivoll from our community needs passage to go get another woman. You'll need to look out for those green aliens you've been drowning, and also some gray and pink ones with three stubby legs."

He whips around to face me. "Those are the enemy."

"Yes, that's right. Ree and Thivoll have been killing them, it sounds like, but there are a lot more of them."

Wroahk turns to the big orange alien, his face suddenly looking far less violent, like he's seeing Thivoll for the first time.

"Tell me you will make sure he is safe and wait for him to return so you can get him back here safely, too."

"I will."

"You will what?"

He gives me his angry face. "I will make sure he is safe." I glare at him. "Safe both ways," he adds.

I give him a sunny smile. "I am going to stay here." The announcement does nothing to improve his mood. He starts to drag me deeper into the water. "No kind hands for three days." He keeps pulling me back, and I have just enough time to yell out a bigger threat. "Three years."

He lets me go and I come out of the water with as much dignity as I can muster before speaking to Thivoll. "He will make sure you are safe. Both ways."

He is making a chuffing sound as he moves into the water.

I turn to Ree. "Was he just laughing at us?"

She smiles. "Definitely."

"Huh. Well, okay, I earned it by ending up with such a *care-chimba*."

We both crack up again.

A thread of anxiety breaks through the stress induced merriment. "I didn't tell him what Thivoll said."

She wipes away some tears. "Was there really a need? Isn't that what Wroahk would do if someone harmed you?"

Valid point. "I like how you think, Ree."

She smiles at me and then we both turn to help poor Rannek settle in.

52

Wroahk

The orange male swims faster without his human and I am sure to follow the agreement by chasing away Many Teeth. He doesn't take the same route as our previous crossing. Possibly to confuse me so I don't know where to find his hiding spot.

Not that I would ever try to follow, but I'm glad I have been threatening enough that he takes the effort. The best defense is the threat of violence.

After he leaves the water, I have a moment of anger that I can't just return to Eli. Then I think about how glorious she was in her anger today. I didn't like anything she made me agree to, but my mating tentacles are all wrapped up in excitement at the memory.

Just thinking about her turning to me with that fierce look on her face when I was scaring that worthless *friend* makes them pulse.

Making her threaten me is a glorious feeling, just like I get when I make a difficult kill. But I think I have figured out something very important. She talks in her own words of making a *deal*, but how this really works is the more things I do that she wants, the more likely it is she will always touch me.

I also know I can't tell her I know this, or she will probably stop yelling at me. I gag when I think of her talking to me like she did that purple coward in the tree. It makes my tentacles wilt, and I thrust the thought of it violently out of my mind.

No. I need to be strategic.

Pondering how best to go about it helps me get through the annoyance of waiting.

I also have more time to think over what Eli said about how her *friends* have been killing the enemy. At first, it caused a surge of jealousy, then I remembered how effortlessly he killed the Many Teeth.

With nothing to do but wait, I think of what Eli keeps saying about this *community* she wants and how it's important to her that it's a form of protection. Now I see the other side of it. There are many more of the enemy out there, and with this *community* comes others, like Thivoll, who will help me kill them.

He isn't trying to take my prey. There are too many out there for me to kill while also protecting Eli. Or someone needs to protect her so I can kill them.

I was prepared to protect this *community* just to make Eli happy, but now I'm excited for my own reasons.

When the large male returns with a silver shell just like the one Elis was in, I see another female inside. He is already protecting more than one human. He will probably protect Eli, too, and while part of me wants to rip him to pieces instead of letting him have my territory, the other part finally understands what she has been trying to tell me.

I don't always have to be watching and protecting if someone else is there to do it with me.

With this thought in mind, it doesn't make me angry when the male is slower in the water as he moves the sleeping female. Halfway across, I even reach out two tentacles and help steady the silver shell, then steadily take more of the weight.

When he rumbles something I can't understand, I somehow know he's pleased, and it feels... good.

Not as good as *kind* touch, but similar.

When he gets to the shore, I can't quite bring myself to help move the silver shell above the water, but instead keep away the Many Teeth.

Then they all talk endlessly as they gesture at the shell before they move it to the cave nearby Eli's cove. It makes me glad that I threw the dead Many Teeth out of it.

The purple coward has retreated up into the forest, so I don't have to look at him anymore.

Once they stop talking, I follow the orange male and his human across the water, this time holding Eli in my tentacles. It's disappointing when she doesn't complain, but I can tell she is tired by the events of the long day.

It's tempting to just go to the bottom with her, but I know she will want to assault me with her words. She never settles at night until she does and it is easier for her to talk above the water. I take us out to the most secluded part of the cove. As far as I can get from any shore and all the ridiculous *friends* that seem to swarm along it in greater numbers every day.

She starts talking as soon as we come up out of the water. "I am so happy. This has been the best day. I mean, not of my life, because that would be sad, but you know what I mean."

I don't and I don't want to.

"Oh! I asked Thivoll why there are so few animals. He said it was from *terraforming* and any dangerous creatures were released as part of making the hunting grounds more of a challenge. That means the Many Teeth are aliens, too."

This might take a long time, so I settle my tentacles into a defensive swirling pattern that keeps us afloat and senses any Many Teeth disturbances in the water.

"But that isn't important right now. Ree and Thivoll went back to their cave to start moving *supplies*. They'll be back at sunrise. I know we talked about this, but I just want to make sure because it is important to me. You'll help me keep them all safe?"

I repeat her words, just like she expects, then add my own thoughts. "I will want their help in return."

Her eyes open wide in surprise. "You do? I mean, yes, I'm sure they would give it, but for what?"

"Killing the enemy."

"Many Teeth?"

"No, the gray ones with pink slime. They were the ones who took me. I want all of them dead. Is that part of *community*?"

Her mouth opens, then closes, then opens again. "I want to say no, it isn't, but I think from what Ree told me that killing all of them is the only way we can make sure we even have a *community* at all."

"You will tell them what I want in return? You will share my *deal* with Thivoll?"

"Alright. Yes, I will. I have one more thing. I think this one will be harder for you, but I need it to live."

I perk up, excited to be moving into more erotic territory. Maybe this will be a fight. My mating tentacles start stroking along her legs in anticipation.

She swats them away. "I have important things to say right now and that can wait."

This is getting more exciting by the moment.

"You can't threaten or kill anyone who touches me."

"No."

She makes that lovely sound of frustration, and I am back to twining myself around her legs. "*Basta.*" Another swat sends a jolt of pleasure through me. "I need more than just your touch."

"*Kind hands* are all mine."

"Not *kind hands*, well... I guess. Huh, there's a translation issue here. Never mind. Not a sexual kind of touch. A *friend's* touch. They aren't the same."

"No."

I spend some more time saying no to her, not paying attention to the increasingly more agitated words she keeps hissing out. Once she gets to the appropriate level of anger, I relent.

"You can touch your *friends*, but not with *kind hands*, and if they ever touch you with violence, I will make sure they have a few Many Teeth at their feet. Is this the new deal for *kind hands*?"

She huffs out a breath. "Fine. Yes, but I think both of us know by now that what we have is more than a *deal*. I don't think that term works anymore."

"Alright. Does that mean you will talk less?"

I almost lose control of the seed in one tentacle when she makes a growling shriek of frustration.

53

Eli

Waiting for them to return is terrible, but it gives me more time to think over how Ree looked. I was so excited about people, and convincing them to stay, that I didn't really properly think through just how different she was.

For one, she had a tail, and I am ridiculously jealous. Surely everyone has wanted a tail since they were a kid, and all I got were hair tentacles.

It's not right.

Little suckers that taste things under the water are not a substitute for being fluffy, though I suppose I don't know that I would have been on board with the black scales. Not that they don't look great on her, or anything, but...

Not that it matters. I have the body I have, and I wouldn't want any of those furry males. If I became like them, how could I possibly be with Wroahk?

He drives me crazy, sure, but he's changed so much. I look over at him, and as always, he's watching me. Letting me know with his eyes that I matter to him. No longer a nobody.

I'm proud of all the ways he's changed. My own changes have been hard, but it's mostly been my body. He's had to work against an entire upbringing to embrace any part of the things that are important to me. Hell, to even stop himself from killing me.

Who else can say someone cares for them so much they would do that?

The yellow tentacles, the gills, this skin, these changes are the only reason we work. A memory of just how well we fit together sends heat surging through me, making the water pump faster through my gills.

Then I remember my new responsibilities and glance back to the cove.

I should probably check on Rannek, but if I do, it won't be without a terrifying octo-shadow, so he'd probably prefer if I just left him alone to guard Amethyst. I also barely looked at her, and now I'm feeling guilty about it.

Well, I can change that when Ree and Thivoll get back from gathering their supplies. I'm bouncing in the water, filled with glee to be listing such a long list of people, as Wroahk makes his grumbling clicks.

He wanted to wait in our cave, but I gave him a verbal lashing along with some tentacles whips, and so here we are, floating near the opposite shore, with no real sense of how long it will be before they arrive.

Surely it can't be too long? I settle back into making plans, cataloging where I know useful resources are, even though some of them I can't eat anymore, and shelter above ground isn't something I can use.

My shoulders sink, the reminder of my changes a harsh juxtaposition to my earlier glee. Wroahk has become surprisingly attuned to my mood, and he reaches up a tentacle to stroke it along my cheek.

It's a reminder I needed. We'll make it work.

I open my mouth to thank him but snap it back closed when I hear movement. A moment later, Ree calls out my name. I try to swim to the shore, but tentacles hold me back.

I narrow my eyes at him, then remember that I have to meet a couple more people and give them a Wroahk-can't-kill-you community pass.

When I look back up, Thivoll has moved onto the shore, Ree grinning on top of his back, surrounded by a bunch of bags, weapons, and who knows what else.

From behind her comes... a dragon.

Well, sort of. Big, blue, spikey, and looking at me with amber eyes. That must be Drasuk.

He's adorable.

My eyes dart up to the shock of pink and black on top of him and my eyes widen. She's beautiful, and also one of the strangest people I've ever seen. She's got some of Thivoll's traits, plenty of Drasuk's, but also a lot more I don't recognize, most notably the white spikes coming out of her skull.

She's holding a gun in her hands, scanning around, and looking at Wroahk dubiously.

"You must be Drasuk and Kira. I'm Eli, and this is Wroahk."

"Hello Eli," Kira calls back. "Nice wiggly threads you've got there."

I move up a hand to my over-excited tentacles, feeling self-conscious.

Ree snorts. "Says the woman posing as a bloodthirsty Statue of Liberty."

I dart my eyes back to Kira, just in time for her to let out a guffaw.

She wipes at her eyes, and I could swear she has some sort of other eyelid. "I'm sorry, Eli. I have a terrible sense of humor, but I really am glad to meet you."

Then she's back to clutching her gun, hands moving over it almost... lovingly.

I shiver. Something tells me this woman might give Wroahk a run for his money when it comes to violence.

Which, of course, means we're instant besties. I've become a brand-new woman, and I know good friends when I see them.

"It's okay."

Ree speaks again. "Thivoll's language might be the better one for us, unless you think Wroahk should still be included. Drasuk knows that one, but he doesn't have translation nanites."

I glance at Wroahk, but his expression is just as mulish as usual. "Honestly, I think he would prefer to not have to listen to us, but I do need to pass on a request first."

From the look of relief on his face, which is so subtle only I could detect it, he agrees.

"Actually, why don't you ask them, Wroahk?"

He shoots me a look that promises later retribution, but all he gets is a grin in response.

One of his tentacles squeezes my ankle, and he shocks me again by actually speaking to the two women. "The gray slimes. I want them all dead."

Kira's eyes light up. "Oh, Wroahk, you are speaking my language."

"No, you are the one using my voice, Kira," he clicks back at her.

She looks over at me. "Another one? I hope he isn't worse than Drasuk or I'm going to need to leave to kill something."

I'm not sure what she means, and she doesn't give anyone a chance to respond before she keeps speaking. "I delight in killing the slimes, Wroahk. We all do, well I guess not Ree, but she has other uses."

Ree rolls her eyes.

Wroahk is looking pleased now, and he speaks up again. "Will you drive them toward the water, then leave so they feel like they are safe? It will make their screams so much sweeter when I rip them apart and scatter them to the Many Teeth."

Ree is looking a bit sick, but Kira has an even wider grin on her face. "Wroahk, Wroahk. I think you and I are going to be very good friends. Let's get everyone settled, and then we can figure out a way to make them scream."

I've never seen the look he has on his face right now. Like he has been given a shiny new toy, and he's not quite sure how to use it, but jumping up and down in excitement, nonetheless.

Except it's Wroahk, so to everyone else, he probably just looks like a shark considering his next meal.

He gets control of himself a moment later. "Deal, Kira. You are community."

Whoa, what? I didn't even have to give them a pass or make him swear to me in words not even the trickiest seelie could wiggle out of.

He even said her name right. Should I be jealous?

My face hurts from all my grinning, which lets me know I really have lost my mind if two people bonding over being murdering psychopaths makes me feel this much hope.

"Well," Ree breaks in, sounding nauseous, but just as in charge as usual. "Is that all you needed to ask, Wroahk?"

"Yes."

Ree winces, then changes over to the growling, harsh tones of her cat-man. "This language is Manticorid, which is Thivoll's species. Drasuk is a drakonid. We'll pass on Wroahk's request later."

I glance back over at Drasuk and give him a big smile.

He doesn't return it, and my tentacles dip down a bit, but then I realize he doesn't really have lips.

"Greetings, Eli," he says. "Are you ready for us to swim across? I would like to return to killing hunters."

Another male with a one-track mind, it seems.

I switch back to Wroahk's language for a moment to let him know what Drasuk said, then answer the dragon man. "Hi. Yes, we can go now, but do you want us to hold some of that above the water?"

"That would be great, Eli," Ree responds, her smile making me feel warm inside.

That dissipates pretty quickly after having to yell at Wroahk for a few minutes until he agrees to be a pack-kraken.

I could swear he doesn't look mad, though. More like... excited? Weird.

My good mood comes right back when Ree, Kira, and I share a knowing look as he grumbles and waves four different packs above his head as we all swim behind him.

Then we all start laughing and none of us can stop the entire way across.

It feels so good to be around people, especially women. There really is no substitute for being around people who share similar life experiences.

Plus, anyone would be a better conversationalist than Wroahk.

Drasuk looks around the clearing when we arrive, then he and Thivoll head out to set false trails and gather a few more items, Wroahk instantly agreeing to escort them, his tentacles almost dancing as they slip into the water.

I show Kira the way to the cave, my mouth endlessly droning on about all the edible plants, which rocks will create a spark, and a few dozen other things. When I take in a long, ragged breath, my lungs already starting to dry out, Ree interrupts me.

"You've been lonely, haven't you, Eli?" Ree asks, empathy heavy in her voice.

Tears spring to my eyes, and I blink them back, not able to afford the loss of liquid. "Yes. I really need people. It has been hard."

Both of them move in to embrace me and I revel in the feeling, but hiss out in pain when their scales shift against my rapidly drying skin.

Ree's eyes sharpen. "You don't look very good. What's wrong?"

"I got his skin, which means I can't leave the water for long."

"Let's get you into the pool in the cave, then," Ree says. "And check on Rannek to see if he's still having a Wroahk-induced panic attack."

My lips shouldn't quirk at her teasing tone, but they do. Now that some time has passed, the image of his wet, purple furred body flying through the air is kinda comical. I doubt he would agree, poor guy.

When we get to the cave, I'm shocked to see that Rannek has Amethyst raised off the ground onto a surprisingly attractive, though rough-hewn, table. Her body is covered in some sort of fabric made of woven reeds draped across the glass.

He's done nothing to make himself comfortable, but he made sure she was and she's not even conscious.

Okay, I definitely feel bad for making fun of him. That was incredibly thoughtful.

My throat shifts to speak his language. "You are amazing, Rannek. How did you make all this so fast?"

His fur ripples and he darts his eyes away. "I will be better equipped in a few days, but it will be fine for now. She deserves better than such hasty work."

Kira's eyebrows have disappeared under her brow plating, and all three of us share a look. If that table is hasty work, the male must make masterpieces.

Ree speaks up first. "She would love it, I am sure, Rannek."

He wipes his three-fingered hands down his fur, his three eyes blinking at the praise.

Oh my, we are going to have to find this cutie another woman, stat. A glance over to Ree and I can see she's thinking similar thoughts.

Kira has moved on to checking out every nook and cranny of the cave as I slip down into the water, a sigh of contentment leaving me as the itching goes away.

"How deep does that go and is there a way in from the lake to there?" Kira asks.

I'm not sure, so I go investigate. I assume Wroahk would have mentioned it, but then I remember that he's let me stumble into Many Teeth nests before.

He's still transitioning from being a solo hunter.

My heart's pounding as I swim down, but after careful checking, it seems there is only a small opening. It must lead to the lake because the water is flowing, but there's no way a predator can come in.

When I report my findings, Kira relaxes a bit, then moves to sit cross-legged facing the cave opening. "You haven't seen any threats on the island?"

"No, but I haven't explored the whole thing. There are these giant alligator things in the lake Wroahk calls Many Teeth, though. They are pretty horrific, and I almost died to one of them my first day here."

"And Wroahk can't exterminate them?"

I hadn't considered that. "Well, probably, but they are also part of what will keep us safe, plus Wroahk, of course. Unless you dump a bunch of blood in the water, or one of them starts hunting you, I think they'll leave us alone. Just don't... well I was going to say don't go into the deep water, but I guess you can't. Nevermind."

Ree speaks up again. "We could always build something out in the water to make sure they can't come up into the cove, plus along the shore edges. The cliffs make this naturally defensible."

Rannek's fur ripples, I assume in excitement. "I can build that. I'll start right away."

He starts to move out of the cave, but Kira holds up a hand. "No. You should wait until Wroahk is back so he can protect you."

His purple fur spikes out, nearly doubling his already massive size.

I come up out of the water and place a hand on his arm, soaking his fur. "He won't hurt you, I promise, but I'll be there with you the whole time, so you aren't scared."

"Alright."

"You can tell me all about your home and I'll tell you about mine. It'll be fun."

His fur settles back down, and I move back into the soothing water.

"Good," I say. "Now, on to more important matters. Such as how you two got tails, and I didn't."

They both laugh.

"Jealous much?" needles Kira.

"Shush," Ree tells her, but there is a similar wicked look on her face. "I'm not going to lie, I wasn't a fan of my new tail and venom at first, but it... grew on me."

She looks at us with a silly look on her face, and I can't help but laugh at her attempt to further lighten the mood.

"I'm a marine, Eli," Kira says while she rolls her eyes at Ree. "Do you know how many genali I would kill for your gills? It's fucking cool. Not to mention I'm pretty sure you could strangle all kinds of things to death with those tentacles."

I pull them forward and up out of the water where they were floating, constantly sending me information about the water I'm in.

They've gotten progressively longer and thicker, and I realize she's right. The ones on the top of my head are smaller and shorter, but the ones near the base of my skull are as thick as my arms and reach even farther.

I haven't been thinking of them as a weapon. I tell one to pick up one of the scrap pieces of wood Rannek left lying near the pool of water.

It's thick, well beyond what I could break with my hands. With just a thought, one of my bright yellow tentacles wraps around it, easily splitting it in half.

"Fuck yes, Eli," barks out Kira, a manic grin on her face.

It's weird. All of this is weird, but that sort of excitement and acceptance feels really damn good.

54

Eli

They catch me up on the things they know about the aliens out there. My eyes get bigger and bigger the more they tell me. How they've been shot, stabbed, throats cut.

We have to eventually switch to English because we're terrorizing poor Rannek. He's settled down at the base of Amethyst's chamber, still taking his role to protect her seriously.

These women are absolutely amazing and my mind races, thinking of their plans. "So Drasuk thinks there must be a space elevator? But we need to find the rest of the women and protect as many prey males as we can before we can get to it?"

Ree nods. "They should all be on this continent, I think, which he said will have been terraformed to not be all that large. We need to kill all the vermin. It will take a while, though, and so I am so grateful for this island. I wasn't sleeping very well in the cave, just waiting for it to be found."

It makes me happy that, even though I had no idea what the heck was going on out there, I still managed to play a key role.

We spend a while longer discussing the changes we can make to the cove to make things more comfortable for them, since no one will want to stay in a cave forever. Ree asks me to convince Wroahk to patrol me around the lake shore on the opposite side of the island once Rannek finishes building protections.

Not just to kill hunters, which Wroahk is going to absolutely love, but to also look for any prey and try to speak to them.

I'm excited by the idea of building a community, though sad that it has to turn into an army soon. She's right, though. Until we take over the planet somehow, they will just keep coming, and at some point they will figure out we are on this island.

With a start, I realize that I put us at risk making that fire. "We'll need to build something to hide flames and only cook at night," I muse aloud.

"That's smart," Kira comments. "Cooking might attract prey, but from what the guys say, none of the hunters have heightened senses."

Ree wrinkles her nose. "Lucky for them. I'd give that one up in a heartbeat."

"What about Silver?" I ask her, then regret it when her face falls.

"All I can do is keep going back and asking the snake man to give her up. So far, he's protecting the area really well. Plenty of dead hunters, most of them crushed. I can smell her cryo chamber, but she must still be in it because even Thivoll can't smell her. I'll tell the male about our island the next time I visit, but pretty much all I get from him is 'moon daughter is mine,' the irritating serpent."

Movement catches my eye and my jealousy spikes again. She's got kitty claws.

What the hell? Why did I land on an island with a shark-octo thingy?

Though, fine... yes, I wouldn't trade Wroahk, even if it means I'm stuck in the water.

Kira glances over. "Silver's safe, Ree. You did well."

Ree lets out a huff.

Wait. I'm stuck in the water, which means I can't be of much help in this whole war campaign craziness.

"I don't think Wroahk and I will be able to help. We can't be out of water very long or it's... really bad."

Ree looks over at me, eyes roaming to take in my features. "We'll figure something out. There's a river not all that far from here and those tend to lead to the sea. We could always keep you covered in wet blankets and have one of the big guys run you."

I let out a laugh. "Oh, Wroahk is going to absolutely love that. Let's not let him know about that plan just yet."

"Well," Kira breaks in, "like Thivoll likes to say, he just hasn't figured out yet that you're the one in charge of him."

I laugh. "Oh, Ree, you get the polite one and the smart one? Look at you."

She really must have picked up a cat trait or two because she... preens. Literally fluffs up her hair like she's trying to make her fur more presentable.

Kira and I share a look and both start laughing. Ree's startled for a moment, then looks down at her hands and joins us.

Thinking of all of our males makes me realize I have another question... fear, really. "Ree?" I say hesitantly. "Uh, you're the nurse. So, uh, can we get pregnant? Because octopi lay eggs and I'm... not into that idea."

Both of their eyes widen. "I hadn't thought of that," Ree admits. "Which, of course, is completely crazy. My mom would be yelling at me so loud right now. It's been so crazy, but that sounds like an excuse a fifteen-year-old would make."

She pinches the bridge of her nose, then keeps talking. "Whatever. I don't know, Eli. I would say no way based on genetics, but those have clearly been altered."

Kira clears her throat. "Not to give the genali too much credit or anything, but I doubt they would sell sex slaves without including contraceptive. I mean, probably one that's easy to extract or, I guess, reprogram or something if it's nanite-based, but I just don't see most buyers wanting a bunch of half human babies."

We all let out a long sigh of relief. It makes sense, but none of us looks fully settled about it, either. I know I'm not.

It's been too much guessing since I woke up on those rocks.

A snoring sound makes us all look over to the big mound of fur near Amethyst. He must be exhausted to be sleeping so early.

Ree's face turns softer. "He's the first one I haven't sent out to do my dirty work. It feels good."

Her eyes are haunted and Kira shifts from her perch enough to sling an arm around her. "You are doing the best you can, Commander."

Ree pokes her in the ribs and then hisses and rubs at her finger. Kira sticks her tongue out at her, the odd yellow and silver swirling of her eyes still managing to show how cheeky she is.

Ree laughs and returns her embrace.

Then they both start purring and I about lose my mind.

"Do not freaking tell me you both... I... got... you... Arg!"

I really could strangle whoever was in charge of doling out this metamorphosis with my hair tentacles until the breath leaves their stupid body, but the snicker I get from Ree, and the fact that it clears the guilt off her face, is worth it.

Completely fucking unfair still, but worth it.

Soon after, the males return, but instead of everyone resting in the last hours of the evening, Kira suggests a different plan.

"Remember that genali camp we planned on raiding?" she asks Drasuk as she leans up against him and strokes the small spikes on his side.

"I do, yes."

She gets back her unhinged grin. "How about we make Wroahk a happy... uh, whatever he is?

"Happy shark man?" Ree quips.

55

Wroahk

The only thing lowering my excitement as we wait lurking under the water is that Eli refused to stay behind. I considered the different ways I could stash her somewhere else as we made our way down the lakeshore, ensuring that we were far enough away from the stretch of water that lead to the island to not attract other hunters, but nowhere is safe right now.

The purple coward is terrible protection and everyone else is out driving the enemy to us.

I'll just have to keep her behind me.

There's no chance to come up with a better plan before I see them, gray flesh jiggling, terror in their eyes as they realize they are trapped against the shore. I fight the urge to surge up out of the water, reminding myself to follow through with the plan.

So, I wait. Keeping myself still and Eli positioned under me so her bright colors don't attract their gaze, thankful my greens and blues are just as well-suited to blending in to this water as my salt water home.

For once, there is no pang of feeling in my chest as I think of it. Instead, I use one of my tentacles to touch Eli's face, a reminder of what is most important.

And then I see it, their relief. They think they are safe now. My mouth opens as I mimic the look Kira had on her face. She is more like the females of my species than Eli, though none of them would have delivered such a prize to me on the same day I asked for a *deal*.

The females of my kind have no concept of *deals* or how good they can make you feel.

I push the thought aside, and enjoy the moment my *community* has given me, tentacles pushing hard against the boulders I waited on to make us fly out of the water. I shift Eli as we move through the air, pulling her body tight behind mine so none of these *guns* they spoke of can hurt her.

There is a whole school of the enemy, all of them screaming out gurgling cries of terror, two of which are instantly cut short as I punch a tentacle through their disgusting bodies.

I keep one tentacle around Eli, and one free to kill each one in my hold, but then use all the remaining ones to snatch up the enemy—the genali—by one of their short, useless limbs. Blood paints the nearby rocks and plants as I pull them apart, dash them against rocks, rip heads and limbs off, all the while roaring out my most intimidating song.

Their screams are just as sweet as I imagined.

Soon, Eli joins her smaller voice to mine, raising it like a torrent of sound as her bright tentacles reach around me, grabbing genali for me to rip apart.

The loud sounds of the *guns* begin soon after, and the moment I see one of her tentacles injured, I stop playing with my kills and finish them, barely stopping myself from tearing into them with my teeth.

As soon as they are all dead, and then crushed some more just in case, I will be claiming *kisses* from my Eli. Right after I punish her for not doing what I said.

An image of how I can use my tentacles to whip her until she pleads with me to fill every one of her holes makes me kill them all the faster.

56

Eli

I'm not sure what came over me. Never in my life have I considered harming something, let alone killing it... well if you don't count Wroahk... and my stepfather.

Huh.

I might have to let go of some warped self-image issues, it seems. Sunny Eli was a useful mask in my previous life. Maybe it's time to see who I am now.

Am I a warrior or something? Because his hurricane call just swept me up into something.

Before I knew it, and without even being able to see around him to the hunters, I had my longer tentacles snatching up genali. Even after the sting of a gunshot raced from the new limb up into my skull, I just kept serving them up for him to kill.

Screaming out my own cry the whole time blood splattered all over us.

Now I'm trying to dredge up some guilt, but it just isn't there. Ree told me some of the things they did when she was on the ship. How Navy died. How there's probably hundreds, if not thousands of human women in slavery right now.

And that's just one species. Apparently, they have stolen drakonids for their body parts, and they've been taking manticorid females.

I thought I would just be the one making the community, keeping Rannek company and helping him build, and I will, but I want to do more. I want to make them pay for what they did to us.

I'm pondering this new reality, still getting jostled by Wroahk as he makes wet squelches out of the few genali he is holding, when I hear a very human whistle of appreciation and surprise.

From the lack of screaming, they're all dead, but clearly he's working through some of his own issues.

Kira starts talking in whale voice, clearly impressed. "I knew you would turn them into pulp. Give me five, Wroahk, my man!"

The jostling stops. "Five what?" comes Wroahk's confused voice.

"You hold up a tentacle... uh, lower, yeah, right there. Now I hit my hand against your tentacle."

I hear a light impact, then there is a long pause. "I do not understand this movement, Kira," Wroahk clicks to her.

"It just means that we did something really well, and now we are celebrating that it was a great plan and we are the absolute best at killing genali."

There is another pause, then I hear another light impact.

"Yes! Just like that."

There are tears of mirth in my eyes as Wroahk moves me from behind him so I can see the rest of our community... and all the gray blood and puddles.

Yikes.

I focus back on Kira, trying to ignore the rest before I start retching, carefully not thinking about the liquid dripping off my tentacles. For one of them, it's my own blood, though the wound already feels a lot better.

Ree is on top of Thivoll's back, looking just as grossed out as I am, but she also has a look of satisfaction on her face.

I'm pretty sure Thivoll is purring. I look around for Drasuk, but don't see him. He must be making sure no one sneaks up on us.

Wroahk still has a tentacle raised and poised next to Kira's hand. Like he doesn't want to let go of the feeling of celebration. When I glance up at his face, I can tell he's just had another epiphany.

Figures that it would take the most bloodthirsty of us humans to more easily help him understand the benefits of working as a group. If I was a less secure woman, the look of wonder as he stares at her might bother me.

Instead, it makes my heart feel full. I was concerned that, at best, all he would ever manage is a relationship with me. I mean, it's a weird relationship, but it still feels like one.

I was afraid that he might simply stop himself from killing everyone else and never progress past that, but I think I'm seeing the development of his very first friendship.

Not counting us, of course. If you can call grumping at each other and having amazing sex friendship.

What am I saying? Of course you can.

Even so, the idea that Kira is his first platonic friend ever is blowing my mind, and it hurts my heart to think about how many years he went without something so simple, so important, but it makes the look on his face all that much sweeter.

He twitches his tentacles, pulling the one held near Kira back slowly. "I enjoyed that, Kira. When can we do it again?"

She grins at him. "To be honest, my dude, probably not very often. We should split up our efforts so I'm more inland and you and Eli check the shorelines. Hunters are bound to come close to a body of water like this."

"And you should find out if the river that way," Ree points off into the trees behind us, "dumps into the lake. It would expand your hunting opportunities."

He looks excited, which kind pisses me off, considering how much time I have spent trying to get him to explore. Then I remind myself that he isn't human. To him, the hunt is the basic foundation of his reality.

I've been putting it in terms of exploring just to leave, but they offered him something that makes sense. I tuck that away as Ree looks us both over.

"Did your body expel the bullets, Wroahk? I see some of them covered in your blood on the ground," she says as she points to one of them.

"Yes, of course."

She raises an eyebrow. "Yes, ladies, we officially got the short end of the evolution stick, just like I've been thinking since I met Thiv. That just looks like a simple flesh wound, Eli. Just get it cleaned off and your nanites will take care of it."

Then they leave to grab more supplies before we all meet back at the island.

57

Wroahk

It took far too long for me to convince Eli to come back with me to our underwater cave. I doubt I would have convinced her had her new *friends* not expressed the desire to sleep.

She's still restless when we get down there. "We should seriously go beyond this lake. There has to be more to see."

How is this still an issue? She has her *community*. They even said they will bring the enemy to us to kill.

"No."

I can sense her annoyance as she droops in my arms, mumbling things I cannot understand under her breath.

I don't like her like that. I want that happy look back.

"Oh, I mean to hunt," she says, cutting her dark eyes at me.

"Not to leave me?"

She turns to face me fully. "Of course not. Wherever you go, I go."

It sends a good feeling through my body to hear those words. She has changed me. From trying to eat her to now trying to understand her feelings and appease her.

She's a troublesome *companion*, but I chose her myself.

I *kiss* her forehead, holding her tighter in my arms. I know she likes when I do that, and she especially likes when I stroke her yellow weeds. Her tentacles wrap around my arm as I rub my grasper through them, feeling and sensing me.

Once I can taste her arousal, I know she likes it.

If they are like mine, the information her tentacles are sending back to her is overwhelming. My excitement rises as I feel her body grow warmer.

"Cold, Eli?"

She likes when I say her name. It makes her squirm and her heart beats faster. I lean in until her lips meet mine and *kiss* her deeply.

I'm now better at *kissing*, according to her. It's almost like tasting her and feeding on her essence. It tells me so much about her.

Her fears, her lust, and her desire for freedom. I can taste all of that and I crave to keep it all for myself. I cannot let go of her now that I've discovered this feeling. My head moves down, focusing on the two organs on her chest.

I've always thought they were odd, though they ask for my touch, given that females of my species don't have them.

I move even closer to them, using my tongue. She moans immediately, her nails digging into me.

"What are these?" I ask, genuinely curious.

Even though she's heavily aroused, my *companion* never misses the opportunity to speak.

"*Mammary gland.* It produces a fluid called *milk*. It is used to nourish our offspring."

"So right now, you can produce this *milk?*" I ask, my mind focused on how best to pleasure her using these.

Every time I touch them, she responds, and so I want to focus all my attention on them. Even now, she's struggling to maintain her speaking.

"N-No, I can't. I'll have to be pregnant for that."

"Hmm. How inconvenient."

Her body freezes. She pushes me away as fiercely as she can, but only gets away when I decide to let her go.

"What do you mean by that?" she questions, offended by my comment.

I don't know why, but I answer her question.

"It seems inconvenient that you can only produce this fluid when you're about to give life. Something so useful, provided only a one certain time."

"Well, it's the way we *evolved*. The *milk* from my *breasts* are only meant for *babies*. If I start producing it at other times, that means something is wrong and I'm going to need a *doctor*."

I just stare at her, waiting until she's calm.

"I am not sure why this has offended you."

"No, I supposed you wouldn't."

She grudgingly returns to my limbs, moving close.

"I need to warm you up," I say, slipping my grasper down to her lower back.

She rolls her eyes but doesn't refuse me. Her moans reverberate in my skull as I *kiss* lower and lower. Then a sharp gasp when my teeth lightly graze her waist.

"Don't do that!" she scolds.

I'm always careful not to harm her... much with my teeth, but it's too pleasant to hear her click out her strident commands. I enjoy watching her writhe and hearing her beg for me.

I never knew I would get so focused on the process, to the point where it's all I can think about when hunting or doing anything. I have grown to depend on her. She's as essential as the water itself.

I want to penetrate her. It takes me all my willpower not to, but I know I can't force my way in. I need her to be ready to take me in and enjoy this experience together.

I also like the part where I taste her.

Her voice only grows louder the more I drink. She becomes less skeptical and aware when our bodies join, forgetting she shares the water with other predators. She's never been conscious of the fact before, so I don't blame her, but I know they lurk.

Let them investigate the taste. I will snap them in half.

I drink her all in, feeling her body tremble in my mouth as she reaches the peak of her arousal. Now I know she's ready.

Entering her almost makes me burst. She has her back to me, her chest resting on the cave wall. I hold both of her graspers behind her back as gently as I can, thrusting in and out at will. She suggested this position, knowing full well that I am capable of breaking her limbs in a moment of carelessness.

This is how much she trusts me now.

Not that long ago, that trust would have disgusted me. Now it makes my pleasure rise.

Seeing the way her body moves from behind just makes me more aroused. My tongue caresses her neck, as I'm feeling an urge to bite her neck and mark her as solely my prey.

I clamp down, waiting for her to tell me no, but instead she moans louder. So I push my teeth into her, the rich taste of her blood filling the water, making my tentacles move in a frenzy.

She reaches her peak again; her scream echoing in the cave water. She starts falling toward the cave floor, but I'm not done with her yet. I hold her back up, propping her legs up against the wall and holding her firmly with my graspers and tentacles.

I push into her faster, tasting her from within, filling her mouth now so I have every part of her. I see her eyes roll back and her mouth stretched wide, the green of my limb exciting to see against her red-brown lips. She no longer begs for me to move faster, only craving me more as I thrust into her.

She's hanging limp when I finally orgasm, releasing my seed in her. She's barely conscious. Now, she looks absolutely delectable.

She shivers in my arms as I spin her. "It almost felt like I was being split into two. *Man*, you are so huge."

"*Thank you*," I say.

According to her, that is what you say when you get a compliment. I'm learning more words from her. For my *companion* who likes to talk, learning how to communicate with her, following our *deal*, seems a small cost.

"Is this what is part of the *deal* for your talking, or for the *community*?"

58

Eli

I take a moment to get myself under control, annoyed to be thinking about deals when I just had my fucking mind blown.

I shift so I can see his face, and then put myself back into the ridiculous mindset of the man I've decided it's a grand idea to spend the rest of my life with.

"*Qué rabia*. Kind hands for all the talking. Kind everything else in exchange for the community."

He stares at me for a long moment with his shark eyes. "Deal."

I feel hollow inside, even after getting him to agree to something that I know goes against his nature. I know he's been struggling with even the simplest concept of living in groups or companionship, but what I feel for him just can't be left unsaid.

Or left so transactional.

The culture of Earth has that vibe in romantic relationships and if the universe was going to plop me into a brand-new planet, it damn well should be a change for the better in at least some ways.

"Wroahk. Have you started to understand what love is from all my stories about my *padre*?"

I get more of his usual impenetrable stare in response. It's likely too abstract for him.

"How about this... Would you feel bad if I were to die?"

"You aren't allowed to die."

I barely avoid rolling my eyes. "Would you feel bad if I left you?"

"I would track you down and drag you back here until you agreed to never leave again."

I huff out a breath, bubbles rising and obscuring my view for a moment. "What if I was with you, but wouldn't touch you or talk to you?"

"You can talk less if that is what you mean."

"*Dios*. Just... *Los cojones*, I can't believe how difficult this always is with you. Forget the deal for a moment. Alright. Imagine this. We are in a little lake together. No one else. Just us. I am sad and won't touch you. Then I leave you. How would you feel? Please, this is important to me."

He stares at me again. I keep my impulse to fill the silence between us at bay with a continual pressure of teeth on my runaway tongue. "Like I lost every territory I have ever claimed and would never find one again. Like I would never again feel the rush of power after winning a hard fight and the sweet taste of first blood afterward."

My eyes are just as full as my heart, adding some salt to the fresh water around us. "That's love, Wroahk. I mean, a very characteristically bloody way of expressing it, but still love. You love me. I love you, too, in my own way. To avoid being sad like I just described, I need to hear it from you."

He shifts me in his hold so I am closer to his face. "I will fight for you until my last breath and provide for you because you can't."

I wait, but the words I need from him don't come. We have a long way to go, but what he said is still huge progress.

But, still... I keep pushing because words are important. They define so much of our lives.

"It goes like this: 'I love you, Eli.' Far fewer words that mean the same thing."

He flicks his tentacle out in a way I've come to understand means disagreement, and my heart sinks.

"No. It doesn't say what I will do for you. It is a word outside my voice that means nothing. I would destroy this world for you. Then I would have to rebuild it with people you can talk to with your endless words so you don't become sad. I will keep myself from ripping your friends into small pieces each and every time they touch you because you say you need it. I will catch the smallest, most difficult to capture food for you and somehow stop myself from cramming it in your mouth for as long as we both live. I will trust you enough to fall asleep with you... someday. I would come pick you up If you were to beach again the moment you floundered. Even if it means I am stuck protecting someone so clearly and hopelessly weak. What would I do if you left me? I would not fight in the next battle when it came, so I would no longer have to feel the empty place where you once were."

My eyes are giant saucers by the end of his long speech and there are tears flowing out into the water. It's the most words I've ever heard from him at a time. Maybe more than he has said in an entire day.

And he's right. Considering how much all of those promises and actions go against his nature, he does love me. Even if the thickheaded octo-man refuses to say it.

And it feels... so good.

My life was shattered at such a young age. No one should have to find out the world is so cruel, so young. Or that safety is an illusion, taken away so easily by the loss of just one person, but now I realize with a start that... the feeling is back. And somehow accomplished by being around easily the most violent person I've ever known or am likely to know.

Sure, the world is dangerous here and we have a long way to go to understand all the things we do and do not like and communicate them. But for the first time since losing my padre I know for certain that I'm with someone who, once he understands my boundaries, even if that is an arduous process sometimes, they will not be crossed.

Not to mention he would destroy anyone who did. My fifteen-year-old self would've never imagined this. It's hard to believe it even now. I hope wherever my padre is he can see me like this. That he knows, as crazy as this might seem, that I feel safe.

The price is having to stay in the water. I'll pay that price and keep paying it. This feeling is worth it.

Wroahk's worth it.

Those dark, impenetrable eyes are staring at me, assessing, wondering what I'm thinking, no doubt. Ready to make another deal. Ugh, that word. Then I think over the words we've been using and kick myself when I realize that it isn't his lack of understanding, but it's because I haven't given him the right concept.

I clear my throat and his eyes sharpen. "We keep talking about deals and agreements, but we've grown past them, haven't we? There isn't a deal, there's respect."

"Respect?"

"Yes. Where we do what the other wants because it makes them feel good and because we know what they don't like and don't want to do that either. That's called respect."

"That is a better word, Eli. There are no deals, there is respect," he says and a weight drops off me, finally making me feel free.

I pull him closer, squeezing him with my many limbs. "We have respect, Wroahk. I'm not going anywhere. No need to talk about empty spaces."

"Good. You would not survive long with those teeth."

I make sure he gets a great view of my useless teeth as I grin maniacally at him. "I love you, too."

59

Preview of Diamond

Kuret

The roar of rage that fueled me becomes a focused hiss as I slow down long enough to lace my hand through his hair so that I can have a proper hold on him.

His arms flail out uselessly in front of his body, but he can only make a wet, gurgling sound when I hit him directly onto the ground, pushing his neck a little too far to the side as I make sure he sees who will punish him.

The sick cracking sound feeds my rage, but it is not enough. Getting on one knee, I pull my dagger out of my boot and drive it into his chest, letting the entire blade disappear into him before dragging it straight across his long torso.

The look of surprise fixed on his face brings a small amount of pleasure, but it is not enough. This male must suffer.

I will make sure of it.

My hand moves faster than my brain as I butcher the male, his dirt-colored blood spraying on my face and body.

Every blow carries a sufficient amount of my built-up rage because things like him do not deserve a single part of them to be looked upon with a single shred of dignity.

I don't realize when my second knee comes down until it makes his head roll off.

Then I stand triumphantly in front of the carcass of the fool I have just butchered, like a common animal covered in his blood, wishing I could bring him back to life just so that I can do it again.

His severed head squishes in my grip as I pick it up and drive my bloodied dagger into one of its shocked eyes. A barking cry leaves my lips when I drag the blade out and push it into his second eye.

I throw the head far away from me and scream again. It is a cry of victory. I have carried out my mission and protected the human like I said I would.

I look down at the pieces of his bloodied body. Every piece for a female he has taken advantage of because predators like him don't just wake up one day and start to hurt the very ones they are supposed to protect.

My hearts are thumping in my ears and, for a moment, it almost resembles the cheers of other warriors. The greatest honor in a man's life is defending a female or someone weaker against a predator, and I have done so.

I can hear Samke's playful laughter, telling me how I cannot escape the donor ceremony now because all the females will be flocking my way, hoping to make a titled warrior their donor.

Speaking of females, I recall the reason I came here in the first place. To rescue the human.

I look down to see her trying earnestly to get away from me by dragging her rear against the ground. Her face is a ghostly mask of fear, as all the color is washed away from it, her bottom lip quivering and tears falling from her beautiful eyes.

Her soft body bearing wounds that mar the perfection of her form, testament to my mistake of believing she was safe.

I turn swiftly to check if there is something else behind me or if the male has magically risen from the dead, but there is nothing there.

Her fully white eyes are wide when I attempt to take a step forward and she scurries farther away from me, further confirming my suspicions.

I don't know what I might have done wrong, and it sits deep in the pit of my stomach that I may have just upset a female for no reason. I take another step and hold out my hand to help her up.

She shrieks and collapses to the ground, her white hair forming a pool that covers her face.

I reach out a hand to reassure her. "He can't hurt you now."

She grunts, wincing in pain, as she tries to speak. "N-no, please."

I stand still and stare at her, unsure of what to do.

About the Authors

This pen name represents a collaboration with the goal of creating stories just like we prefer: spicy slow burn, strong character arcs, and all about the... shall we say delectably different.

Ky is our public face...

the one of us who posts on social media, who decided it was *smart* to get a PhD in History (and so now regales you with the book related historical mythology in our newsletter), who tends to have all the wild ideas, the writing voice we follow, and who keeps all of it moving (sheesh, that's a lot... thanks, Ky!)

On a typical day you can find Ky hanging out with her own Mr. Delectably Different, loving on her fur babies, or convincing her two kids that she really is funnier than they'll admit.

She's a musician, sculptor, graphic designer, and lover of weirdness. Most of the time, she's either working her 9 to 5, writing, or running out in the wild.

Legends Start Somewhere

Myth Awakened: Vimala and Jentoll

Vimala

I was once a courtesan for kings... until a rival sent an attacker in the middle of the night. One moment. One coward with a blade. I lost everything.

My beauty no longer sustains me, but I refuse to simply fade away. And yet it is hard to maintain hope after so much loss. Will this otherworldly avatar of Vishnu be my salvation?

Jentoll

I've given more than enough to my people. To my failing empire. I gave an eye. My tail. Pieces of my sanity... far too much precious time. And now it's crumbling to dust. Falling to a far different sort of rallying cry. One for peace.

Let the next generation bear that task. This is my chance to flee. To find a new home.

**Two wounded hearts, both seeking refuge.
Will they find it in each other?**